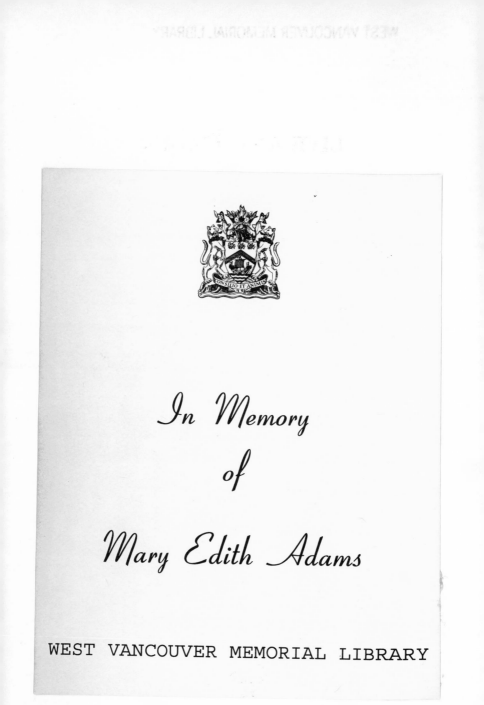

In Memory

of

Mary Edith Adams

WEST VANCOUVER MEMORIAL LIBRARY

LIVE AND LEARN

The Novels of Stanley Middleton

A Short Answer
Harris's Requiem
A Serious Woman
The Just Exchange
Two's Company
Him They Compelled
Terms of Reference
The Golden Evening
Wages of Virtue
Apple of the Eye
Brazen Prison
Cold Gradations
A Man Made of Smoke
Holiday
Distractions
Still Waters
Ends and Means
Two Brothers
In a Strange Land
The Other Side
Blind Understanding
Entry into Jerusalem
The Daysman
Valley of Decision
An After-Dinner's Sleep
After a Fashion
Recovery
Vacant Places
Changes and Chances
Beginning to End
A Place to Stand
Married Past Redemption
Catalysts
Toward the Sea

LIVE
AND
LEARN

Stanley
Middleton

HUTCHINSON
LONDON

1 3 5 7 9 10 8 6 4 2

This edition first published in 1996 by Hutchinson

Random House (UK) Limited
20 Vauxhall Bridge Road, London SW1V 2SA

Random House Australia (Pty) Limited
20 Alfred Street, Milsons Point, Sydney,
New South Wales 2061, Australia

Random House New Zealand Limited
18 Poland Road, Glenfield, Auckland 10, New Zealand

Random House South Africa (Pty) Limited
PO Box 337, Bergvlei, 2012 South Africa

A CiP record for this book is available from the British Library

Papers used by Random House UK Limited are natural,
recyclable products made from wood grown in sustainable forests.
The manufacturing processes conform to the environmental
regulations of the country of origin.

ISBN 0 09 179220 7

Typeset in Times by Pure Tech India Ltd.,
Pondicherry, India

Printed and bound in Great Britain by
Mackays of Chatham PLC

1

'What time is it, mate?'

The question was rudely asked by one of four young men who blocked the narrow pavement in front of him. The voice sounded hoarse so that he had difficulty at first in understanding what was said. Three white scruffs and a black youth in a baseball cap stood there, or rather rocked slightly on the balls of their feet. He glanced at his wrist-watch.

'Ten minutes past eight.'

'Ten minutes parst eight.' One of them mimicked his long vowel, and sniggered.

'Hand your wallet over,' another ordered. 'And your watch while you're about it.'

Their grouping seemed to him almost ritualistic, not threatening as yet, but likely to burst any moment into aggression. A boxer in his corner, standing ready for the bell.

He did not wait, but rushed between the middle two. They staggered at the impact, one was knocked flat, and he was past them. He felt a heavy blow thwack across his shoulders as if from a truncheon. Now he chased fiercely along the poorly lit street.

'Get the bastard.'

He moved confidently, sure of his prowess. A glance established that the youths still pursued him, but not together. Baseball cap was out in front. A stone whizzed past him, rattled along the pavement.

Forty yards on he turned right for no good reason, not slackening his pace. He could hear no sound from behind, stopped, turned. The yobbos regrouped on the corner, and came on after him again.

A high wall dammed the street. He had chosen a cul-de-sac. The youths must have known.

'What's up?' The voice of a man in shirt sleeves in spite of the winter evening standing at a small, wrought-iron gate between privet hedges at the end of a path.

'Muggers.'

Shirt-sleeves opened his gate without a sound, signalled him inside, closed the gate with oiled quiet, urged him with a slight push between the shoulders towards the open front door. Inside, there was no light on; shirt-sleeves took him by the arm again and guided him to the bay-window of the front room. They stood together. It was difficult to see out into the road because of the height of the hedge, but they had no sooner reached the window than one of the group appeared in the space over the gate.

'He must 'a gone in 'ere, somewhere,' they heard. 'One o' these houses.'

'Goo in an' ask 'em.'

Nothing happened as the two listened. Shirt-sleeves crept towards the front door, opening it slightly and, bending, listened. From further down the street broken glass crashed.

'The bastards must have put a stone through somebody's window. Typical.'

He opened the door more widely, without a squeak, poked his head out before tiptoeing exaggeratedly along the flagstones of the path. No sound. The two peered down the street. Only one of the three sodium lamps worked. No one else made an appearance, not even the owner of the broken pane.

'I'd just wait for a minute or two,' the householder said, 'to give them the chance to move on.' From the corridor he opened the door to his living room, letting light out for the first time. 'In you go, and sit down.'

'Thank you.'

'Not at all.'

The visitor, a tall, strapping young man in his late twenties, chose a not very comfortable chair on the far side of the hearth.

2

'Thanks,' he said.

'And your name is?' The enquiry seemed too early, almost impertinent.

'Winter.'

'Are you going to report this to the police?'

'I suppose it would be sensible. Not that they could do much. But it might tie up usefully with something else.'

'And it might not.'

Jonathan Winter looked over at his host.

'It was kind of you to let me in. Fortunate you were at the gate.'

'What would you have done if I hadn't been there?'

'Scrambled over the wall at the end. Or turned into a front garden, or a path, or even if the worst came to the worst made a rush at them and then run back to the main road.'

The host considered this, flattening his grey hair with the fingers of his right hand.

'You're big and broad enough,' he answered. 'But you don't know with these thugs. They might carry knives. Were you concealing anything valuable?'

'No. Wallet with a pound or two. Cheque cards and so on.'

'How far had they chased you?'

'From the Market. Dean Street.'

'That's quite a way. They must have meant business.'

'I bowled one of them over when I started to run.'

The host, who had not yet sat down, marched from the room into the corridor and returned carrying a shotgun. It looked to Winter's uncultivated eye to be clean, oiled, ready for use, exceptionally nasty.

'This is what I keep to welcome them.'

'Is it loaded?'

'It is.'

'Isn't that dangerous? You hear of accidents.'

'You hear of accidents with carving knives, but I still keep one.'

'You would have used it?'

3

'If they had tried to force their way in.'

'Would it do much damage?'

'I'll say it would. Could kill. But there were four of them on to two of us. And I'm elderly. And you were there as a witness. An ideal opportunity to use it.' He patted the butt. 'But we were inside too quickly for them. They must have been pretty confident to tackle a big chap like you.'

'There were four of them.'

'Yes.' The host returned the weapon to its place in the hall, saying with confidence over his shoulder, 'Oh, yes. I own a licence for it.' This time when he returned he sat down, stretched his short legs in front of the gas fire. Jonathan explained that he had been to a selection committee of teams for his club's rugby fixtures over the Christmas and New Year holidays. He usually used his car, but had decided against it, so that he could have a drink.

'Do people want to play in the holidays?' the older man asked.

'There are three first team games, and we're preparing for a cup-match in the middle of January. There's strong competition for places. We've quite a good side. The Old Morleyans.'

'That's an old school team, isn't it?'

'It was originally. It's an open club now.'

They talked for perhaps ten minutes when the older man said, suddenly, 'I've enjoyed the chat. It'll be safe for you to go now. I'll let you out the back way. Brings you into Player Street. My name is Hookes, with an 'e', George Hookes. And the number is 32, just in case the police ask.' He stood. Jonathan zipped up his anorak. They moved into the corridor, through a long unlit kitchen and out into a yard, down a short flight of steps and along a straight, made-up path for thirty paces through the back garden. One could just about see. Hookes led the way, with the shotgun nonchalantly under his arm. He unlocked, then unbolted the back gate which was approached by three steps down and looked about the street.

'The coast is clear,' he announced, comically. 'Up to the top, right there and you'll be on Player Street.'

'Thanks again.'

'Not at all. Call in on me. I might even come to watch you play rugby.' Hookes raised his gun purposefully skyward, sighting it. 'One of these fine days. Don't mention this to the police.'

Jonathan met few people on the streets, and soon found himself at the centre of the city. On his way to the bus a couple begged from a shop doorway. He fiddled in his pocket, handed over a pound.

'God bless you,' the woman said.

'He's done so,' he replied, but the remark was wasted.

Back at home by nine he rang the police. They listened politely, seemed in no sort of hurry, agreed with him that there was little they could do, but thanked him for his trouble. He left his name and address.

Sitting down with a mug of soup, he found himself worrying about the evening's incident. He did not quite understand why. He realised that he could easily have been felled by a blow to the head instead of across the shoulders. Then he would have been at the mercy of the muggers. They would have stolen his wallet, which would have meant time-wasting with his bank, but that could be easily managed. An ill-delivered blow might have fractured his skull, killed him or left him seriously incapacitated, a prey to kicking. He nodded to himself, hardly believing these possibilities. He sat safe in his flat. And then the eccentric Hookes snagged at his mind. How old was he? Middle-fifties, perhaps? Educated voice. Decent furniture. One or two interesting pictures on his walls. Deep, colourful, newish carpets. But ready for invaders, Hookes had placed a loaded gun in the hall. Why was he at the front gate as Jonathan passed? Was he on the look-out for trouble? Did he actively court it? That was unlikely on a quiet side-street. Yet first time out, in shirt sleeves on a frosty night, he'd netted a fugitive. 'Keep on the path,' he'd warned. Had he lined his garden with mines

5

or man-traps? It all seemed unlikely, and Jonathan grinned at his fancies.

The phone rang.

Jonathan's father called from the other side of the city. He sounded disgruntled, but brightened at his son's account of the attempted mugging.

'I shall see the Chief Constable at the end of the week, and I'll mention it. He won't know anything about your case, but they may be watching your quartet in that part of the world. It does no harm to know somebody's keeping a beady eye on them.' His father, a solicitor, might easily have meant the police rather than the criminals. 'Were the police helpful? They were. I see. Good. Good.'

'And how are you?' Jonathan asked when they'd cleared the situation to his father's satisfaction. The old man wouldn't like to mention a topic to the Chief Constable, or anyone else, even at a social function, with only half the facts at his command.

'I've felt rough today.' The adjective surprised.

'Flu?'

'No. I had a dream last night, first thing this morning, and it upset me.' Again this was unlike the old man. 'Usually I forget what I've dreamt, on the rare occasion when I can remember it in the first place.'

'Get on with it. Don't keep me in suspense.'

'It was so very unlikely.'

'Aren't they always?'

'Are they? I don't know. I'm no sort of expert.'

Jonathan realised that his father deliberately held back on his story to ensure the maximum drama or enjoyment for himself. The son, therefore, said nothing, breathing evenly, not averse to this sort of contest of silence.

'I dreamt,' Harold Winter began, then stopped. 'It was ridiculous, and yet it seemed so real, believable. I was addressing a quite large group of professional philosophers at a university, I guess. I'm not sure of the venue or the subject.'

'Not the law?' the son suggested. 'The philosophy of law?'

'That may have come into it, but it was not the topic. And though I can remember speaking, and that my speech was in three parts, I can't remember what it was about. Except some aspect of philosophy.'

'Why had you been asked to address them?'

'That baffles me. I seemed to recognize one or two of them, but they weren't people I know in real life. I have had dealings with one or two academic philosophers. But not any of these men.'

'Were there any women there?'

'To the best of my recollection, no. Thirty or so men.' Again a long pause as if Winter senior considered ways of expressing himself. 'As I say, there were three parts of my talk. The first seemed the longest, the most important, and in it I outlined my ideas, though I haven't the foggiest notion now what they were. In the second I talked about the application of judgement to the topic. I seemed most confident here.'

'Did you realize you weren't master of your subject? While you were talking?'

'Yes. I felt vaguely uncomfortable. It was as if I was giving an account of some medical condition which I'd read about in a newspaper. I knew what had been written but I dared not make additions or glosses or cite illustrations, especially as my audience consisted of experts. They listened politely enough.'

'And when you had finished?'

'Discussion time. There were one or two low-key, uncomplimentary remarks, one of which made no sense to me at all. And then a man in the middle got to his feet. I understood him all right. He said I had wasted their time, that all his first year students would have made a better job by far of addressing the subject, that I ought to have been thoroughly ashamed of myself talking such elementary, illogical rubbish, that I had made a fool of myself in public, that I had come disgracefully unprepared, and so forth. He was objectionably rude.'

'Who was he? Anyone you knew? In real life?'

'No. Though I can see him clearly. He wore a beautifully cut, rather sporty suit, and highly polished brogues. He had a good head of hair, parted on the left, a square, red, handsome face and large, black-framed spectacles.'

'Voice?'

'Slightly nasal. He kept pointing a finger at me.'

'And then?'

'We broke for lunch, or coffee. No vote of thanks. We went out. In the interval one or two spoke to me, and they all said the same thing: that this man shouldn't have spoken to me like that in public. But no one came up with a word in favour of my lecture, not even that I'd raised an interesting point or two, if only by chance. Nothing. They were sorry for his rudeness, but tacitly agreed with him.'

'And?'

'I felt low, Jon. I knew I'd done badly. I'd let myself down.'

'Can you account for the basis of it all? Had you gone into court lately only half-prepared?'

'Not really. Very often we start a case with only a partial story, but this seemed quite unlike that. In the courts I know my way round, can sort difficulties out, put a brave face on it. But this was different. Here I stood talking; I couldn't think why. I was even unable to say what the ideas were that I was putting forward. I just appeared there and read my piece, lost, but hoping somehow I'd get away with it. I didn't. I felt utterly disheartened.'

'And you can't account for the content or setting of your dream?'

'No.'

'Did you tell Alma about it?'

'Yes.'

'And what did she say?'

'"What do you know about philosophy?"'

'And you answered?'

'I answered, "Nothing. I know nothing." I think that's what so disturbed me. First, that I'd allowed myself to be manoeuvred into giving this talk. And secondly, that I

8

can't remember anything I said, so I can't now try to correct my errors or trivialities. It was so bloody humiliating.'

'What did she conclude?'

'She thought it was unimportant, that I'd get over it in a day or two.'

'As you did?'

'As I did.'

'But you've had second thoughts?'

'I've tried to dredge up some explanation for myself.' His father cleared his throat. 'It's this. I wondered if it wasn't an unconscious account of my life. I'm getting old.'

'Fifty-eight. Comparatively young.'

'Yes. I shall be thinking of retirement in six or seven years, and time passes by so quickly.'

'Well?'

'I begin to wonder if this dream isn't a symbol of my life. That what I've done is nothing, no, worse than nothing, just wrong or misconceived.'

'But I'm sure,' Jonathan said, 'you could give me a lucid account of how you've spent your time. You've defended and prosecuted fairly, seen to it that your barristers are well briefed in the higher courts, sorted out all sorts of private problems and transactions, put time in on good causes at your own expense, and yet made a decent living, brought up a son, given me a good start, looked after my mother, cheated nobody, returned a fair day's work for a day's pay and all the rest of it. You're an honest and respected man. Your fellow practitioners, the Law Society, the hospital trust, the lot, think highly of you, ask you to speak on their behalf in tricky situations. I don't see how this adds up to failure.'

Jonathan could hear his father humming to himself at the other end of the line.

'Ah, but.' His father paused, hummed again. 'That's where the philosophy comes in.' Again Jonathan was given time to work it out for himself. With no answer forthcoming, Winter senior resumed. 'It's not a matter of giving their money's worth to my clients, or looking after my wife and child, or even doing good works.' Again the lacuna.

'What is it then?'

'From a philosophical point of view I've achieved nothing.'

'Not so. The world is, marginally, you may say, better for your time here. But better.'

'I wish I could believe it.'

'What you need is a doctor and his packet of pills.'

'Is that the best you can do?'

'I think so. If you feel no more cheerful, get down to the surgery. Prozac for the present.'

'I'll come to watch you play on Saturday.'

'Yes. We shall get thoroughly thrashed.'

2

On the following Monday Jonathan Winter locked his Honda in the university car park. A colleague, overcoat flapping, waited for him.

'Ready for Christmas?' Jonathan got it in first.

'Doesn't entail much for me. I've an efficient wife. I directed the decoration of the Christmas tree.'

'And it looks good?'

'The kids paid no attention to my instructions, so in fact it does.'

Christopher Lowe straightened the flaps of his tweed coat, rebuckled the wide belt, fiddled with his spectacles and lifted, then replaced, his brown, racing-correspondent's trilby.

'I hate these bloody mornings,' he said.

'You're not out with your family?'

'No. Gisela's shopping. The girls are away on a day's riding. So it was a case of sitting at home moping or doing it up here. I see from the paper this morning that you won on Saturday.'

'By the skin of our teeth and good goal-kicking. We did quite well. Tackled 'em off their feet.'

Jonathan never lost his surprise at the widespread interest in his rugby playing. He turned out regularly for the city team, the three counties, the Midlands; matches in which he appeared were reported in *The Times*, the *Guardian*, the *Daily Telegraph*, the *Independent*, and read and remembered by his colleagues, even by the professor. He appeared with and against international players, could comment at first hand on their prowess; this seemed highly regarded by middle-aged, scholarly men who'd not for years even aimed as much as a kick at the cat. Rugby Union was part of the body of culture.

Jonathan breathed deeply. The morning air struck damp, though not cold. Mist shrouded the factories and cemetery in the distance, thinned the outline of poplars on the edge of the University Park.

'I could work just as well at home,' Lowe said, 'and I don't know why I don't.'

'No distractions here.'

'None there today.'

They walked at a fair pace downhill into the smallest of the Arts Faculty buildings, and paused the other side of the imposing glass door.

'Tom Taylor was mugged in the street on Saturday night. Had you heard?'

'No. Is he hurt?'

'Bruised. *Amour propre* injured. Luckily he wasn't carrying anything valuable. Not five minutes' walk from his home.'

Jonathan outlined the attempted attack on himself.

'I wouldn't tackle anybody your size,' Lowe argued.

'There were four of them. And they had a truncheon, at least. Possibly knives.'

'Two within the week,' Lowe mused. 'Why?'

'We wear old-fashioned raincoats, and ties, and don't walk very fast.'

'None of that applies to you.'

'No.'

They laughed, walking away from each other. Jonathan admired Lowe, who was, he claimed, a historian of literature, not a critic, nor a moralist. He lectured brightly, stuffing his students' heads with facts about wages, size of families, cost of books or schools in Dickens' time, and asked the pupils to apply this knowledge to what they read. 'I sometimes think,' he'd trumpet lugubriously, 'I ought to see what they can deduce about, let's say, employment in London from the novels rather than the other way about, but they don't read carefully enough. They'd get nowhere. And t'other way round, they at least read the novels. Some of them.' A clever, useful man,

Jonathan concluded, and quite willing to have his brains picked.

Jon parked himself in an armchair in his room. He was about to spend his time before Christmas re-reading *Hard Times*, pencil and notebook in hand certainly, but seated in a comfortable chair, not at his desk; he saw himself as a reader, a common reader, not as a scholar. He stood up to move the chair a yard nearer the radiator. The phone rested on a small table by his side; some fool was certain to ring, but he'd welcome the interruption in this period of not-quite work. He liked these 'reading days', when he did not set out to excavate points for research, merely to enjoy, to liven his mind. Only in a few short sessions during the holidays, two or three days, perhaps four times a year, could he manage this. He'd finish *Hard Times*, but these free-and-easy periods couldn't cover *Middlemarch* or *War and Peace*.

Again, the colleagues who knew about these 'free' days admired him for it. They invariably took up a book with a purpose, like examination candidates, searching out matters they could quote, use, make texts from; if they read freely he guessed it would be the tittle-tattle of the posh Sundays, or, at greater length, Dick Francis. This 'pose' of his, of sitting down with a classic of the language, and reading it, or, purporting to do so, as if he were a sixth-former pulling an unknown book from the public library shelves, was not comprehensible. A 'pose' they could understand: a learned man making out he knew nothing. But a simpleton sitting down to enjoy himself in a field where he sweated and strove for advantage for the rest of the year seemed ludicrous. The book and the half-dozen articles he'd written seemed as cramped, constricted, carefully argued as they could wish. When he spoke to them about George Eliot and the work he was writing, he seemed exactly as they were, a scholar, conversant with modern literary theory, so that this deliberate change to the ordinary man confused them. God knows there were eccentrics enough about the university, but his version struck out on an unusual line, the equivalent of playing rugby football, and playing it well at a high level. Nobody copied him; a classical historian, a bachelor, who claimed that for the past twenty years he had read *A Christmas Carol* every year, beginning on the Eve, and reading late. But he had no special expertise, and perused the book in an edition the size of a church Bible, a glass of claret at his elbow.

Jonathan had read for an hour and a half, had turned on his kettle when the telephone rang. James Towers, the professor.

'You're the only one in,' the professor said.

'Chris is here.'

'He's not answering his phone.' Towers coughed, cleared his throat. 'May I come round and interrupt you? I'll try to be brief.'

'The kettle's boiling. See you straight away.'

Professor Towers was a solid man, broad across the shoulders, of medium height, with black eyes in a sallow face. He seemed to fill the doorway of Jon's room as he stood, dark-suited, unsmiling. His white collar could just be seen above the rim of his high-necked pullover, giving him the appearance of a clergyman, high church perhaps, utterly serious, not to be trifled with. The voice with which he wished his junior good morning was extraordinarily deep, but mellifluous, without roughness. To the seated Jonathan, Towers seemed a large figure, but as soon as the younger man stood to make instant coffee, the professor was diminished to his five feet eight.

'All very neat and tidy,' he beamed, 'in here.' He did not receive his mug by the handle. He laid the coffee down to point at the one open book in the room, on Jon's table. 'What's that?'

'*Hard Times.*'

'Um.' The professor hummed, and nodded, as if thoroughly satisfied, a Buddha within reach of enlightenment. He would say no more on the subject unless Jon raised it. 'I had to exchange a word with someone.'

'Aren't the administrators in this morning?'

'I've not enquired. I want to speak to a member of the human race.' At this Jonathan closed his eyes and bowed his head. 'I'm worried. About Ian Gormley.'

'Oh, yes.' Gormley was a colleague, elderly, near retirement, disappointed in himself. He rarely spoke to Jonathan.

'He came in to see me yesterday, and wept about the death of his cat.'

'He was perhaps fond of it.' Jon liked to plague his superior with these truisms.

'I'm sure. He would be less distressed by his wife's death.'

'He still has his wife?'

'I can see I'm interrupting you.' Towers assumed saintly patience.

'Finish your coffee. What's wrong with Gormley?'

'He acted in a way that seemed, well, almost hysterical. Now, don't give me any of this talk of my admiration for the stiff upper lip. It was at my home. I thought Lesley might well hear the noise. Fortunately she didn't. Or she says she didn't. It was embarrassing. Even you must see that.'

'Yes. But if it got it out of his system . . . And he does his work adequately.'

'Ah, but does he?'

'Have you had complaints?' Jonathan asked.

'Not quite. The students don't find him exactly encouraging. Oh, I know what you'll say. "Gormley expects his pupils to have read something, and if they haven't he calls them to account." And I faintly approve of that. But he has published nothing in the last ten years; no, longer. Has made no attempt. Now, that counts heavily against him these days. You know it does.'

'He's sixty-ish. You can't expect . . .'

'It's not what I expect. It's what's demanded. It's already been suggested to me that he should be employed on a part-time basis only, so that his lack of research won't tell against us. He's not keen, even though he'd lose nothing financially by it.'

15

'What's his objection, then?'

'A feeling of rejection, that after a life of honest effort we cast him off in his old age.'

'That's the truth.'

'Of course it's the truth, but that's the way universities are run.'

'Would you like to get rid of Gormley? Be honest now.'

'I suppose I would. If it could be done without blood. You don't approve of that, do you?'

'No. Gormley has hardly anything to say to me,' Jon answered. 'He read my book on Hardy's verse, and pointed out two very minor errors. I'm grateful for that, I suppose. I'll correct them in the next edition. He's done it more than once. That must mean something. On the other hand he delivers his lectures on time, and his tutorials. He marks exam papers and essays according to his lights. He's a bloody nuisance at faculty meetings, but he wastes less of your time than others at the professorial colloquia you have to attend. And he'll leave in a year or two.'

'So you advise patience?' The professor grinned sarcastically.

'I'm taking my usual holier-than-thou line. If I were in your place I'd think exactly as you do. But I can't help realising Gormley knows a great deal.'

'But what he knows is not what students, or colleagues, are interested in, nor is his sort of knowledge what is examined these days.'

'We must have a variety of opinion.'

'When I talk to you, Jonathan, I begin to wonder who is head of this department.'

Jonathan Winter smiled.

'And the conclusion of the matter?'

'There's no telling.'

Professor Towers shifted his cup an inch, examined it, stood up, thanked his junior in an absent-minded way and, saying he must get on, left the room. Jonathan took the mugs to the kitchen outside and swilled them. He did not exactly enjoy ribbing Towers, but found he could not resist the temptation to do so. The professor was not himself a great propounder of moral law, dubbed himself a pragmatist, would not claim prescriptive powers for life from the study of literature, but laid himself open to chastening by naive confessions such as this morning's. He would have not the slightest intention of paying real attention to what Jon had advised, still less of following it, but he had offered his colleague a means of making a fool of him, shunting him into factitious vulnerability.

Jonathan reflected that he had done neither himself nor Gormley any good. Next time he applied for a post elsewhere, or a promotion here, Towers would remember, and damn him. If he submitted a book, the press might well consult his head of department, who while disclaiming expert knowledge, 'not my period', would blow bitterly cold on Jon's behalf. On the other hand he was not sorry that he had chidden his professor, even mildly. It made life interesting, and might even break open the fount of compassion. That seemed unlikely. Jon did not care, he decided, what happened to Gormley. In Towers's place he would have been just as unsympathetic, as flint-hearted.

Gormley shuffled along the corridor towards him, nodded sourly as they passed. Jon, ten yards on, was surprised to be called back.

'Winter. Winter. One moment, if you please.' Gormley had no time for first names; it was bad enough to remember the really distinguishing mark.

Jon turned. Gormley spread his hands.

'I wonder if I might ask a favour of you.' A wait.

'Yes.'

Gormley took a few steps towards his colleague, spoke breathily.

'I have completed my book on Shakespeare.' That was news. 'And I understand that any day now the proofs will arrive. I wondered if you would do me the kindness of reading one of the copies.'

'With pleasure.' The immediate acceptance took Gormley by surprise. He expected hesitation, negotiation.

17

'It is not a long book. Two hundred and fifty pages, perhaps. I realise that it is not exactly your subject, but . . .' But, Jon interpreted to himself, you can spell and punctuate. 'Everyone has some knowledge of Shakespeare, however vague, and you seem a person of balanced views and wider reading than some that I could mention, so I'd be grateful for your opinion.'

Jon translated this again: You will read it carefully. You will not argue over much with the views expressed. It will be a cheapo task.

'What's the book called?' he asked.

'*Shakespeare's Obsessions.*'

'A good title.' Gormley wrinkled his nose in distaste. 'Who's publishing it?'

'Oxford.'

'Did they ask Jim for an opinion?'

'Towers' views would carry no weight with them, I hope. My name on the title-page would be enough to elicit an unfavourable opinion from him.'

'Is that quite fair?'

'Meticulously so. The man is not only overwhelmingly ambitious, but also ruthless in disposing of opposition. He sees me as an obstacle to his plans, and the publication by Oxford of this book will remove most of the ammunition he hoped to use against me.'

'Against . . .?'

'Come, Winter. You know as well as I do that he's trying to get rid of me. This will scotch that little game.' Gormley cleared his throat, made what almost amounted to a bow. 'I'm grateful for your cooperation. I will let you have the book as soon as it arrives. And if you could complete the task rather quickly it would be to my advantage.' Again the slight obeisance, an about-turn which almost had the man over, and Gormley was shuffling away.

Jonathan grinned.

On his way home at four o'clock Professor Towers stopped him on the corridor.

18

'You didn't tell me Gormley was publishing a book on Shakespeare.'

'I didn't know.'

'He tells me that you have offered to read the proofs.'

'I have. I had just washed out your coffee cup when I met him and he told me about the book. I was surprised. I had not heard of it. And you had insisted to me not five minutes before that he had done no research for at least ten years.'

'Are you giving me the exact truth, Jonathan?'

'Are you calling me a liar?'

'Just think. Had he mentioned any such project before? In however disguised a way?'

'He lectures on Shakespeare. No student has reported on his conclusions. Not to me, anyway. And he's said nothing himself. I was utterly surprised that he asked me to look at the proofs. He won't rate my critical comments very highly.'

'I wonder if he hasn't looked out some old idea he dropped years ago and tarted it up?'

'If he has, he's not only completed it but got Oxford to accept it. Didn't they consult you about it?'

'They did not. I am surprised, but they did not.' Towers pulled a bitter face. 'Well, thank you, Jonathan.'

Jon Winter watched the professor walk away, and un-clenched his fists.

19

3

Early in January Jonathan climbed angrily downstairs towards his car. He had just left a committee meeting of the Old Morleyans R.F.C., where the chairman had told him that he must make up his mind whether he would play full-time for them or give first choice to the City club.

It was clear to him now that he had enemies. This did not surprise him. He had replaced at centre three-quarter the son of the chairman who had made a vendetta of it. The playing members of the committee had nothing against him, for he had acted exactly as they would. The City had invited him to join them, and had argued that it was the duty of all good players to support the senior side. Jon had immediately offered to resign from the committee on the grounds that he would only rarely see other members play, but they had insisted that his views as an outsider would be valuable. His name was on the list of the players entered for the Corbett Cup, and though he himself had voted for the inclusion of the chairman's son in the team for the next round, he had been outvoted. The chairman had made his usual speech on loyalty and duty, had referred again to the occasion sixteen years ago when in a ferocious 'friendly' against the City the O.M.s had won.

Jonathan closed the door on the meeting in bad spirits. He would play in the next round of the Corbett, and then resign. The chairman called out from behind and stopped him in the main doorway to the street; this had meant the older man had had to hurry down a long double flight of stairs to make this meeting possible.

'I hope,' the chairman, Alfred Perkins, had breathily said, 'that you don't think that my remarks in the meeting were in any way personally intended.'

'I see.'

'I have the good interests of the club in my mind.'

Jonathan nodded solemnly, lips drawn-in thin. Perkins looked away from the grim face. Jonathan made no answer. Perkins breathed heavily.

'Well, if you're going to take it like that, there's no arguing with you.'

The young man stood his ground.

'I wanted you to know my point of view,' the chairman said.

'I do.'

'With respect, you do not. We made you welcome to the club when you came to the city three years ago.' Still no reply. 'It's not as if you are so outstandingly good that you can guarantee to yourself your place in the City side. They'll drop you smartly enough if they can tempt somebody better down from the big London clubs, or the universities. You know that, don't you?'

'Yes. It seems proper. The club comes first. You constantly remind us of that.'

'You're a sarcastic . . .' Perkins bit back his noun.

'Alf,' Jonathan used the Christian name with some difficulty, and immediately he felt easier in his mind, 'you'd better listen.' Again Perkins started back, affronted. 'I understand quite well what it is you're saying, and why.'

'I'm not sure of that.'

'No. I guess you're not. But let me offer my piece. You're a good chairman of this club. You put time and money into it. Nobody more so. And you've brought about some good results, both on the field and off.' Perkins looked surprised, gratified, suspicious. 'You're different from me. When I came to this city, a friend, a rugby player, an ex-international, recommended the Old Morleyans to me as suitable for my level. You, your club made me welcome. But then the City Club and the County and the Three Counties began to call on me. I made no approach to them.'

'I know that.'

21

'But when they picked me I chose to play. The City is the pre-eminent club, and we should all do what we can to further their ends. Rugby's a competitive game. I'm keen to play at as high a standard as I can manage. But rugby's not the be-all and end-all of my life. In a few years' time, when I'm over the hill, you won't find me turning out in the O.M.s' fourth, nor acting as fixtures' secretary, social committee member, vice-chairman or anything else. They're useful people, essential even, but I shan't be numbered amongst them. This is a game, a pastime, not a religion for me. I'll play to as high a standard as I can and after that I'll fold my tents like the Arabs and slope off.'

'Once you've no more use for us?'

Jonathan was calm now, even cheerful, because he felt he was right, reasonable, just even.

'Yes. I've had no complaints before. It's a pain in the neck when a player you want chooses to go off elsewhere. But given your arguments about loyalty to the game, even you'd have to defend me. It's more important for rugby-football that the best players play for the City or County than for the Old Morleyans. This upsets you. It's made worse by the fact that I keep your son out of a regular place in the Corbett Cup side, but I put it to you that if you were offered some superior place in the R.F.U. hierarchy, and you thought you could do some good, you'd be off like a shot to fill it, at some cost to the O.M.s. And you'd be right.'

Perkins, mollified, patted Jonathan's arm, a stout man touching a tall.

'Perhaps I've misunderstood you, Jonathan,' he said. 'I'm not exactly at my best.'

'How many of us are?'

Perkins ignored the pleasantry.

'I'm off now,' he said, ponderously, 'to visit my father. He's dying. Cancer. He's fought it for two years now, but it's spread.'

'I'm sorry. I didn't know.'

22

'He's at home. That's a good thing. He gets MacMillan nurses and all the rest; they're very good. He's in no serious pain, only discomfort, utter weakness. He can't do anything for himself. He doesn't eat, but just lies or sits there, not a bit of flesh on him, and he was a man my size.' Perkins slapped his paunch.

'How old is he?'

'Seventy-two.' Perkins moved his mouth round. 'It's past the three score years and ten, but it's not old these days. And I see him there. He's no voice left. He understands what people say, and that it only needs a bit of a chest infection and he's done, gone.'

'Is he clinging on to life?'

'No. I don't think he is. He'd be glad to go, I reckon. He's doing no good to himself, to my mother, to anybody. He has no religious beliefs. He's stuck there, weak as water, waiting. He can barely get his tablets down him. He isn't angry; he's too weak. But he sees me there, and he looks at me. I hold his hand, but he's ashamed of that.'

'Was he a rugby player?'

'No. Soccer. I didn't take up with rugby until I went to grammar school. Have you ever been ill, really bad? No, I don't suppose you have at your age. I have, and I'll tell you one thing. However bloody you feel, there's always this, well, belief that you're going to get better. With the old man it's not so. He's going to die. And he can only hope it's going to be painless. He can't fill in the time. He's too weak to sit upright, or look out of the window, or listen to the radio. He doesn't eat. He sips water and tries to swallow his morphine or whatever. And looks at my mother, poor woman.'

'Is she fit?'

'For her age, yes. And for the strain. He doesn't want to go to a hospital or hospice, and she doesn't want him to. They're an obstinate pair. Always have been. But they consider each other. It's a bastard; in't it a bastard?'

Jonathan stared at the stricken face. Alfred Perkins at this minute, he surmised, saw as little as his father staring

23

out of the window. Jon put a hand out, and diffidently Perkins took it.

'Thanks for bothering to come down to speak to me,' Jonathan said.

'It's nothing.'

That was not so, Jonathan guessed. It had taken it out of this man to chase after his opponent, and explain his position. Of course, the committee didn't want a disgruntled centre-three playing in the Corbett Cup, but they'd guess he'd do his best, for himself if not for them. Perkins, with his paunch, his broken veins in cheeks and nose, his club tie, his breathy over-weight, presented no picture of virtue, but he'd spoken up in spite of personal trouble, or because of it, and Jonathan Winter found himself touched and at a loss. They shook hands again. Two men in a marble-floored hallway by a swing door, neither sure what was happening.

Out in the street it blew cold. Jonathan made for the car park, stood there staring down from the third concrete floor at the damp roads, the trees, the sparse clumps of moving pedestrians. All aggression had left him, all bile. He hovered like an angel, smiling at his conceit, and spoke out loud,

'So in a voice, so in a shapeless flame
Angels affect us oft, and worshipped be.'

The verse had nothing to do with his present euphoria, but added to it. Alf Perkins was no angel. Jon clapped the rough-cast wall, its small pebbles with flat hands. Laughing at himself and his delight he walked over to his car. Grandfather Perkins was no whit better, or worse, for this moment of pleasure. He drove home, singing.

He had no sooner made himself comfortable in an armchair in his flat than the telephone rang.

Emma Ashley.

'I'm just ringing to ask if you'd like to go to Purcell's *Fairy Queen* with me. On Saturday evening?'

'Yes, thanks very much. I'm playing at home.'

24

'It's out at Gunthorpe Hall. This is a kind of run-through, and they're drumming up a small audience. It's an amateur production, but I think they're really good.'

'When do they mount it properly?'

'May, June? For a week.'

'And they're having a dress rehearsal in January?'

'Not dress. Orchestral. There's money behind this. And the man who's organising it likes happenings, events. So he's laid on an orchestra, and now a select audience to keep them going.'

'And next week?'

'Next week back to dull rehearsal. But on Saturday at the real venue, with the real orchestra to spice them up.'

'Won't it have the opposite effect?'

'Possible. But not for me to say.' He could imagine Emma with her lips clamped close, seriously considering his suggestion. A solicitor, she could give the impression of intense consideration. 'You and I will form part of the small, select audience.'

'And how or why do we find ourselves amongst the elect?'

'Friend of the musical director. He's a client of the firm. And you, a friend of a friend.'

'I've made a note,' he grumbled, happily.

She rang off, having made Saturday's arrangements perfect.

Back in his armchair he considered Emma, her proposition and her person, with pleasure. Was he serious about her? He was. In love? A vague phrase, but his feelings passed muster. What an expression. Now heaven walks on earth. Well done, Orsino. Always ready to go overboard. He walked to his shelves and picked up his Arden *Twelfth Night*, reread Act Five.

Enjoying himself he stood by the shelves, reading. The telephone rang again. This time, Ian Gormley.

'I hope you'll excuse my intrusion on your privacy,' Jonathan didn't answer this. 'I felt I owed you an explanation. You were kind enough to offer to read the proofs of

25

my Shakespeare book. I expected them in the Christmas vac, when you'd perhaps a little more time to spare. But they haven't yet arrived. And this is a university press. I wonder if your offer still stands.'

'Yes. I look forward to reading them for you.'

'Well, oh, well, ye' . . . , yes, most kind.' Gormley wriggled amongst syllables, put out by the directness of the answer. The man clearly distrusted someone who offered to do something for nothing. 'As soon as they arrive, I will. . . .' His words trailed off. 'Has Towers said anything to you about it?'

'He blew me up on the day you asked me for not telling him about the book.'

'And not since?'

'Not really. He did ask me vaguely once if I'd seen anything of it.'

'Was he suggesting, do you think, that I'd invented the whole story?'

'I shouldn't think so.'

'Why not?' Gormley pounced, out of character.

'Because Towers doesn't think you're mad. And that's what you'd be to announce a book, title and all, from Oxford if it didn't exist.'

'Do you think he's rung the Press?'

'To check up? One of his pals there? I wouldn't put it past him.'

'No. No.' The voice over the phone exactly mimicked Towers's organ tone. Jon grinned at Gormley's unexpected imitation. 'Well, thank you very much, Winter, for your kind offer. I'm most grateful. I hope I haven't interrupted anything of importance.'

'No. I was just reading Shakespeare.'

'For any particular reason?'

'For my pleasure.'

'Oh.' Clearly that was not the answer Gormley wanted nor expected. 'What exactly?'

'*Twelfth Night*. Act Five.'

'Any particular reason for the choice?'

' "Now heaven walks on earth" came into my mind and I was just making sure where it came from.'

'Do you know what springs to my mind?

> O thou dissembling cub. What wilt thou be
> When time has sow'd a grizzle on thy case?'

'Not applied to me, I hope,' Jon said.

'No. Not at all. To the deteriorating world. You choose Heaven, and I Orsino's justified (is it?) anger. That's the difference between us. Thank you, Winter, again, and goodnight.' He replaced the phone with a plastic clatter.

Jon grinned to himself. They were all twisters, deceivers to Gormley. He'd be older than Alf Perkins by about ten years, but better preserved. But they lived contemporaneously in a world that had served both badly. He picked up the play and replaced it on his shelf. *The Fairy Queen* next. He ought to have asked Gormley about that: it was the sort of thing he knew, though he'd no interest in music. He would offer names like the quick opening moves of a nervous draughts-player: Betterton and semi-opera. Jon wondered where he'd dredged those from. They were hardly the talk of departmental meetings or common-room exchanges. Neither were Lacan, Foucault, Derrida and Kristeva. Nor Shakespeare and Dryden, for that matter. He laughed out loud. The world proved not too bad a place. The phone rang again. Emma. Could he take Elizabeth Rhodes with them to Gunthorpe Hall on Saturday? He could. And bring her back? Yes. She, Emma, had introduced Liz to him at a concert last autumn, if he remembered. She lectured in the music department, and, a bit of a battle-axe by all accounts, she had enthused to him at their meeting about the beauty of Purcell's suspensions. He'd mischievously offered her Browning in return.

> What! Those lesser thirds so plaintive, sixths
> diminished sigh on sigh,

Told them something? Those suspensions, those
                                        solutions – 'Must we die?'
Those commiserating sevenths – 'Life might last!
                                        we can but try!'

'Yes,' she'd said grimly. 'What's that from?'
' "A Toccata of Galuppi's". Know him?'
'Yes. Later than Purcell. Eighteenth century.'
That put him, Robert, Henry and Baldassaro in their
places.

4

On Saturday evening Emma rang his bell. Outside it snowed slightly, rare, hard flakes in the wind. She and Elizabeth Rhodes pushed into his hall, stood scarfed and cheerfully complaining about the weather.

'It's beautifully warm in here,' Emma said.

'The car's ready in the street.'

'Yes. We saw it.'

He put on his overcoat, and a plain grey muffler. They trooped out silently. Once they were in the car, he asked Emma, who occupied the seat next to his, if she knew where they were going.

'Roughly,' she answered, to annoy him.

'Haven't you looked it up?'

'Yes. But I don't know whether I can remember.'

'Haven't you brought the map with you?'

'Do you think I'm quite cracked?'

She produced and flourished the map, tightly folded, and issued him preliminary instructions. He guessed she could name and number every road they'd use, have distances to hand, have considered alternatives.

'How long's it going to take?' he demanded.

'Twenty-five minutes. At most.'

They drove off into the night. Liz had not spoken except to ask about her seat-belt. Emma issued her directions in good time so that they turned into the half-opening of the drive to Gunthorpe Hall in a little over twenty minutes. They could see from the windscreen that it was now raining hard, and windy with it.

'I'm glad it's not snowing.' Emma said pacifically. 'This is bad enough.'

'It's January, you know.'

29

They drew up on the rectangle of land in front of the main doors, which were approached from two sides by shallow steps. Four classical pillars added distinction and helped support a sheltering porch.

'I thought they'd have left it flat so that they could drive their coaches right up to the door,' Jon ventured.

'Tough birds, the local aristocracy.'

'Is it still occupied by a family?' he asked.

'Not really. They're negotiating with National Heritage, I believe.' This from Liz in the back seat.

Emma pointed out where they should park. He backed neatly in, turned up his headlights to illuminate the hall.

'A bit grim,' he ventured.

'Nothing's at its best on a night like this.' Surprisingly, to him, from the back seat.

He turned his lamps off, and the grey block of the frontage all but disappeared. One light, dimly steady, glimmered from a half-open door under the portico, and another from an upstairs window at the far end. Jon opened his door.

'Still raining,' he reported.

'We're in good time.'

'I've an umbrella in the back,' he said. 'When you're ready I'll escort you across one at a time.'

They gathered on the dry concrete, by the half-opened small door let into a larger one.

'Lift your feet,' he warned.

Inside, in a tall space, lit or darkened with one bare bulb, they stopped.

'At least it's not raining in here,' Jon said.

'Nor exactly warm,' Liz Rhodes answered.

Once their eyes were accustomed to the lack of light, they discovered an elaborate double-door with what they surmised to be a decorated pediment, and touched then shoved harder for entrance, failing on the left side but succeeding to the right. A swing door, without the ornate knob they expected, lacking the heaviness so tall a structure demanded, it easily opened to the push of Jon's shoulder, and they were inside, in a hall, a ballroom more strongly illuminated than the foyer but dull, dim still. The windows on the far side were concealed by heavy curtains but the walls were bare, discoloured, without pictures. Floodlights were grouped on the floor at one end pointing presumably at what was to be the stage. Music stands were lined with a rough accuracy and beyond these were a straggling double row of chairs, some occupied. There was no sign of actors, singers, musicians. One man strolled from one end of the room to the other to disappear; two in overalls wrestled on the floor with what seemed an electrical appliance and a mesh of cables. Talk, such as it was, dribbled from the spectators.

'We're ten minutes early,' Emma muttered in excuse.

Another man, in denim, with a long pigtail, all incredibly neat, marched past, stopped, stroked his sleek head and greeted Emma.

'Get yourselves seats,' he ordered. 'We shall be starting soon.'

'Has it gone well?' Emma asked.

'Now and then. We've been here since the crack of dawn. But, yes. I suppose it has. Snag is, we have to clear all this bloody lot away before we leave.'

'That'll need a pantechnicon.'

'Two, actually. Parked somewhere. Anyhow, make yourselves comfortable.'

He left smartly, swinging his arms in a military fashion as if he tried to act out, amateurishly, some part.

'Who's that?' Jon whispered.

'Adrian Gaul. An assistant director. He's the man who invited us.'

'God bless him.'

They found and occupied three chairs some yards from the rest of the audience, who watched their manoeuvres without much interest. No sooner were they down than the swing-door gaped and a large group erupted into the room, talking, yelping, laughing, apparently much at home.

31

'Get yourselves chairs from the back,' one of their number commanded. They obeyed in a rowdy, disorganised way.

'Who are they?' Jon asked Emma.

'Looks like the annual outing of the Three Crowns,' Liz answered. Certainly they gave the appearance, both stiff and venturesome, of a coach party. They settled some ten feet behind the existing straggle of seats and formed themselves into a rough rectangle of scraping chairs, shouting with raised, cheerful voices.

'Let battle commence,' a voice sounded from amongst them.

'The above have arrived.' Another joker.

Nothing happened from the stage side so that the hilarity subsided to some small extent. Liz Rhodes shrugged, pulling a sour face.

'Pissing about,' she said. 'That's the blazon of amateur dramatics. One minute's work for every ten wasted.'

At ten minutes to eight a dapper figure appeared, peremptorily clapped his hands and called for silence. He apologised for the lateness of the start, but claimed this was the fag-end of a busy day to them. They intended only to perform the first three acts, all they had time for. There would be no dialogue and, moreover, no scenery, a great loss in a production of this semi-opera, but they would have to put up with it until such time that he could put it up. It took time for the coach party to latch on to that, but they clapped his wit in due delayed course.

He explained that Act I consisted of a meeting of the Fairies from *A Midsummer Night's Dream* and their mockery of a drunken poet and his companions. He then bowed. The orchestra dribbled in. The conductor made for his stand, tapped it and they were away. The playing seemed beautiful to Jon, precise, lively and vigorous.

'Good?' he asked Liz.

'Very. They know what they're doing.'

The fairies entered, dressed, undressed sketchily for their rôles, but again they sang with verve. The drunks tottered,

32

the female fairies cavorted leggily around, pinching and prodding, while the poet hollered and confessed mellifluously. He seemed more intent on a beautiful sound than conveying either comedy or pain, but it did not much matter. The short act, about twenty minutes, was well received, clapped beyond reason by the coach party. Poets and fairies bowed together, and strolled off unconcerned. The orchestra sat, chatted to each other and the conductor.

'Did you enjoy that?' Emma asked.

'Yes. They're well rehearsed,' Liz replied. 'It's a bit difficult to know exactly how these comic scenes would be handled originally, but these people have aimed at consistent style.'

'The coach party enjoyed it,' Jon said.

'Bring on the dancing girls.' Emma, smirking.

Jon queried Liz about the author of the libretto. To his Betterton she added Elkanah Settle and said Hazlitt thought Dryden responsible.

'That's a great name, Elkanah,' Emma mused. She seemed delighted with music, singers, players, the audience, the occasion. 'He was the father of Samuel.'

'How do you know that?' Jon, equally pleased.

'I paid attention in the R.I. lessons.'

The second act began almost casually. The producer explained that they were offering little of the original dialogue this evening, merely the music. This scene would show Titania lulled to sleep by allegorical figures: Night, Mystery, Secrecy and Sleep.

'One or two of Purcell's better-known songs.'

'Allegory inspired him?' Emma mischievously inquired.

'Purcell was like Mozart. He could set the joke on the back of a match-box and make music of it.'

Again the scene was lovingly presented when the figures sang to lull Titania to sleep, no attempt at dramatic presentation was made. The fairies listened as entranced as their Queen; this was a divine concert. Neither human nor supernatural being could want more. Puck squeezed the

33

juice into eyes as the spirits danced. The orchestra finally downed their instruments as men and women justified.

The conductor spoke to his leader, illustrated some musical point with a movement of his hand, nodded warmly at the violinist, smiled broadly, laid his baton on the stand and made towards Elizabeth Rhodes.

'I didn't know you were here,' he said.

'Adrian Gaul asked us.'

'Yes. Good. How do you find it?'

'Excellent. You make Purcell sound as I think it should.'

'It's not Brahms,' he said.

'You go steady on Brahms,' she answered. 'I won't hear a word against him.'

'I'm sure.'

They talked, technically, for a minute or two, but not seriously, as if both realised that the work received condign treatment. Purcell, both musicians considered, demanded homage. Liz praised seriously, overstressing nothing.

She asked about the spoken dialogue.

'Ah, that's a difficulty we haven't resolved,' the conductor said. 'There's something like two and a quarter or two and a half hours of music only. That's making for a very long affair. Half seven to ten without breaks. And you need intervals if you're going to provide the sort of scenery and fancy effects we ought to have.'

This led to a discourse on money. The idea was that at the beginning of June, on a Saturday, there'd be a gala presentation of the opera, afternoon and evening, with a champagne picnic between the two halves. Tickets had already been sold out at fancy prices, and royalty would attend. Prince Charles, he hoped. The sale had been so successful that they were considering a second performance of the complete words and music, though this brought problems. For the rest of the week, Monday to Saturday, there'd be a shortened version, eight to ten, that sort of length with an interval. Tickets were going well for that, but they, the conductor addressed all three, could see what difficulties it caused with the cast. He had pretty well prepared the short form, had even trimmed the complete version, and the accountants had, by dint of begging for sponsorship, covered the enormous costs.

'For an opera years out of copyright and an amateur cast and an orchestra giving its services free you'd be amazed how much money this runs away with. It's supposed to be for charity, but I'll be surprised if there's anything above 2p left.'

He spoke cheerfully.

'I've always been determined to do this. And the right circumstances just came together there. No professional theatre, except the big opera houses, could put it on, and I don't think they would. But what with one thing and another, the Prince's presence, and then some affluent American coughing up just at the right time.'

'And your people?'

'First rate. From the director downwards. He has a thing about Purcell. It's something to do with his first wife's death. I hope to God they manage to arrange the big Sunday as well, though it will ruin the rehearsal for the shorter version. But I can't expect everything.'

He stood there, shaking his head with Medusa-locks, smiling like a drunk.

'I suppose I ought to start again.'

'Cheer up,' Liz said. ' "If love's a sweet passion why does it torment? If a bitter, oh, tell me whence comes my content?" '

' "Since I suffer with pleasure, why should I complain?" '
He sang the line.

'Exactly.'

The producer, or his minion, signalled readiness, and the orchestra were away without fuss on the very duet that Liz and the conductor had quoted. Again the performance, as with the whole act, was satisfying, well-prepared. A scattering of puzzled applause, with an aleatory crescendo from the coach-party, briefly acknowledged by the conductor, and it was over. Three men in overalls began, with an ardent discussion, to dismantle what little was there.

35

Spectators left, some carting chairs to the back of the stage. Jon and another strong man tidied and piled. Nobody thanked them, noticed their good deed.

Outside the three made their way to Jon's car through the cold darkness. Already a pantechnicon stood outside the main entrance. The rain had ceased.

'That was something,' Emma said, to Jon's surprise.

'It makes me feel better about human kind,' Liz said from the back. 'John Bankes, the conductor, is a real find. He teaches at Leicester University. And Paul Dent-Parker, the producer, is even more lively. That pair will put on a first-rate performance, be it the long version or the shorter, because they're frightened of nobody, have been here just long enough to know their way around, and not be at the beck and call of every amateur singer and player. They're competitive, and they'll audition until they get exactly what they want.'

'What if the talent's not there?' Jon asked, manoeuvering into the drive.

'There's plenty of potential, make no mistake. And they don't owe anybody anything. Most operatic societies are riddled with feuds, and spoilt by has-beens who demand rôles every year. Not so, with this. The singers are keen, and youngish. It's élitist, that I can tell you. But that pair, John and Paul, won't waste a minute.'

'So this is unusual?' Emma asked.

'Very. Especially with two people of their quality.'

'Have they worked on Purcell before? Together, I mean?'

'Yes. They did *Dido and Æneas* at Leicester.'

'Did you see it?'

'I did. It was superb, and ran for a fortnight. And then they took it to York for a week. People used to drive up there after work every day. That's dedication. And absolutely necessary. They wouldn't do it for anybody less gifted than those two.' Liz paused. They were now on a wider road, headlights undipped. 'But I will tell you what puzzles me.'

'Go on,' Emma said. 'I didn't think anything did, or ever could.'

'It's this. There must be behind them an administrator of their class. A thing as large as this performance in an out-of-the-way venue needs hundreds of phone calls, leg-work for weeks, coaxing and threatening. You can't get royalty just by ringing up. Especially to opera done by amateurs. Somebody knows exactly how to pull strings.'

'And who is this genius?'

'When they did *Dido* one of the assistant-registrars at Leicester did the work. And very good he was. Efficient. He's still there, and working for them. But they say it's our Chief Executive. He's clever, first rate, cunning and can use the services of the County Council within reason. His wife is also mad keen, a singer and a forceful personality in a ladylike way, and she's friendly with a very good young woman in the Leisure Services. All these have come together. Like a dream. And Gunthorpe Hall's pretty well on the intersection of three counties. It's bits of luck combining like this that make these marvellous occurrences.'

'Will they manage this second long performance on the Sunday?'

'They will. And the following Saturday.'

Jon now made progress along a wide main road. Strangely there seemed little traffic. He dropped Elizabeth off at the complex of university teachers' flats.

'She's a fanatic,' Emma said.

'But quiet with it.'

'They're the worst sort. I bet she'll do the editing down of the score for them. John Bankes is an old pupil of hers.'

'What's he do for a living?'

'Lectures in music at Leicester. She told us.'

'Is he a Purcell expert?'

'I don't think so. More of a contemporary man. Has got a chamber orchestra together in London to do modern works.'

'Is he a composer?'

'I think I've heard him say that he is. But he has a good many irons in a good many fires. Liz loves him.'

'Literally?'

'No, you oaf. Not like that. I don't even know what her inclinations are. But he's the most talented person she's met, and she wants to keep an eye on him so he won't fritter his gifts away.'

They went into Emma's new, small town-house for coffee. Emma, as usual, made conversation, pressing him about the rugby club. He gave an account of Perkins's attack and retraction.

'It seems unimportant,' she declared. 'Children squabbling. I don't mind it so much in operatic societies because the basic occupation is good, is adult. But kicking a ball about.'

He shook a finger at her. This topic appeared at least three times each winter. Both enjoyed it, especially he because he could not justify to himself the enthusiasm he lavished on the game. He tried to explain himself to her often enough, but had not yet convinced himself.

'It's quite different from my stay-at-home, sitting-down everyday work,' he claimed. 'It's physical.'

'Manly? Brutal? Barbaric?' she gibed. 'Macho?'

'If you like. But within civilizing bounds. At least so far. Sometimes I think it'll hurtle over the edge, and somebody will be killed.'

'People get killed today. We're dealing with a case now.'

'Yes, but by accident.'

'I'm afraid every time you go off to play. And you've often appeared on Sundays with a black eye or pieces of sticking plaster on your cuts.'

He did not know if she was serious. At work she would be efficient, and assiduous, prepared to go the further mile in a client's interest. She did most of the conveyancing for the firm, but during the two years since he had known her had suggested that there was less and less work for her to handle, and that soon she would be parading at the job-centre.

'Why don't you take another speciality up?'

'Tobias won't let me.' That was the principal. 'He put me on to that because that's where the vacancy was when I joined the firm. And he says there's still enough work for me, provided I'll turn up in the courts now and again, and grub about among law books for somebody else.'

'Do you like that?'

'Like what?'

'Grubbing about in law books?'

She laughed, giving him the impression that she inhabited a saner, remoter world than his.

'A solicitor's life,' she began, amused still, 'is not a giddy round of excitement. It's mostly dull, but the work needs care. Conveyancing is not difficult; people have been known to do it for themselves, though I wouldn't think that's very wise for the majority. But one must be careful. Over forty per cent of complaints about solicitors are about conveyancing. Not surprising, you may say, because the only time many use a solicitor is for buying a house.'

'What are you complaining about, then?'

'The property market has been very depressed. I thought I might well be out of a place.'

'And?'

'There's been a slight improvement lately. I've been kept busier. The outlook is healthier. We're all more optimistic.'

'And that means,' he spoke slowly, word separated comically from word, 'you'll soon, you hope, be engaged full-time on your speciality, and no longer the office drudge.'

'Well,' she drawled, then stopped, and smiled. 'Tobias thinks I'm good as a researcher. I've ruined my own case.'

'Whatever happens, it's for the worst.'

Emma nodded at sardonic and lugubrious length. Jon watched her, the neat head of dark hair, the pale skin and blue eyes, the trim figure, shapely hands.

'Emma,' he said.

'Yes?' Raised eyebrows.

'Will you consider marrying me?'

She covered her surprise, if she felt any, and assumed a mock-judicial air.

'Yes,' she said, in the end. 'I will consider it.'

'And when shall I get my answer?'

39

Again a pause, and quiet concentration on her part.

'Now,' she answered. 'Any minute.'

That appeared too preposterous for satisfaction. He dug the nails of his left hand into the palm. He waited. She, in no hurry, said nothing. He ran his tongue across his lips.

'Come on, then,' he said.

'Yes,' she answered brightly. 'I'll be glad to marry you.'

When he thought about this afterwards, her attitude seemed brittle, as if the minute postponements were more important than the acceptance of his proposal. It could not have been so, he decided, and perhaps demonstrated his or her nervousness. At the beginning of the evening he had no intention of making his declaration; he had considered it many times, but had seen no reason for hurry, had waited for snags to show themselves.

They kissed, and decided on the day when they would choose the ring. They sat silently, overawed at what they had done. In the end she instructed him to stare into jewellers' windows so that when the day came he'd have some notion of what was what.

He helped her wash and put away their coffee-cups, and left the house at eleven-fifteen both subdued and elated. Her last question from the door step frightened him.

'Is this going to be a long engagement or a short?' she had asked, in her court-voice.

'I hadn't thought. It's taken all my courage to pop the question.' She pulled a face at him. 'What do you think?'

She stood suddenly on tiptoe.

'We either mean it or we don't,' she said and kissed him.

5

Ian Gormley gave Jon two days only to read the proofs of his book, muttering specious excuses about some legal expert holding on to the copy for a fortnight when his decision could have been arrived at inside twenty-four hours. Jon did not know whether to believe his colleague, wondering whether Gormley had deliberately kept the book back to forestall any criticisms Jon might offer. This seemed unlikely enough, for Gormley would hardly consider him qualified to pronounce either on Shakespeare or Gormley's conclusions about the poet.

'I'll barely have time to check the commas,' he said.

'That will be useful, and what I want from you. That's what I want exactly. To put it under the eye of a literate man.'

'Have you let the Prof read it?'

'Certainly not. I can do without his nit-picking.'

'Isn't that useful, though, to turn an antagonistic critic on to the work?'

He thought for a moment that he'd gone too far, that Gormley would snatch his precious pages back and make off with them. Instead the old man sniffed, shrugged, laced his fingers together, wrung then loosed them, and said, 'Yes, but only if the opponent has a modicum of intelligence.' He stalked off, walking quietly on his toes, as if pursued.

Jon read the book carefully over the weekend. He was not playing rugby, but had promised to go with Emma, herself away on Saturday, on Sunday evening to show her engagement ring and her fiancé to her parents. He picked her up at six-fifty and explained as they drove how he'd spent his weekend with Gormley's *Obsessions*.

41

'Is it good?' she asked.

'Yes. He's clever, in that he points out things that you think you would have noticed, given time. He doesn't miss much. The critics will argue it's all very obvious.'

'But it isn't?'

'No, not really. Or at least not obvious to the sort of people who'll profit from the book.'

'You, for instance?'

'Yes. And most students. And many general readers if they bother with books about Shakespeare these days. But the experts will dismiss it. And the theoretical kings. And the feminists. Those who are politically correct. Anybody with an axe of their own to grind.'

'And will Gormley mind?'

'I guess so. Like hell. He'll despise them. But he'd love praise. To hear people discussing his book favourably on television would be heaven to him.'

'But they won't?'

'No. It'll cut no ice. Or at least I don't think so. One's never sure about these literary matters. Somebody with clout likes it for whatever reason and praises it in some influential way or place and it begins to catch on.'

'You'd review it favourably, then?'

'Yes. But I shan't be asked. Not my line.'

They drew up outside her parents' house, a manse next door to a Victorian Methodist chapel.

'Half seven. Just right. They'll have counted the collection and locked up.'

Emma's father was the minister of the church.

'We should have come earlier and heard your father preach,' Jon said.

'No, thanks.'

Emma sounded firm. She had no time for religion, her father's or any other's.

'Did you ever live here?'

'No. They moved about the time I left home?'

'Will they stay till he retires?'

'I don't suppose so.'

Emma's mother answered the door. She in no way resembled her daughter, being stocky, red-cheeked, with untidy curly grey hair. She kissed the daughter, and admitted on enquiry that she was well. Emma held out her ring for inspection.

'Give your son-in-law-to-be a kiss,' she ordered. Jon bent a long way to make this possible. 'How's dad?'

'Worn out with two sermons.'

'Were they any good?'

'I've heard worse.'

Their coats were now hung neatly on the pegs, but Mrs Ashley seemed in no hurry to move them out of the hallway.

'You're very large,' Mrs Ashley said, grinning at Jon.

'It's the rugby,' Emma answered.

'Do you play rugby?' Mrs Ashley, amazed.

'Ma's got you down in her book as an intellectual, and that doesn't quite tally with rough games. How's Di these days?'

Diana was Emma's older sister, who had married out of Methodism, and was the wife of an Anglican clergyman in Yorkshire.

'Well. Busy. Occupied with the children.' Diana had three.

'Has she drawn the line yet? Three's sufficient. She should send her husband in for a vasectomy.'

'I'll tell her you said so.' The mother looked shocked.

Mrs Ashley shepherded them into the living room, a place of dark furniture and draughts. Emma's father rose, slowly, from his armchair. He seemed more like his daughter in that he was pale, tallish and delicately built. He kissed her, and she introduced her fiancé.

'This is Jon,' she said briefly.

'Hello, Jonathan,' her father answered; he held out a well shaped hand. They shook. 'I'm not at my best on Sunday evening. Especially in winter.'

'Virtue has gone out of him,' Emma said sotto voce.

'Tea or coffee?' Mrs Ashley asked. 'I'll cut some beef

sandwiches. Daddy's always hungry when he comes back from service. He hardly eats a thing all day on Sunday and then he's ravenous.'

Emma accompanied her mother to the kitchen. Mr Ashley stirred in his chair.

'It's not a long journey here, is it?'

'Something over half-an-hour. Emma wouldn't allow me to speed. She said you wouldn't be back.'

Ashley inquired about the make of his car, and motoring talk ensued. This did not take much time, for neither man was unduly interested. They could hear laughter from the women.

'You work at the university, don't you?' Ashley changed tack. 'It must be pleasant up there. I spent a few days at a conference there some six years ago. We stayed in a hall of residence. Stewart's. It's a beautiful campus. One of the finest, I guess.'

'Yes. It's large.'

'And your subject is English, I believe? I get this information at second hand. Emma tells her mother over the phone, and she passes it on to me.'

'Inaccurately?'

'Certainly not.' Ashley bridled. 'The fault might well lie with me. I am often preoccupied.' He gently stroked his lined brow. 'You'll have a speciality, I guess, these days?'

'Victorian Literature.'

'Anyone in particular?'

'I'm writing a book on George Eliot. It's nothing out of the ordinary. An introduction for students.'

'Do they need an introduction? I should have thought that a young person of eighteen upwards and clever enough to win a university place could pick up, let's say, *Adam Bede*, and make out what was going on.'

'In one sense perhaps they can. But they'll also be expected to place the novel historically, or know what critics have said about the book. They'll also be expected, and in a moderately short time, to have read *The Mill on*

44

the Floss and *Middlemarch* and to be able to say if these books are different, and in what ways. They are asked such questions in their finals as "Is George Eliot the most important character in *Middlemarch*?" '

'I see.' Mr Ashley stroked his chin. 'That seems perverse, if I may say so.'

'I don't doubt it. But English Literature at a university doesn't merely consist of reading a book, and then being able to give a summary of the plot, or a brief account of the doings or attributes of the characters. There's the text. The lexis. Why did the author use these particular words in these particular ways?'

'I understand, I may be wrong, that modern critical theory has dismissed the author as of no account.'

'None of our students is taught to think in that way. But of course a writer is a result of his circumstances, and that bears thinking about. Shakespeare, for instance, isn't dealing with original plots. Moreover, it would appear that when he was writing *Antony and Cleopatra* he had North's *Plutarch*, the actual book, there in front of him. Unless he had a phenomenal memory, which is, I suppose, possible. But when he composed Enobarbus' famous speech "The barge she sat in" he clearly saw or remembered North's Plutarch's account, used it, changed it into magnificent poetry.'

'And?'

'The students need some help. At the bottom end they may accuse him of "copying", but even higher up the line they may think there's something not quite right in having to lean like this on another literary work.'

Emma returned with a tray, coffee pot, cups and saucers.

'Am I interrupting anything?' she called.

'Interesting. Most interesting,' Ashley murmured, to himself rather than to his daughter.

'What is? Don't keep it to yourself.'

Mrs Ashley followed with a huge plate of sandwiches. 'Beef,' she said. 'With mustard,' pointing, 'or without.'

45

'What are you two arguing about?' Emma asked John.

'Literature. Literary plagiarism.'

'And did you reach any conclusion?'

'We'd hardly posed the initial questions.'

Mrs Ashley, smiling, poured the coffee.

'I hope you haven't puzzled Daddy too much,' she said to Jon, 'or you'll be appearing in his sermons for the next six weeks.'

'Oh, he won't mind that,' Emma said. 'He likes nothing better than to be the cause of conversation.'

Emma seemed uncertain, dashing in with remarks out of her unease. Her father watched her like an examiner.

'Have you shown your ring to Daddy?'

Emma did so. Her father held her left hand in his, fiddling with his right at his glasses.

'Very handsome,' he pronounced. 'Rather more beautiful than the one I could afford for your mother.'

'Oh, I don't know.' Mrs Ashley held her ring up to the light, as if seeing it for the first time. 'It's what it stands for that counts.'

'But how do you judge that from a material object?'

Ashley ate heartily, but managed to insert questions, observations and, once, a quotation from Shakespeare:

Love looks not with the eyes but with the mind.
Therefore is wingèd cupid painted blind.

Jon noted not only his error but the care taken to make the incorrect line scan properly. He made no comment. As Ashley ate, he became more jovial, or less saturnine, even laughing occasionally, though mainly at his own witticisms. Emma and her mother clearly got on well with each other, conducted snippets of conversation in which the men were not expected to participate, and once joined forces to argue with the father. He capitulated immediately, saying in Jon's direction he had no defences against women-power.

There seemed to Jon an air of constraint, as if Emma and her mother thought that at any moment the father would lose his temper, jump up and set about them. They spoke, on this account, with circumspection, as if certain topics or tones were to be avoided.

'You'll be a great admirer of Tyndale, I take it?' Ashley threw questions like this unexpectedly.

'Yes. But it's an opinion formed from what I've read about the subject rather than my own detailed knowledge.'

'You don't study the Bible, then?'

'No.'

'And do your students? Is there likely to be a question on the translation of the scriptures in your examination papers?'

'It's quite possible. And they might be asked, I guess, to compare a passage from the Authorized Version with a modern translation. But I don't know how many students would attempt to answer. Or, indeed, if anyone lectures on the topic.'

'Your students would not be expected to know the Greek original, or the Hebrew?'

'No.'

'No, of course not.' Ashley spoke unctuously waving his hands pacifically, as if he realised that he'd gone too far in gibing at the ignorance of the students or their tutors. Emma and her mother listened to this passage in silence, eyeing the men suspiciously, expecting an outburst. Jon guessed that this part of the conversation would be re-examined by Ashley, re-expounded to his wife, once the visitors were out of the way. Jon did not mind; if his father-in-law set out to prove that there were stretches of ignorance in his prospective son-in-law's knowledge, then he was on to a winner; the point would be conceded at once. He wondered how Gormley would have taken it. Not kindly, squashing his opponent with a few killing lines from Homer, sarcastically translated, or from St Paul's Greek, left in the original, unconstrued.

Mrs Ashley had collected their plates and rushed out to the kitchen to return with a delicious deep apple pie and thick cream. This, after fatherly murmurs of delight,

47

silenced the company. Ashley and Jon had two helpings. Jon congratulated the cook, who said the apples came from their own trees. Father, feeling that more should be stressed on this festive occasion, responded with a quotation, half-sung:

' "Ma, I miss your apple-pie. Ma, I miss your stew." '

This he delivered in a kind of chant, and with immense satisfaction, as if he had demonstrated that he was in no way alienated from popular culture. The mother produced, polishing, four wine glasses and a bottle of Schloer.

'We've got nothing stronger, I'm afraid,' she mumbled apologetically to Jon. 'We're teetotallers.' Her husband said nothing, took his glass and wished the couple happiness. They drank together. He said he hoped they would be as fortunate, as blest as he and Barbara had been. Jon was surprised at Mrs Ashley's name, though he did not know why. He thanked his parents-to-be, kissed Emma and, arm round her shoulder still, bent to kiss her mother. Barbara smiled, and he understood at once how attractive she must have been as a young woman.

They sat, glasses in hand, while Ashley recalled some matrimonial triumphs and disasters he had known. He could deliver an anecdote very neatly, Jon decided, chose his words with care, reached his climax on time and did not over-prolong it.

Jon offered to help Barbara Ashley with the dishes. She accepted his offer and led him off to the kitchen, where he was given a tea-towel.

'I'm glad,' Barbara said, once the washing-up was begun. She left it at that, unembarrassed.

'Good,' he said.

'That you're engaged to Emmy. And that you get along so well with Daddy. He can be awkward. Nobody's good enough for his daughters. He doesn't look on Anthony, Diana's husband, with much favour. He loves intellectual talk. He had to struggle for his education. He took his honours B.D., you know.'

'I see.'

Mrs Ashley, rushing round the kitchen, putting away utensils, continued to talk.

'Daddy'll be questioning Emma about you. Not that he'll get much change from her. She'll tell him what she wants to, and no more. She's always been like that. Diana was more compliant, or sly. Emma hasn't much time for religion, and isn't afraid to say so. That makes Daddy uncomfortable, or cross, because he worries that if he can't convince his own children how can he convert others. Are you a believer?'

'Well, no, not really.'

'Oh, I don't mind.'

'I don't think about it all that much. I ought to. Religion comes in to my teaching, but it doesn't concern me. I can see what the excitement was about, but the battle's over as far as I'm concerned.'

'Would you mind, then, getting married at Daddy's church. He'd like that.'

'No. It'll be up to Emma, won't it? Would you like it?'

'Yes. I think I would. Yes.'

'We'll see what can be done, then. Though if Emma's taken against the idea, there'll be no shifting her.'

'I know. I know.'

When they'd finished their chore, they returned to the living room to find Emma explaining some careful point of law to her father. Both seemed relaxed, very friendly, pleased with each other. Mrs Ashley smiled broadly.

The young people spent another three-quarters of an hour in the house before Emma gave the word to go. They congregated in the cramped hall, and spilled out, talking still, into the chilly front garden. By the light of a street lamp Jon read the father's name on a notice board behind the iron-railings of the chapel. It was in gold letters, brighter perhaps because more recent than the rest of the text. 'Minister: Rev L. L. Ashley, B.D.' They kissed, shook hands, even spoke loudly in the deserted, chill street.

On the way home Emma sat quietly as if it had all proved too much for her. Jon said he'd liked her parents. 'Congratulations,' she answered, sarcastically.

6

On the following Tuesday Jon received a letter from the
secretary of the Old Morleyans Rugby Club reporting that
the committee had reconsidered their decision to keep his
name on the list of players for the Corbett Cup and that
therefore were now willing to accept his resignation from
the competition, which he had offered at the former meeting. The letter, well-typed, was awkwardly expressed as if
Simon Gruber, the secretary, had not agreed with the
content of the message he had been ordered to send. They
thanked him for his much appreciated services to the club.

The letter had surprised Jon. Since Alfred Perkins had
pursued him that evening he had thought the subject
closed. He had himself considered it unfair that his name
should be included amongst those for the Corbett Cup, had
said so, had pleaded the cause of those excluded so that his
superior skills could be placed at the club's service on these
special occasions. It was wrong, but he'd been outvoted.
Next season he'd withdraw altogether from the club, he
had decided.

But now the committee had changed its tiny mind. He
wondered why. He could hardly imagine that Perkins, after
his first volte-face, would have been the instigator of a
reversal of policy. And yet somebody had felt strongly
enough about it to raise the matter at the next meeting, and
then to persuade the committee to change its opinion.

That evening he rang Brian Clarke, one of the selectors,
and a player still, to ask about the decision.

'Ted Wareham,' Clarke said immediately. 'We'd had a
long drawn out meeting and then right at the end Wareham
raised this question. He said he'd been thinking since the
last time, and it had worried him. Selecting you might just

51

heighten the chances of winning the Corbett Cup, but he didn't think we would get beyond the semi-finals whoever played. But in the long run and in the best interests of the club, he had come to a conclusion, it ought to be a guiding principle, that players should not be fetched in solely for special matches. Blah, blah, blah.'

Clarke had argued that they'd discussed this topic at length only a week or so before and that they didn't want it worked through all over again. Wareham objected, with another long spiel about rugby as a team game and a lot of other high-sounding cobblers, which wasn't apparently very well received. It was proposed and seconded that the matter should be put to the vote, and to Clarke's surprise Wareham's view carried the day. Harsh words were exchanged, but a legitimate proposal had been passed and the secretary was instructed to write a letter. Tim Fletcher, captain of the First, and the Corbett Cup side, had been furious, leading off about geriatrics making fools of the rest of them. 'I've got to go on the field and play the sodding game,' Fletcher had shouted. 'And I want to do it without my hands tied behind my back.' But that was down in the bar. He hadn't said anything in the meeting, but Clarke claimed that everybody had imagined that Wareham's idea would have been voted out.

'How did Alf Perkins vote?' Jon asked.

'Oh, for Wareham. What do you expect?'

'I see I'm not popular,' Jon said.

'The bloody players want you in the team.'

Again Jon felt unduly disturbed by this decision of the committee. He immediately composed, though only in his head, a cold letter to the secretary indicating that he was surprised that the committee had changed its mind with such remarkable speed, and asking for a return of his subscription, but later he neither wrote nor considered writing to them. A dignified silence would best put the vacillating idiots in their place. He remembered Alf Perkins puffing after him on the stairs to apologize, with his talk about his dying father. The whole matter was incomprehensible to him. He thanked Brian Clarke, who was now steadily cursing himself into a rage, and rang off.

Human beings were oddities.

When he had returned Ian Gormley's proofs he'd received hardly four words of thanks. Later in the day Gormley had appeared, the first time ever, in his room. Jon had imagined that he'd come to hear the reader's comments on the book, but this appeared not to be so. His colleague merely said that Jon had found only one error that Gormley himself had missed, and had failed to notice something quite important on two occasions. Gormley had frowned all the time he was talking.

Jon ironically wished the book every success.

Gormley said that success was unlikely because the book had been too careful in its maintenance of high scholarly standards. Its appeal would be to two or three fellow experts. Jon begged to differ, saying that the book would be more than useful to students.

'I hope you are right,' Gormley had said. 'But you obviously have a higher opinion of the present generation of students than I have.'

With that he had curtly thanked Jon again for his efforts, and had turned at speed and let himself out of the door.

He discussed these two matters with Emma.

'Men are like children,' she opined. 'Games of football are not important, and yet here are men driving out at night to sit round uncomfortable tables and working themselves into a lather. I could see some sense if they were trying to raise money for the starving in the Horn of Africa or the former Yugoslavia. That could save lives. But this, this is just throwing and kicking a blown-up piece of leather.'

'And does Gormley's book fall into the same category?' Jon enquired.

'Not quite. I approve of scholarship. It adds to my sort of life, if only distantly. And incidentally gets your department a high rating on university lists, and so helps to keep your job safe.'

'As long as I add to the pile.'

She enquired about his George Eliot book. He hoped, he said, to get the first chapters out of the way at Easter, and complete it in the summer. He was on top of it.

'My mother rang last night,' Emma said. 'Unusually.'

'What did she want?'

'Nothing much. Just to say how much she and Daddy had liked you. They have discussed it at every meal since Sunday, have reached their conclusion, and Daddy has, I expect, instructed her to let me know that they approved of you.'

'Good Lord.'

'That's their way. They live in a more gently-moving age. Daddy's job allows it.'

'Did they want to know when we were getting married?' Jon asked.

'Yes,' she said, 'they did.'

'And you answered how?'

'I told her that we hadn't made our minds up yet, that you had a book to get off your hands, and we didn't want to hold that up. It sounded silly, but I think Daddy approved.'

'What about this summer?' he asked.

'If that's what you want.'

'Did she say anything about being married in your father's chapel?' Jon queried, lightly but without smiling. Emma compressed her lips.

'She did.'

'And you said?'

'That if you had no objections, I hadn't.' Emma grimaced. 'I think that pleased her. She was afraid I'd object.'

'Why?'

'She and Daddy believe that I'm dead set against all religion, and so I'd refuse.'

'You must have given them some reason to think so.'

'I must. I did.'

'And won't they think it hypocritical of you, then, to be married in church when you have no religious beliefs?'

'They wouldn't put it like that. They'll think that I think it will add to their local credibility if I appear in white. Diana was married in Southwell Minster. To an Anglican clergyman.'

'Did your father resent that?'

'I don't honestly know. I'd say not. They gave him some small part to play in the service. No, I think he'd be pleased. He quite enjoys pomp and ceremony, given half a chance.'

'Do you get on well with him?'

'I don't go to see them very often. I'll ring my mother now and again. But I feel slightly awkward, as if I'm getting in Daddy's way. We don't argue much these days. We've both learnt more sense. And so I'll get married there.'

'Did your sister never have religious qualms?'

'Di? Not that I ever heard. I guess she now feels slightly superior as an Anglican, but I don't know. She gets quietly and efficiently on with her own way.'

'Unlike you?'

'Unlike me,' Emma answered, 'in this one case. And what my father is like is your rugby committee. He thinks he knows best.'

'But he doesn't?'

'He has some experience to draw on. Again like your committee. They can think back twenty or thirty years not just to last Saturday's game. What they don't see is that times have changed.'

'Go on,' Jon said, pleased. ' "I love to cope her in these sullen fits / for then she's full of matter".'

'Who's that?'

'Shakespeare. *As You Like It*. Duke Senior about Jaques. With a change of gender.'

'I've never read it,' she said. 'I don't know about rugby, but my father regards religion in some form or other as an essential element of society, of culture. As he would regard Shakespeare and Milton and Tennyson and Wordsworth. A formative influence. But more so. Young people don't see it like that. You say so yourself. Students regard the cinema as more relevant to their lives than these poets. Pop music is a central strand of their cultural thinking.'

'There was pop music in your father's time?'

'Of course. But nobody would have credibly claimed, especially in universities, then, that Irving Berlin or George Gershwin, say, were the equivalents of Bach or the great Viennese composers. Even Gershwin was surprised when Alban Berg said he admired him. "It's all music," Berg told him, and Gershwin could scarcely credit his ears. You blame the enormous increase of students, with little of the old background, who bring their own preoccupations, and insist on their relevance and centrality.'

'Rightly?' He had often put similar arguments to her.

'I can only speak for myself as an amateur. I find Woody Allen more interesting than, let's say, *She Stoops to Conquer* or *The Rivals*. Whether people in a hundred years' time, when society's differently organized, will agree with me I don't know. I have a feeling that Goldsmith in some way writes better than Allen, but that may just be a rag of prejudice left from what my father and my school teachers drilled into me.'

'Ah, yes,' he said. 'I wondered where your father came into this.'

'He'll regard you as on his side, an expert in the great vista of Western culture. You may not be an expert on St Paul any more than you're a whizz on Sappho or Pindar or Sextus Propertius, but at least you've heard of them, think they were gifted in their times. So, in a way, you're an ally, and worthy, therefore,' she grinned broadly, 'to be received into the bosom of his family.'

'He realizes, does he, that nowadays an expert on Shakespeare or George Eliot is regarded as about as important as an expert in Melanesian languages, something that might be worth studying for its own sake, but not making much difference to Mr and Mrs Coalminer or Steelworker?'

'There'll soon be as few of them as there are scholars of Greek poetry if we go on as we are doing,' Emma objected.

56

'That's right. And soon there'll be a nice little niche in academe for those few who know all about methods of mining deep coal 1850–1990. So much for the Vanity of Human Wishes.'

Emma smiled, poking out a finger.

'But my father regards religion as a centrality. Scientists make no attempt to tell us why we are here, or whether the universe could start without some outside, self-creating being or force to press the button.'

'Does he believe in evolution?'

'I guess so. It's all part of God's plan. He has no difficulty with that. His God is sophisticated, like Einstein's.' Emma was frowning, as if pursuing some difficult thought. 'This business of a work of art being irrelevant or politically acceptable is tricky because it's not very easy to make out a case for the intrinsic artistic value of a work. In what way is *Fidelio* or *Rigoletto* or *Così fan tutte* better than *Porgy and Bess*? Is *The Coffee Cantata* in some way a more admirable human production than *The Boy Friend* or *Cats* or *Oklahoma*?'

'Even Tolstoy found that hard.' Jon said. 'And came up with some daft answers for himself. "Count heads", he said. And if more people prefer "Ain't misbehavin'"" to Mozart's "Violet" or Schubert's "Hedgerose", there's your answer. It's the greater work of art.'

'But that'll change from period to period.'

'So it will under the old system of comparison with a canon of established classics. Shakespeare's out one minute or Pope or Shelley, but back they'll come from time to time, and that makes me think that has something to do with their value. They're not just flashes in the pan. I remember talking to my grandfather, a clever old man, who left school with matric at sixteen and worked himself up to be a full-blown solicitor, telling me that I didn't understand how highly Shaw or T. S. Eliot were regarded in his youth. There's nobody like that now. The papers find a new genius every month, but it's not statistically likely.'

57

'If a writer or composer finds some sort of favour in different times then he or she is likely to be good? Is that it?'

'Yes.' Jon enjoyed these exchanges. 'Not everything. I think the difficulty of the preparation may have something to do with it. Not always. To be a Bach you have to pass all sorts of tests in competition with other gifted musicians to be highly regarded. In our sort of society you can be hyped or televised into fame.'

'You're blaming society? I suppose that's right. Even with us the pressures of society determine to some extent what the law decides, even when it seems clearly written and not to be altered. But society gradually fritters it away into something different.'

'And better?' he asked.

'Possibly. But there's always argument. About capital and corporal punishment, for instance. Of course, we have statistics and research these days. And they help to determine law in a way that was never the case a hundred and fifty years ago.'

Jon often wondered about these probings into literature or sociology. That he and Emma could, after a marvellous sexual encounter, sit primly there with cups of coffee and these debating-society topics he ascribed to Emma's upbringing. Her father would approve of such exchanges of ideas. Jon stopped himself. Would the Rev L. L. Ashley, Bachelor of Divinity, be delighted if Emma put lucid, cogent arguments against the existence of God? Jon doubted it. She'd probably already done so. The old man would then be wounded in some emotional heart, which could not allow logic to be the final arbiter, some centre where essential truth resided inviolate, and that truth was emotional, felt, not to be worked out. Basically he was on the same level intellectually as someone jigging to the sound of the Pet Shop Boys. All the rest was superstructure, decoration, fancy-work. He put this view to Emma. She smiled, looked very like her father and answered, 'Daddy would say that he arrived at his truth intellectually, after a strenuous mental combat, and now it's part of him, and his best part, and best preserved emotionally because he wants to use it dealing with people.'

'But the attacks on his religion have changed. When he started it was with rifles if not with bows and arrows, but now it's with nuclear weapons.'

'Oh, he wouldn't object to a re-jig of intellectual arrangements, now and again. He'd approve, say it was vitally necessary. Though I'm not absolutely sure. His mind's made up. For good and all.'

Her voice spoke steel and her face was set. Jon slightly feared her as one who would come to an inexorable conclusion, however unpalatable, if her argument led her there.

'And your mother?' he asked. 'Does she question her religion.'

'No. It's there. It doesn't bother her. It's like Shakespeare to you. Always present. Sometimes she thinks about it, sometimes not. Sometimes it's a comfort. She doesn't question it. She's not that sort. She's clever, just as clever as Daddy, but she's not the sort temperamentally to run up against the system.'

'Does she never feel down?'

'Yes, of course she does. Just like everybody else. But if things seem grossly unfair or violently evil, she'll compare herself to a child snatched roughly away from danger by a caring parent. The child, scared by the parent's action, is in no position to assess the situation. But it's for the best. The child doesn't know that; the whole world suddenly seems to him to be suddenly and nastily unfair, and that his loving mother loves him no longer, but that's not so. To tell you the truth, I wish I had my mother's temperament.'

'I like you as you are,' Jon said.

'You're another,' she answered.

He saw from the local newspaper that the Old Morleyans had lost their rugby tie in the Corbett Cup. The score, 13–8, flattered their opponents, according to the report,

59

but the O.M.s had played very badly. They had missed, the reporter named names, a powerful second row forward and their experienced fly-half, both injured, and Jonathan Winter, unaccounted for, at centre three-quarter.

He met Brian Clarke in the street.

'We lost,' Clarke said, without prologue. 'It was a shambles.' He gave a cursing account of the game.

'Did you play well?'

The swearing increased. Clarke pulled at his face with lugubrious fingers. Fletcher, the captain, had set about Ted Wareham publicly after the match. The next committee would be war.

'You'd miss Bill.' The fly-half. Jon spoke placidly.

Brian Clarke kicked the pavement as if to crack York stone. Words had escaped him. He stumbled away.

Not a hundred yards on Jon noticed Alfred Perkins approaching. Perkins had obviously seen him and had veered left, turned his back to stare into a shop window, intent on not speaking to him. Jon stood passively at his back.

'Hello, there,' he called out.

Perkins turned ungracefully, nodded, jowls shaking. He looked thoroughly sheepish if not frightened.

'Oh, hello. I didn't see you.'

Both waited, Saturday's match looming ugly between them.

'I meant to ask you,' Jon began, voice low and steady, 'what sort of progress your father was making.' The odd expression betrayed his unease.

'He died on Sunday evening. About, oh, nine o'clock. He'd been pretty well unconscious for the last day or two. But he went easily enough. Stopped breathing.'

'Were you there?'

'No. We'd been to my daughter's, up in Yorkshire, Skipton. She's just had a new baby.' A smile blubbered his face, and he shifted his feet. 'A little girl.'

'Your first grandchild?'

'Oh, no. The fourth.' That strengthened him. 'We got

home about ten, and there was the message on my answer-phone. I went round. And Aileen. Though we were tired.'

'How is your mother taking it?'

'Well, to say, well. She knew it was coming. But when it actually does you don't know what the effect will be. She's staying with us till after the funeral. That's on Friday.'

'I'm sorry,' Jon said woodenly, 'but I suppose it's for the best. There wasn't any hope.'

'No. There wasn't. We all knew that. He did, as well. But it's amazing. I still think, and it's only a few days, "I'll tell my Dad about that" or "My Dad'd like that." It's odd. Not an educated man, you know. Made his own way in the furniture business. But straight as a die. Honest as the day's long.' Perkins was breathing heavily as if he'd chased upstairs. His podgy hands hung loose. A button on his overcoat was undone. Breath pumped.

'Are you all right?' Jon asked. No answer at first, merely the struggle to breathe, then a nod.

'Shall be.' He gasped for air. Spoke finally in explanation. 'The old ticker plays up.'

Jon waited for recovery, and, when he had judged the moment, said, 'I'm sorry about your father. You'll miss him.' He put out a hand. This would be the second time he'd shaken with Perkins.

'Yes, I shall. Mark yo', he could be a bloody nuisance sometimes.'

'Not unlike the rest of us.'

'Uh. Mm. Ye'. Ye'.'

'Let me know if there's anything I can do for you.'

Perkins looked at him with a spaniel's eyes, held out a limp hand. The pair shook again. Jon smiled, and moved away. When he glanced back Perkins waddled along the middle of the pavement. Ungenerously he thought Perkins would have travelled to Yorkshire for lunch, and so missed the Sunday morning inquest on the cup-match. Thrashed Saturday, granddaughter Sunday, lost Dad Sunday night. Jon pondered Perkins's praise of his father. Straight.

Honest. What would he know about that? Or want to know?

In a cold world Jon quickened his pace, not uncheerful.

7

The young couple fixed the date of their wedding, July 17th.

Mr Ashley insisted on talking to them about the marriage ceremony, and this led to some argument between him and Emma. Both snapped, but Jon was pleased to see the pair tempering their arguments to the other shorn lamb. Ashley clearly understood that Emma paid him some sort of compliment by agreeing to be married in his church. He wasted money on advertising the engagement in the *Daily Telegraph*: Dr Jonathan F. Winter, only son of Mr and the late Mrs H. R. Winter to Emma C. D. Ashley, younger daughter of the Rev. and Mrs L. L. Ashley.

'Who's this aimed at?' Jon asked her.

'Himself. Flashes your doctorate. His acquaintances will learn from an insertion in the *Methodist Recorder*.'

'You like him, don't you?' he asked.

'*Amo atque odi.*'

Mrs Ashley had no fears, it appeared. Jon seemed a reasonable man; he accommodated himself to her ideas.

'We're holding the reception in the Sunday School room,' she purred. 'That is if you agree. Just a minute, now. It will mean there'll be no alcohol.'

'The wedding will be heady enough for me.'

'But what about your friends? Won't they miss it?'

He shrugged.

'There was strong drink at Diana's wedding, but that was at a hotel.'

'What's the advantage of our abstinence?'

'It'll save money. Methodist parsons aren't all that rich. And the food will be miles better than anything you get in a hotel.'

'What are we eating?'

'That's a secret.' Mrs Ashley spoke almost childishly. 'I have to have my bit of excitement.'

'I hope you've discussed this with Emma.'

'She'll trust me. I know what you think. Chapel meals are bits of wet ham with limp lettuce and a tomato, swilled down with thick cups of strong tea from an urn tasting of last week's disinfectant. Set your mind at rest.'

Jon put his arm round her shoulders and kissed her. He had never partaken of a chapel meal in his life. She seemed almost foreign to him in that her underlying assumptions about everyday living were different from his. It needed no uncouth language to stress these differences. And yet he would have said that Emma's views appeared similar to his own. One generation had altered attitudes radically.

Jonathan's father greatly approved of Emma.

This seemed slightly unexpected in that Jon thought the old man would look on women solicitors in much the same way as Dr Johnson regarded women preachers. H. R. Winter sometimes questioned Emma, in the guise of consulting her, about points of law. She managed, in her fiancé's opinion, to hold her own, and once this efficiency had been established Winter senior raised his tricky matters with an educational intent. His daughter-in-law would not be caught out if he had anything to do with it. He considered her firm respectable, her principal decent, and said to Emma, 'To tell you the truth, I never expected Jon to marry a local girl.'

'Why not?'

'I thought he'd marry some hoity-toity miss from Cambridge.'

'Just like you,' his son interrupted.

'I was born in Lancashire,' Emma claimed. 'I went to school mostly in Yorkshire, and my parents live in Derbyshire, so I'm not exactly local.'

'Next county. And all north of the Trent.'

'You never advised me to do my wife-hunting in these parts.'

'I never advise you about anything much, because I know I'd waste my time. If you'd taken my advice you'd have been a solicitor like me, not a university lecturer. My father made it clear what career he wanted me to follow.'

'And you've never regretted it?' Jon pressed.

'Ah, that's another matter.'

Jon's father lived in the spacious house where his son had been born, and where his wife had died. The place, with five bedrooms, was far too large for one man, but he employed a house-keeper who lived in, a Mrs Franklin. When Mrs Winter had died, six years before, rather unexpectedly though she had been ill for some months, Harold had almost immediately installed Mrs Franklin, who had helped about the house during his wife's incapacity, and had lived in a small flat of her own about half a mile away. This move led to gossip. The malicious claimed that Alma Franklin had been Winter's mistress, his first love, his childhood sweetheart. The latter seemed unlikely as one would have guessed from her appearance that she was Harold's junior by at least fifteen years. A good-looking, well-spoken woman she had never seemed short of money, and at least gave the impression that she had worked for Mrs Winter more as a friend or companion than a hired servant. She would not have disgraced Winter as a wife, but the subject never arose. She had her own bed-sitting room and bathroom at the top of the house, although she took meals with her employer and sat with him on his free evenings. The late Mr Franklin was never mentioned, but one of Jon's cousins, a talkative middle-aged woman, daughter of the oldest Winter child, had confidentially informed him that Franklin was a brilliant surgeon, considerably senior to his wife, who had made substantial financial provision for her. 'There was plenty in the kitty, I can tell you. But she's a bit of a mystery woman,' the cousin concluded. 'Very much on top of her life. She's let her flat out. She's very comfortable with your father, and enjoys living in that

65

fine, big house of his. She knows her way about, make no mistake.'

Jon had concluded that the cousin disliked Alma Franklin. Probably her curiosity had received short shrift.

One evening at the end of March Harold Winter took his son aside. They stood in front of the gas fire in the father's study. A large oil-painting of some sort of battle, or military manoeuvre, on a bright day by a winding river in the eighteenth century hung in a wide, gold frame above the mantelpiece. Jon examined, as he had always done since childhood, one or other of the redcoats. Not the general, who stood on higher ground, but one of a marching troop, or of a square kneeling or standing with rifles raised, but pointing against no enemy. The whole picture, made up of finely worked-out detail, from leaves on the trees to spurs on the tiny horsemen, shone bright but wooden, failing reality, rather a natty collection of inlaid pieces, all neat but aesthetically feeble. The picture showed to advantage, Jon decided for the dozenth time, when most of the lights were off.

'I've been thinking,' his father said. He spoke ponderously, as if his vocal cords could barely produce the words.

'Yes?'

'Your wedding, now. Your wedding.' Having roughly established the area of his thoughts, he swayed about on the balls of his feet. 'My present to you.' He enjoyed keeping his listeners waiting. 'I think I'd like to do for you what my father did for me. Of course, it will entirely depend on you and Emma. It will be your decision.'

'Yes?' His monosyllable encouraged his father, he hoped.

'There are drawbacks, but then there always are.' Harold Winter smiled, spread his hands, determined to be charming. 'I wondered what you would think if I gave you this house as my gift.'

'That's very generous of you, Dad. I'm a bit taken aback. Where will you live?'

66

'This place is far too large for me. But it is an ideal family home. Largish, but in every way convenient. Your mother had her wits about her when she chose it, when we left my father's old pile. It will take some money to keep it up. But, I presume that you are paying a mortgage on your present flat, and I suppose Emma's doing the same. So that will be there for you to use.'

'It's a marvellous offer,' Jon said. 'I just am lost for words.'

'Don't bother to go looking for them then.'

'But where will you live? Won't you need to do a fair amount of entertaining at home? Your colleagues, or your clients?'

'I'm fifty-eight years old. I shall make no great effort to advance either my career or my status by feeding large numbers of people at once. If that happens, a most unlikely occurence, then I shall hire a room or rooms in a hotel or at the university or some convenient place. But I want you to think seriously about this. Consult Emma.'

'What about Mrs Franklin?'

'She's capable of looking after herself. And if she weren't I'd take it upon myself to see that she was properly dealt with.'

'Thanks, father. I'm staggered. I really am.'

'My old man, also a widower at the time, made over his house to us when we were first married. It helped us considerably. I still own it. I might even go back there. He went off and bought one just as large, but that was typical of my father. He was a good lawyer, but he lived as though one couldn't make provision for one's future.'

'Can one?'

'You can't exactly decide the date of your death, unless you're raving mad. But you can make sure that if you continue to live, you'll do so in a certain, solid, prepared-for style, not as if your next week's wages don't exist. He was the son and grandson of miners.'

'And before that?'

'Farm labourers, I imagine.'

67

Emma was as overwhelmed as Jon at the offer of the house.

'Can we afford it?' she asked. 'It will take some looking after.'

'We're both earning.'

'But if we start a family?'

She mentioned the offer to her mother and father, and asked them to give the place a careful inspection when Harold Winter invited them for dinner. They arrived in Lionel Ashley's ten year old Vauxhall, which appeared not quite up to standard on the broad, gravelled drive, as if it belonged to a window cleaner, or plumber's mate. In the same way, Winter's new, well-cut suit contrasted with Ashley's decent, ancient, slightly shabby clerical grey. This did not in any way seem to embarrass Ashley, who treated Winter as an equal. Mrs Ashley freely exclaimed on the beauty and size of the house, and the richness of the furnishings, and on his generosity in offering it to the engaged couple. Her openness, relished by Winter, was as acceptable to the rest as Ashley's sturdy independence. The evening grew successful, warmly so.

Mrs Franklin served the meal, but ate with the family. She had extended herself with thick vegetable soup, roast duck and orange sauce, iced pudding, cheese, coffee. She and Harold Winter sat at either end of the long, polished table.

'I understand that you don't drink wine,' the honest host said, expansively. 'So we shall drink Alma's home-made lemon.' Ashley nodded, as one greatly favoured. 'Of course,' Winter brightened his voice, 'neither Jesus nor John Wesley would have refused wine.'

'No,' Ashley answered. 'Jesus also wore a seamless garment, but I do not. One has to follow him in the important matters.'

'And wine-drinking is not one of them. I see. You don't know what you're missing.'

'No. And that makes it easy for me.'

As they sat over coffee and Alma had refused Ashley's offer to help her with the pots saying she would use the dishwasher, Harold Winter asked Emma if they had made up their minds about accepting the house. It was typical, Jon thought, not only that his father raised the matter in public, but that he put the question to Emma and not to his son.

'Almost,' Emma answered, like a shy schoolgirl. 'I've nearly finished my sums.'

'A cautious girl,' Harold said to Ashley.

'A solicitor,' he answered.

'And that's synonymous with caution, is it? You'd be surprised. I could tell you some stories.' Winter turned beamingly to Barbara Ashley on his left. 'And if you were in Emma's place, m'dear?'

'I'd accept without a qualm.'

'Even if you couldn't afford it?'

'I'd work it out, like Emma, and see if we could struggle through. You see, I've just had houses thrust on me. We moved, and there was the manse. Furnished. Allegedly ready for use.'

'Were they acceptable? Good?'

'On the whole. You knew the hazards of the particular job. Rather old-fashioned and draughty. Well-worn furniture. You looked at the manse when you visited the church for a trial. If it was hopeless you didn't go. Not that Lionel ever turned down a call on those grounds. At one time Methodist parsons moved strictly every three years. That was in abeyance, really, by the time we were in the system.'

'Didn't it ruin the continuity of the children's education?'

'In some cases I guess it did. Not always. And the Salvation Army were worse. They moved their officers round even more rapidly.'

They sat after the meal and talked at length, Harold Winter asking their indulgence while he partook of a medicinal glass of whisky. The younger people did not join him. The senior Winter enjoyed his guests, questioning them closely on their way of life, busy as an anthropo-logist, and as tactless. Clearly he did not understand how highly educated people like the Ashleys could willing-ly accept such a limiting style. He said as much to Jon when he cornered him on his own just before the guests left.

'I guess they've never known anything any different,' his son answered. 'And besides he's doing what he's chosen to do.'

'Which is?'

'Preaching the gospel.'

Winter frowned, poking at his moustache.

'You've not got religion, have you?' he asked his son.

'No. No fear of that.' Jon poked a finger out at his father's chest. 'What if I had?'

'Your mother was religious. She never went to church, but she used to pray, and tell me about it.'

'You should have let her go to church.'

'I didn't stop her.'

'No, but I bet you didn't encourage her. You could have gone along with her now and again.'

'That would have been hypocrisy.'

Jon pulled a long face, and nodded his head like a father listening to a barely specious excuse from a child. Then the two men laughed, and Winter punched the broad arm of his big son.

When Jon met Emma in two days' time she reported that her mother had telephoned to say how much she and her husband had enjoyed the evening at Harold Winter's. Daddy had declared Winter a clever man, who knew his way about the world. They had especially appreciated his decision not to serve wine, which showed he'd gone out of his way to make them feel at home.

'Saves money,' Emma had said.

'How can you say such a thing when he's offered you such a magnificent wedding present?' her mother had objected.

'Ah, yes. We haven't decided about that yet.'

70

Her mother had been shocked, especially when Emma had added that she thought they could just about afford the upkeep of the house. Her daughter had answered shortly that she and Jon would discuss it again.

'But how can you refuse?' her mother had pressed. 'I wish we had the money to offer you presents like that.'

'I'm surprised to hear you say that,' Emma had answered primly. 'An evening with a plutocrat has gone to your head.'

They'd argued, Emma told him. Her mother was capable of giving as good as she got when she bothered. She'd also enquired about Harold's housekeeper.

'That Mrs Franklin said hardly a word,' she'd ventured. 'What's her place?'

'Oh, Alma. She's the housekeeper.'

'But where's she come from?'

'I don't know anything about her. A doctor's widow. She's worked with the family for many years. While Jon's mother was still alive, and he was at home.'

'How old is she?'

'Forty perhaps. I've no idea. Why are you so interested?'

Mother and daughter had enjoyed the exchange. Mrs Ashley was pleased, Emma guessed, that her daughter was so independently minded. She had yielded up her own advantages to stand by her husband in his work of serving the Lord, but she, from the side-line, as it were, approved the fact that her daughter had no such pliable ideas.

After she had given Jon an account of this conversation, he said, 'What are we going to do about this house?'

'Tell me what you think, and then I'll say my piece,' Emma answered.

'Have you made up your mind?'

'Oh, yes.'

'Then I don't think we should take it.' Jon spoke slowly.

'Why not?'

'I don't really know. One shouldn't look a gift horse in the mouth. But it's a kind of puritan prejudice on my part. One ought to make one's own way.'

'But your father accepted just such a present from his father.'

'Yes, he did. But I'm not my father.'

'You don't think he'd use it as a hold over us in some way?'

'You're not beginning to see *The Rivals* as relevant to your life are you? Sir Anthony Absolute rides again? Lording it over me?'

'He's just generous, is he?'

'Ye', I think he is. He likes you, and would enjoy doing you favours.' Jon put hesitation deliberately into his voice. 'On the other hand . . . '

'Well?'

'He wouldn't completely upset his lifestyle just to please us. I can't believe that.'

'Then what is he doing?'

'He perhaps has come round to seeing this house as a burden. He can afford it, and a dozen like it if it comes to that, so there must be some other reason apart from expense. Perhaps it's Alma; he wants to get rid of her, and this is a good excuse to buy her off.'

'I thought you were going to say he wanted to marry her,' Emma interrupted.

'I've seen no signs of it. But if he has such designs,' Jon giggled, 'and he can be a crafty old sod when he sees fit, then he's perhaps offering us an early bribe, because she'll inherit at least half his money when he pops his clogs. And I shall be that much the poorer.' Jon shook his head, comically mocking himself. 'Anyhow, what do you say? About accepting the house?'

'I think we shouldn't,' Emma answered, confidently.

'Bloody hell.' He leaned over to kiss, then squeeze her to him. 'Still, I was morally certain your answer would be "No". '

'So? What do we do?' She snuggled into him.

72

'Tell him, and be damned.'
'Are you sure?'
'No. But I never am.'
They made love, infinitely pleased with each other.

8

Jon met Tom Fletcher, captain of the Old Morleyans First, after a meeting of the City and County Rugby Association.

'Bad luck about Alf Perkins,' Fletcher announced, holding up his pint to the light.

'I've not heard,' Jon said, not very interested.

'Dead.'

'Who is?'

'Alf. Ten days ago. Buried last Tuesday.'

'They didn't mention it tonight.'

'I don't know why not,' Fletcher answered. 'It's been in all the papers even though you didn't notice it.'

'Was it sudden? Unexpected?' Jon asked.

'Yes. Though he looked like a heart case to me. Middle of the night, apparently. They whipped him off to hospital, but he died there.'

'He wouldn't be all that old?'

'Fifty, perhaps. Julian's twenty-five. I do know that. But he's been struggling with his business. Keeping his head just above water. I did hear him say they were beginning to do better now. But it's been hard work.'

'And his father died recently after a long illness.'

'Yes. Not that Alf spent much of his time on the old chap.'

'He spoke to me about it,' Jon said, 'and he seemed quite upset.'

'You surprise me. But perhaps he was getting to an age where he saw it coming up to his turn.' Fletcher pulled faces, examined his pot again as if it contained the secret of the universe. He slopped his beer gently from side to side. 'I didn't like him much. You're not supposed to speak ill of the dead. But he'd go behind your back to get his way.'

'He put a great deal of time in for the club.'

'Well, yes. Though I don't know why you're praising him. He had it in for you. Him and that crafty bastard, Ted Wareham. They made a pair.'

'Alf thought I was doing Julian out of a place.'

'Well, you were, because you were the better player. That's the bloody idea of competitive rugby. But Alf wanted his way, and was determined to get it by whatever means.'

'Like most of us.'

Fletcher frowned at him.

'You're a funny bugger, Jon,' the captain said. 'I suppose it's all this time you spend in bloody universities. You're out of the world.'

Jon sent a brief note of condolence to Julian Perkins, Alfred's son, who replied asking if he could call for ten minutes to see him.

Julian appeared by arrangement, sat down, refused a drink and began immediately.

'I wanted to thank you for your letter. I was surprised, really, because I guessed you thought my Dad was trying to run you out of the club. And I suppose he was.'

'I didn't mind,' Jon answered. He wondered if that were true. 'There was something to be said for his point of view.'

'He wanted me to play, and that was the top and bottom of it.'

'I don't blame him for that. Besides, you practise with the club more than I do. You know the moves. You're less likely to do something unexpected than I am.'

'You're a better player than I am by far.'

'Kind of you to say so. I'm not so sure.'

Julian Perkins looked across at Jon, plainly puzzled. A handsome young man at twenty-five, one could see that he might easily put on weight like his father unless he watched his lifestyle carefully.

'My Dad was a tremendous worker,' he said.

75

'What was his line?'

'Architectural woodwork. Fine doors and window-frames, staircases. That sort of thing. It's pretty cut-throat with recession, and he's up against some of these large factory corporations.'

'Didn't he use machines?'

'Of course. But the whole job was not done by machine. He used real craftsmen. In these last two or three years he's had to do jobs he wouldn't have looked at before to keep his men employed and the business running. He worked like a dog. Twelve hours a day, and then off to a rugby meeting. I'd give him a hand on Sunday mornings. I'm an accountant, you know. He'd start at seven; I'd join him later, and then after we'd worked we go down to the O.M.s' clubhouse at twelve. He fought like a tiger to keep the place running.'

'And is it doing better now?'

'Yes. In the last six months he was overrun with work. People have a bit more confidence, and aren't afraid to invest a bit more to get their jobs done properly.'

'Did he actually put his hand to, let's say, making a door?'

'At the start, yes. And still would if they were pushed. And he used my grandfather when they first began. He'd done his apprenticeship as a joiner.'

'He died quite recently, didn't he?'

'Yes. Not that he and Dad always saw eye to eye.'

'About work?'

'Partly. Grandad saw Dad as one of the boss class. I guess he knew how hard he'd worked at it, to get where he was. And I guess he didn't see a great deal of sense in it. Any more than he did in the time Dad gave up for the rugby club. "You'd do better to put a few hours in on your wife and family," he'd say. Not that he scored very highly in that line himself.'

'What will happen with the firm now?'

'His partner will carry on. They've full order books for three or four months. Horace Simms is quite efficient. He'll keep the ball rolling. He's not the worker my dad was, but he's been at it long enough, and he'll manage.'

'Your mother will be all right?'

'Yes. Dad saw to that. She might sell the house, but only because it's too big. She thanks you, by the way, for what you said in your letter.'

Julian Perkins left almost immediately, puzzled, not at ease with himself. He'd done his duty by his father, and found no rancour in his father's enemy, and wondered what he'd worried himself about. He could barely trust his view of the situation.

Jon, pleased with himself, drove over to see his father. He had decided to refuse the house.

By the time he rang the doorbell his euphoria had vanished, for he feared his father's anger at the decision. Alma Franklin answered the door, saying that Harold was in his study.

'Anybody with him?'

'No.'

'Is he busy?'

'I don't think so. He's listening to some CDs he's just bought.' Alma pointed upstairs, from where they could hear unrecognisable music. The doors of this house hung solid. She tapped the internal phone, had to wait for an answer, to announce the visitor.

'You're to go up,' she said. 'He's not been very well, but I expect you know.'

'No, I didn't. What's the trouble?'

'Waterworks. And he's had a bad chill.'

'Has he seen the doctor?'

'He's very sensible for a man. If I make the appointment, he'll keep it. And take the medicine.'

'Is he talking about retiring at all?'

'No. Why should he?'

Jon thanked her, not without irony. She laid a red-nailed hand on his sleeve, and with the other indicated his known way. He walked up the stairs, looking down at his feet on the dark-red and navy pattern of the carpet. Mrs

Franklin, or her understrappers, kept the house in fine order.

He tapped at his father's room, was invited in. As he swung the heavy door open a blast of sound greeted him. His father seated in his polished leather armchair, on a cushion, operating a remote control, turned the sound up violently.

'Sound an Alarm' ricocheted from the walls of the room. Harold Winter, face rubicund, laughed out loud, though unheard in the blast. He reduced the volume, to moderation, placed the control squarely on his table, pointed Jon to a facing chair, and questioningly raised his decanter. Jon refused the offer, sat down, stretched his legs.

'Who's singing?'

'Walter Widdop. It's taken from an old 78.'

'Good voice.'

'Your grandfather had this same recording. Heroic.'

'Oh, yes.'

Harold suddenly put a stop to the solo, uncrossed his legs, and asked, 'To what do I owe the pleasure of this visit?'

'We've come to a decision about the house.' Jon spoke steadily.

'Ah, yes. The house. Yes.'

'We've decided against accepting your offer.'

Harold's eyebrows shot up, and then he composed his face. He nodded, very slowly, almost in approbation. He rubbed a hand across his chin, rasping the bristles. He always claimed to appreciate plain speaking.

'I see.'

'We're extremely grateful. Your offer is most generous. Perhaps that's it. I'd thought it over, and I came to the conclusion that I ought to make my own way. You know. Buy a house I could afford. Anyhow, that's what I concluded. But I would have fallen in with her view if Emma had, had decided the other way. I was almost certain she would have done.'

'Why?'

78

'She'd spoken about your generosity, what a marvellous wedding present it was, so I was surprised when she came down against it.'

'Did she say why?'

'She's a bit of a puritan. By upbringing. We both have this feeling that we ought to stand on our own feet.'

'So if I died you'd refuse any legacy I left you?'

'No. Not at all. But this must be a considerable sacrifice to you. This is a beautiful house, beautifully furnished. You ought to enjoy it while you can.'

'Can you honestly say,' Harold asked, smirking, 'that it never crossed your mind that I wanted to get rid of the place?'

'But you could easily sell it if that was all you wanted.'

'Has it never struck you that I'm rather fond of you and your Emma? That I'd like to make you an appropriate present?' He put on a parsonical voice. ' "If ye then, being evil, know how to give good gifts unto your children" . . . '

Jon was invariably surprised at his father's knowledge of the Authorized Version, presumably drummed into him at school, for he had no religious conviction, and did not attend places of worship today. 'Or is it the old saw: "I fear the Greeks, even when they bear gifts"? You wonder what the crafty old devil's up to? Is that it?'

'I did consider it,' Jon answered. 'Nobody would want to leave a place as good as this. And it must have associations.'

'Your mother and I were very happy here. The house was her choice. And she saw to the decoration and furnishing. She chose the pictures and changed them about. And that's all the more reason to make it over to you.'

'We realise . . .'

'Oh, I'm sure you do.'

'You're not angry, are you?'

'No. Surprised. That you're daft enough to rebuff me in this way. And disappointed. I thought I knew how to please you both, but apparently I'm mistaken.'

'We're most grateful. It was the perfect present.'

His father scratched an eyebrow.

'I see.' He waited before continuing. 'I'll need to think about it. It really does alter the situation.' Harold Winter rose from his chair, took three or four aimless steps, leaned on a wall-to-ceiling bookcase where he lifted down and opened a book. He appeared to read, three-quarters turned away from his son, then slowly closed the volume and replaced it, straightening the rest of the row. He swung, rather gracefully, to face Jon, and stood for a moment with his hands clasped in front of his genitals. His eyes seemed no-coloured. He took in a mouthful of air, ' "He was the greatest composer of all",' he said.

'Who was?'

' "I would uncover my head, and kneel at his tomb".' Harold looked at his son as if expecting an answer, and on receiving none rubbed his high forehead. 'That's what Beethoven said about Handel.'

'Did he?'

'Handel.' He pointed at his pile of black boxes. 'The man who wrote "Sound an Alarm".'

'I know.'

Now Harold walked, feet wide apart, to the huge bay-window, as yet uncurtained though it was dark outside. With his back to his boy he stood, unmoving, breathing heavily. Otherwise silence prevailed, the son sitting staring at the carpet, the father out to the strings of lights on distant main roads. Digging his chin into his tie he slowly shuffled towards his chair, subsided into it. There he collected himself. To his son he seemed like an actor playing, not very convincingly, an old man.

'That alters the situation,' he said, without emphasis, to himself.

'I'm sorry.'

He raised his well-manicured right hand to check further interruption, and then sat unspeaking. In the end, it seemed long enough, he sighed gently.

'I'm going to make a suggestion.' He lifted his face, smiled slightly. 'No, that's wrong. I'm going to tell you what I'm going to do.'

Jon now watched his father intently.

'I'm going to make this house over to you whether you like it or not. You needn't take it. Emma will explain how you stand legally about accepting it. But I hope you won't be obstinate enough to leave it to rot. More than anything in this world I want to give you this house. I thought long enough, I can tell you, about what I could and should do for you. I know it's awkward now you've made your minds up otherwise, but it would please me so much. What do you say?'

'Well. . . . '

'You'll have to consult Madam. I know that. But how do you answer for yourself? Will you take it? Speak now. Under which king, Bezonian? You can change your mind later. You're committed to nothing. This is a preliminary decision.'

'I expect we'll take it. Once Em knows how much it means to you, she'll agree.'

His father advanced on him right hand forward. Jon stood. The two men shook, and Harold threw out his arms to hug his son. The old man had some difficulty as he was so much shorter, but he pressed with vigour.

'Your mother would have been pleased.'

'Good. Good.'

'She used to say to me when you were at university, "I wonder who our Jonathan will marry." She'd have liked Emma.'

Harold seemed loath to release his son, and Jon, embarrassed, allowed his father to cling on. He remembered Alf Perkins weeping. Both were hard men in their fifties, but sentimental. He wondered why. Perhaps they felt the best of their life was over, and they must live through other people, and thus he explained the shakiness of control over their emotions. In Perkins' case this was certainly so, though the man did not realise it at the time. Harold Winter had different expectations. He had power, and money, ruled quangos, expected clients to follow his advice, chose his own ways in leisure, arranged his life and that of other people without trouble to himself. And here he stood, embracing his son on a half-promise, not unlike a child.

Jon refused a drink, saying that he was driving, and left soon after. His father's ebullience had vanished, but Harold walked downstairs from his second drawing-room and along the length of the laurelled drive and out into the street to wish his son goodbye.

Emma heard his news by telephone that evening, and said that he was to please himself. Slightly surprised, even annoyed, he said he'd give her the right to sleep over her decision. She laughed.

On the next day she laughed again when he asked for her answer.

'You want to take it, and that's good enough for me. We'll have it. I'm not so foolish as to cross two of my closest male relatives so early in the proceedings.'

'Will you ring my father and announce our decision, then?' Jon demanded.

'If that's what you'd like. No trouble.'

'I would. And he'd like it even more. He's fond of you. He really is.'

'What would your mother have thought of all this? Presumably, if she had still been alive, they would have continued to live there.'

'She did her best to fit in with what he wanted. Or to give that impression. I imagine she knew how to handle him. He spent a great deal of time at his work, and I imagine that my mother received scant consideration if he had to choose between an important job and something she had arranged. But he knew this, as she did, and when it came to, let's say, holidays and the like, he let her have her head.'

'Did you see much of him as a child?'

'At weekends. He didn't play golf. He stayed about the house.'

'Doing what?'

'His work. He brought work home. And he pottered about the garden.'

'But by and large you were reared by your mother?' Emma smiled at the quaintness of her phraseology.

'By and large,' he mocked. 'By and large.'

'The mother's boy.'

'Personified.'

She reported later that she had contacted Harold by phone, and that he had invited her to visit. They had spent an hour together as he led her round the house and garden.

'I want you to know what you're taking on,' he said. 'I do not want to feel that I've changed your mind for you unfairly.'

'I was wrong,' Emma said, 'to refuse in the first place.'

'Do you think so?'

'It was a generous gift. The best I've ever had. But Jon and I are the same in that we feel we have to earn what we own. Especially something as beautiful and valuable as this house. I can barely begin to tell you what your gift means to us.'

'Jon doesn't say much,' the father said.

'The way he was brought up by a canny lawyer.'

'Sheila, my wife, was very quiet, but I prided myself that I knew how to please her. And then she'd speak.'

'Was she legally trained?'

'No. Her father was in the wholesale furniture business. In a large way. And after she left school, she was eighteen and didn't want to go to the university, she joined the firm. She married me when she was twenty-three.'

'Did she enjoy working for the father?'

'Not particularly. She'd be efficient. Knew about the money side. But he didn't delegate much responsibility. Not her way. Though she continued to work for him for the first two years or so of our marriage. Until she became pregnant with Jonathan. She never went back, though I think her father would have liked her to.'

'Did he retire?'

'Not really. He went into the office on the day of his death, when he was over eighty. He outlived Sheila.'

83

Emma enjoyed Harold Winter's easy sentences, interspersed with descriptions or provenance of furniture, pictures, books, ornaments he proposed to leave behind, with their permission.

'But won't you need these in your new place?'

'The other six houses I own are all furnished, and three of them would suit me admirably. They're smaller than this, but I shouldn't be cramped. One of them will become vacant next month, so I can get it ready for my occupation. I shall take Alma in with me. I value my comfort, and she knows my little ways. I'll give you a list of the bits and pieces I propose carting off. It won't be a great deal.'

'It's exciting,' Emma said, 'but I can't help feeling I'm robbing you.'

Harold Winter smiled, spread his hands histrionically. 'That's exactly as I'd want you to feel. I'm a bit of a sadist.'

'I don't think so.'

Emma kissed him.

'I approve of you,' Harold said. 'If I had drawn up a description, or prescription,' he laughed at himself, 'of his bride-to-be it would have tallied exactly with you.'

She kissed him again, and they walked round the cooling garden, watched from behind curtains by Alma Franklin.

9

In June sunshine Jonathan Winter walked out of an examination meeting with his professor.

'I shall be glad when this term is over,' Towers said, sighing.

'More than usual?'

'Yes. I'm getting old. When's your wedding?'

'July 17th.'

'Not long. Will she move in with you, or you with her?'

'Neither.'

Jon explained about his father's house. Towers showed immediate interest; he loved matters out of the ordinary. He expressed his envy with some vigour.

'And when will your father move out?'

'About a fortnight before the wedding. But he's leaving the majority of the furniture.'

'Some people fall on their feet.'

'We were very doubtful about taking it,' Jon mumbled.

'Your ideas and mine are different.'

'I'm sure of that.' Clear and forthright.

The two men walked in the direction of the car park, along an avenue of huge lime and horse-chestnut trees.

'When's Gormley's Shakespeare book coming out?' the professor asked.

'I'm not sure. I think it was put back, for some reason I can't make out.'

'Has he, er, retained a proof?'

'No idea.'

'I'll ask him. Not that he'll be pleased. He'll think I want to borrow it for some nefarious purpose. Was it any good?'

'I thoroughly enjoyed it.'

'Ah. Is that the same thing? Is it in any way original?'

'Not in a newspaper sense,' Jon answered. 'Gormley would regard himself as qualified to write the book because he had not only read the texts carefully, and most other critics, but has known for years works by Shakespeare's contemporaries. So he doesn't set out to prove that Marlowe and Shakespeare were the same man, or that the poet died in "the old religion". He takes up ideas that appear in the text . . . '

'Such as?'

'That villains can conceal their evil intentions and are often good looking, or that society is likely to thrive when a hierarchical order is observed.'

'Everybody knows these things.'

'Everybody, let's say, who has studied for a degree in English. Or did so up to a year or two ago.'

'Then, young man,' Professor Towers leaned on the vocative, not perhaps knowing that a football manager used the words to someone he considered inadequate, 'what's the point? If most of us know it already.'

'I'd say that Gormley refers to all the places where Shakespeare touches on these matters. And he knows when to stress what the poet writes and when not. And why does he know? Because he's read about fifty times more than the average student. Or the average lecturer. And remembered it.'

'Wittgenstein used to say that any assistant lecturer knew more about the history of philosophy or the ideas of his predecessors than he did.'

'He was an original. He wanted to go where Plato had never been. And he wouldn't have been of much use to the average undergraduate, not as a teacher. Gormley is the other way about. He wants his pupils to be sure that they understand what Shakespeare was making his characters say.'

'I see that,' said the professor. 'I suppose that's what is meant by scholarly.'

'Exactly.'

'Do you think that Gormley understands what, say, a post-modernist critic is driving at?'

'Whatever else he can do he can read, and understand, and remember what he's read. I've never heard him pronounce on Derrida, for instance, so I don't know whether he'd consider him of any importance. Probably not. But he's not said so to me.'

'You sound as if you admire him, Jon.'

'Of course. He's doing what all good university teachers should do, he's preparing his students to be able to read a wide range of literary works.'

'That's not the only thing, is it?'

'No, but it's the first.'

Professor Towers seemed cheered by this statement, and left his subordinate to clamber smilingly into his car. Jon wondered why he bothered to lecture his senior. Towers claimed he was 'a Leavisite of sorts' whenever he talked to Jon, which was not often, about literature. His books were workmanlike in that he had not forgotten how to read, but he had no new ideas himself. He was careful enough to be accounted scholarly, and caustic and catholic enough to be feared and admired as well as widely read. Ask him for a resumé of a work of Foucault, he was there at once, and expounding with a clarity perhaps not always obvious in the original. He could give you, moreover, a reasoned criticism of the text. If, to catch him out, you switched and asked him to say why Shelley would be worth reading in the twenty-first century, he would do so, quoting at length, ready for carping on your part. This was, in Jon's view, exactly what a professor of literature should be like, but what he did not know was if the man admired Hardy or Pope or Leavis or Lacan. He maintained his distance. Jon watched the professor glide away in his Daimler Jaguar into the brightness of the afternoon. He could work for worse, he guessed. He had already done so.

The Old Morleyans wrote to ask if he'd play for them in the two annual charity cricket matches against a rival cricket club. Jon had to refuse because he was attending conferences on both dates. The secretary rang to ask if the club had annoyed him, and whether he would renew his membership next year.

Jon politely explained, he'd already done so in his letter, why he could not play on the Saturday and Sunday chosen. He said he did not think he'd join the club next year; he saw no advantage to anybody.

'So you are annoyed,' the secretary barked. He was a small, energetic man, with flopping hair, a lap-dog. 'Don't be afraid to speak out, man.'

'I've nothing against the club. It's made up of human beings.'

'I know that Alf Perkins and his cronies had it in for you. I said so at the time.'

'Listen, Simon. It's all very kind of you. Why are you bothering to ring me up? I've told you I can't play cricket for you on the two days you've chosen. I have a job to do, and it sometimes impinges on the weekends. I'm so busy, in fact, that I shan't be playing cricket at all this season.'

'Doing what?'

'Finishing a book and getting married.'

'I didn't know.'

'Both have been announced in the public prints. Now perhaps you'd answer my question. Why are you ringing me up?'

'I don't like loose ends. I've only done this job for eighteen months.' He'd been assistant secretary for ten years before that. 'Alf Perkins's death will mean changes. Perhaps in a large way. I'm poking round. Peering in. Questioning. I admit it. I don't want this club to run into trouble by default.'

'That's not very likely,' Jon breathed at him.

'You may say that, but . . . .'

'But twaddle. If the standard of rugby is to be anywhere near decent, there has to be competition. Between us and our rivals. And in the club itself, between players for places. That will cause trouble. I don't see how you can avoid it. You appoint a coach, and he picks, perhaps with advice, his best Fifteen. That's not always easy. Mere ability on the field isn't the only criterion. Your coach has touchline critics. Their judgement is never put to the real test. Their Fifteen doesn't appear on any field.'

'What are you . . . ?'

'What am I trying to tell you? Nothing that you don't know. In any sporting club there are tensions. Some people thrive on them; some drop out. You can try to talk your way round them, and you may even succeed from time to time. But feelings are involved; people get worked up; words are exchanged; fists fly.'

'And where, may I ask, does this leave you?' The voice whined sarcastically.

'I'll tell you.' Jon saw no use in beating about the bush. 'I'm twenty-eight. I shall never get any better. At the very luckiest I shall play for the county for another two or three seasons. I've had a great deal out of the game. But remember, Simon, that's all it is, a game. And mainly for our own entertainment. We're not yet league professionals, putting on a weekly public show. And I realize, at least I think it's the case, that there are other things I prefer to do. I'm not playing cricket regularly now, only the odd knock-up game. And next season, though I'll pay my subscription to the County, I probably shan't play. It takes up too much time. Time I can ill afford.'

'What will you do?'

'Get on with my job, and cultivate my wife.'

'Plenty of married men play.'

'Muddied oafs. Flannelled fools.'

The secretary rang off, after a time, none the wiser. Simon Gruber, of German ancestry, now thoroughly English, except that he was known in the club as Adolf Schickelgruber, was a thoroughly decent man, and worked hard for the benefit of the players. He'd do well to take up string quartets, or the local music clubs, operatic societies, artists group and use his administrative skills there. But he preferred to do his bit towards the cultivated society amongst the broad shoulders and the cauliflower ears of the Old Morleyans.

Jon announced to Emma that he would probably play no more serious rugby, and she made fun of him.

'Why, half the women spectators go just to admire your legs.'

'I'm getting to be an old man now.'

'Twenty-nine next,' she mocked. 'I'll oil the bath-chair.'

'I've enjoyed my rugby . . . '

'But you'd sooner bow out while you're at your best.'

He whirled her over his knee and pretended to spank her. His speed and strength surprised her, but he was not sure he'd done right. Emma laughed with him, but not exactly wholeheartedly.

'I'll take up karate,' she said, face reddening.

She discussed Jon's games-playing with her parents, whom she now visited more often.

'I can't understand all this admiration for games players,' her father said. 'I can see that young men like to win and retain the admiration of their peer groups, but Jonathan doesn't seem to be a person of that sort.'

'He was very good at games at school, and won a varsity blue. He's not allowed it to stand in the way of his career. It's a hobby. If he collected first editions, or painted or played the piano you'd think that appropriate.'

'But what has he got to show for it? There's nothing more ridiculous than seeing these old men on television with their rowing caps and cricket blazers on. They ought to have more sense.'

'That's not like Jon.'

'A colleague of mine, quite clever, used to carry about in his wallet a yellowed cutting from the local paper about a match he'd once played in and scored fifty. He was at the university at the time, and the other side had two former test match bowlers in it.'

'How far back was it?' Emma asked.

'Thirty years perhaps. But he still retained this bit of fragile paper, and he'd fish it out and show it to people.'

'Yes, but was it sensible?' Mrs Ashley asked.

'Perhaps not. I was never much good at games.'

'Jon now thinks that he'll have to put more time in at practice and training to keep anywhere near the standard he needs. And he won't do it. He prefers to do other things.'

'That shows judgement,' her father praised.

'I don't understand men,' her mother answered. 'Was he any good at the other sort of football?'

'I've no idea. He's never said.'

'What about this house of yours? When do you move in?' her father enquired.

'Harold moves out on the seventh of July. That gives us nearly a fortnight. Alma will clean it up, he says. Or see to it that it's done. And we don't need carpets, curtains and so on. And most rooms will have more furniture in them than ever we'll want.'

'It must be a wrench.'

'I'm not sure. He insisted on giving us the house. He owns property elsewhere.'

'You don't call him Harold, do you?' her mother asked.

'He asked me to.'

Lionel Ashley retired to his study while Emma helped her mother in the kitchen.

'Daddy doesn't understand Jonathan's interest in games,' her mother said.

'No. I see that.'

'But he really likes him. He loves it when they talk about literature together. He's always saying now, "I must ask Jonathan about that", or "I wonder what Jonathan thinks" about some translation or other. It's good.'

'He's too narrow,' Emma answered.

'Who is? Daddy? What makes you say that?'

'When he talks about games, I often wonder if he's ever considered his own position. Here he is preaching to a handful of people every Sunday, or a few women on Thursday afternoons, and attending meetings and preparing occasional people for exams. That seems about as far removed from the concerns of the majority of the population as playing rugby football on Saturdays.'

'Where two or three are gathered together in My name . . . '

'It's no use quoting Biblical texts at me . . . as well you know,' Emma said, grimly.

Her mother looked worried, her mouth a thin line, her hair thin and untidy.

'Don't you go saying things of that sort to your father.' She called him 'father' to her children only when the situation was serious. 'Heaven knows he suffers enough disappointments these days without your help.' She paused, rushed crockery into a cupboard.

'Go on.'

'Do you think he doesn't realize he's only speaking to a small handful of the faithful? And they don't want their minds or their habits changing. And they seem no better than anybody else, with their petty bickerings and selfish concerns. They come complaining to him, and want him to take their side. And he reads and studies and prays and goes round to them when they're in trouble. But when he's on his own he feels so down. He wonders if he's not wasted his life.'

' "If God be for us, who can be against us?" ', Emma said, comforting.

'How do you know that?'

'It's a soprano solo near the end of *Messiah*. Handel's *Messiah*. Where does it come from in the Bible?'

'Romans, I think. But that's not how it feels to Daddy when he's all on his own. He wishes he was like Jonathan, able to write books. To reach more people.'

'Why doesn't he try?'

'He has. He spent years on one about St Paul, but nobody would have it. He got the impression that they'd only accept things from people in academic posts. They praised it, but it went no further. He's done a little pamphlet on prayer that was published, but nobody paid much attention to it. It wasn't even reviewed in the

92

Methodist Recorder. And he's written a few hymns, but they've not found their way into any official book. "They fall between two stools," he says. "They're neither Charles Wesley nor happy clappy." '

'And this bothers him?'

'Of course it bothers him.' Barbara Ashley sounded exasperated. 'He set out with great hopes, and where does he end up? In an out-of-the-way Derbyshire village.'

'Most of us deal just with one or two people only. Lawyers, teachers, surgeons. They all deal with just a few at once. Jon's books aren't read in every household in the kingdom. Just by a few hundred or dozen students and their teachers.'

'But they attract notice in the right quarters, don't they? Academic journals?'

'You'd be surprised.'

Emma said that she hadn't realized that her father suffered from depression of this sort.

'Not always. But he's a clever man, and so he can't help realizing that he's not facing, addressing what people think of as the great causes of the world. The civil wars, the famines, the refugees.'

'Do you think,' Emma asked, 'that if he had his time over again he'd not be a minister, but a charity worker or something of the sort?'

'I suppose it's possible, but he holds his religion very deeply.'

'Does he never have any doubts?'

'He's compacted of doubts.'

'That's a fine phrase.'

'That's why he's so good. When your father dies there'll be a great, gaping hole left in the world. Not many will know about it, but it will be there none the less.'

'I wish somebody would speak about me like that.'

'You have to deserve it first.' The mother laughed, face red. 'But Daddy's a big baby sometimes. Like all men.' She straightened her face. 'And what's your Jonathan going to be?'

'He's always been clever, and good at games. And he has a job he likes at present. But he says the next bit is the real test. He's published one book based on his Ph.D., and another small pamphlet he calls it on Victorian drama, and now he's nearly finished his study of George Eliot.'

'Is that good?'

'I've not seen it. But that's the problem. He's worked hard on it. He's read a great deal. But he says he's not sure he's not just stating the obvious. I tell him that's important. It's what we're always trying to do in legal judgements. But he says literary criticism's different. And he thinks that even when he's got it right in his own judgement, there'll always be some critic popping up to say he's disregarded Marx or Foucault or somebody who would have given it real weight or direction.'

'And so?'

'Well, he's got to keep publishing, just as Daddy's got to keep preaching and praying. It's that which counts. His career depends on it, and the reputation of his department.'

'What about teaching the students?' her mother asked.

'That's like visiting the sick and elderly for Daddy. It has to be done; it's supposed to be done, but it doesn't score very highly with those in authority. The only people who know about it are the poor and needy in Daddy's case, and the students in Jon's, and their voice isn't much heard.'

'So when he's finished this book, he'll have to set off on the next.'

'Yes. And the next. And the next. By that time he'll be chasing a chair.'

'He'll be . . . ?'

'A professorship. That will be partly luck, depending on what's there, and on who's retired or died. And, as he speaks now, he's a bit of a snob. He won't go anywhere just to be able to call himself "professor". So it's all very tricky.'

'If some time away.' Her mother sounded sensibly cheerful.

'That's true.'

'And will it be your job to keep him publishing, and applying for jobs, and all the rest of it?'

'I suppose so. Just as you have to keep Daddy up to scratch in the pulpit or at meetings.'

'Will marriage make a difference?'

'That's a moot question. Did it make much difference in your case?'

'We didn't sleep together, you know. Have sex.' Emma marvelled at her mother's bluntness. She had never spoken this freely when she and Diana were children.

'Marriage is more than sex, isn't it?' Emma asked, only half seriously.

'Yes. As you'll very soon find out. But we considered sex more important than you seem to.'

'In what way? Ways?' Emma's court-voice.

'To young people nowadays it's just a form of pleasure. Like drinking wine or dancing or taking a holiday. To us it represented the giving, the yielding of the one partner to the other.'

'The woman to the man, you mean?'

'In one sense, yes. And I know you feminists hate that. But in a quite serious way, it was partnership. Mutuality.'

'My word, we're stretching the vocabulary today.'

'So it should be for what I'm trying to tell you.'

Emma looked at her mother's flushed face, untidy hair, wet red hands, and tried to think of her as a young woman. She had seen photographs in which Barbara had seemed quite a different being from this housewife set about with many cares. Her father had not changed all that much; in his early manhood he had always seemed a person apart, a minister, a thin, dark, intense, saintly, touchy creature. Emma tried to imagine them in their honeymoon bed, virgins, ignorant, but in some twisted, unnecessary, self-denying love half a step into the kingdom of heaven.

Barbara Ashley stopped, wheeled suddenly, flashing a silver-new baking-tin.

'It was an achievement. I don't know if this is the right

metaphor, but it was like climbing a craggy, dangerous mountain as opposed to walking on a pleasant beach.'

'Both can have their attractions,' Emma answered, determined not to make it easy for her mother.

'Of course.' Barbara seemed to catch and throw an explosion of sunlight into her daughter's eyes with the tray. 'We didn't know nearly as much as you do. We didn't have manuals of instruction. We had to stumble our way. And the pleasure, such as it was, had up to this point been forbidden, was connected with sin. And that's what made it remarkable.' She stopped again, flicked a tea-towel over the tin, as if she could not help herself. 'I'm not advocating virginity for all young people today, but it meant something for us, for me. Don't think there weren't temptations. Or young men who tried it on, or fornicators and adulterers, and illegitimate children. And don't think that some weren't emotionally crippled by their restraint, and that hypocrisy didn't abound, but it seemed, and I'll use the same word I've already used, important. As it doesn't now.'

'Worth waiting for,' Emma said, primly.

'That makes it sound like a bar of chocolate rather than climbing Mount Pisgah.' Barbara Ashley laughed suddenly, almost raucously, loud. 'I'm very old-fashioned.'

Emma threw her arms round her mother's neck, and kissed her vigorously, with happiness.

'I guess you could give me advice,' the mother said. 'I must sound like a child to you.'

'Unless ye become as little children . . . '

'Ye shall not enter into the kingdom of heaven.'

They finished the verse together, laughing, floury, pawing one another.

'Where's that from?' Emma asked, once the excitement had subsided.

'St Matthew.'

10

The weather proved superb for the wedding. Relatives
dressed to kill walked round the Winters' house dropping
crumbs and compliments. It had been decided late in the
day to hold the reception in the newly-weds' home rather
than the chapel school-room. Barbara Ashley sat seemingly
overcome, but Jonathan's father looked after her, comforted her, showed her the nooks and crannies of the
garden, the attic rooms. Alma Franklin kept an eye on the
caterers, who did their part to perfection. Mr Ashley and
the Rev. Dr Anthony Gregg, Diana's husband, did not
confer together all day, but from time to time converged
and exchanged serious words cheerfully. All agreed that in
these changed times, when the booking of a hotel room
determined the date of a marriage, that the chosen venue
here could not be beaten. Wine was drunk, but in moderation. Conversation flowered, but no singing. Speeches
were decorous and short. Lionel Ashley's, with quotations
from Milton, Shakespeare, Holy Writ and Bernard Shaw,
'every man over forty is a scoundrel', and Wilde, 'it is
somewhat too sensational', outsoared the rest. Jonathan
confined himself to four sentences and was loudly ap-
plauded. Professor Towers, impressed by the house and
grounds, smiled his way into favour; his wife, Jonathan had
not noticed before, was a beautiful woman. It is amazing
what public occasions reveal. Ian Gormley had had to
refuse the invitation, being away on some urgent family
matter, but had sent a leather-bound eighteenth century
edition of *Pamela* in four beautiful, highly polished vol-
umes.

'Have you read it?' Emma asked Jon.

'No. But I shall now.'

At three in the afternoon the newly-weds set out for London, where they would stay overnight before they flew to Italy for ten days.

'Where did you go for your honeymoon?' Emma had asked Barbara.

'Bournemouth.'

'Was it good?'

'Yes. The weather was disappointing, though, for August.'

Emma envied her mother. She would have made something of it if she had spent her honeymoon in a coalshed.

Their own time in Italy touched excellence. It was too hot; the drains stank; every street was crowded; they had to queue and wait, but the hotel provided a comfortable bed and they enjoyed chasing and choosing their meals. Next time they decided they would stay at one place, and earlier in the year, but this time they used the train service twice. Their faces, arms and legs were burnt red, and the classical past beat about their heads like the ferocious sun. They collected books and brochures, cards and pictures and both madly used their cameras.

'I shan't remember it otherwise,' Emma said.

'The bits you don't photograph are what you should remember.'

'You're a dirty old man.'

The time in Italy passed like a quick dance, a whirl, all-demanding on the limbs, but offering only a blur to the dazzled eye and brain. They arrived home dark-red and exhausted.

Their new house seemed welcoming. Alma Franklin had seen to it that the refrigerator and freezer were well-stocked, and surface dust removed. Clearly she had been in every day to draw blinds. The lawn had been mown, and the flower beds tittivated and watered.

To Jon's surprise his father did not put in an appearance. He left a friendly, decorous note welcoming them home, and mentioning that as part of his wedding gift he would continue to pay the gardener for a year. 'I don't want to sack him, because he's a good worker. You'll learn a great deal from him in a limited way, and after a year it's up to you. If you want to keep him then I'll keep coughing up.' The note ended with an expression of his own happiness and a rather formal series of congratulations. It seemed, somehow, appropriate.

Harold Winter lived only five minutes' drive away, had settled well, so he informed them when they telephoned, and was about to visit America for a fortnight. If they wanted anything, advice or assistance, they were to ring Alma. She would be at home; Harold said he had no idea what she was doing for a holiday. Nothing, he hoped, while he was in New York and Boston.

Emma thought it a good idea to invite Alma over for a meal while they were away from work. Mrs Franklin did not seem unwilling, agreeing to come on Saturday evening.

She seemed, on arrival, subdued, in both dress and manner, not nervous, a junior school headmistress on her own territory. She made fun of Harold Winter's American jaunt, saying bluntly that he wouldn't enjoy it. He had met some American lawyers and they had pressed him to visit them, to attend a conference. 'He hadn't been drinking,' she claimed, 'because it was only after several invitations in writing that he decided to go. But these days he makes snap, or nearly snap, decisions that run against the whole pattern of his lifestyle.'

'Such as what?' Jon pressed.

'Well, I don't know whether I should say this, but giving you this house is one example.'

'Do you think he regrets that?'

'No. I don't. The opposite, in fact. But until recently he would have gone over it, sorted out pros and cons, and put back the final decision time after time. It was his wife who, for instance, made him move from the place his father gave him to this. The old man, William Winter, would buy up and sell property without a tremor. That's why Harold's got his present home, it's one of the pieces of bricks and mortar in his father's investments.'

'Is it suitable?' Emma asked.

'Very. It's smaller than this, not so grand, but large enough for a single old man and his housekeeper.'

'But this house is beautiful,' Emma objected.

'So it is. And that's why it should be in the hands of young people who know how to appreciate it. Usually one can't afford such a place until one's older, and set in one's ways, and so you don't get out of it what's there for the taking. Except for these yuppies who've made rapid fortunes on the stock market, and who are buying up some of these lovely old houses in the south. But I don't know whether they'd appreciate their places, as you could and your husband or even his father. They'd regard it as an asset, something that could easily be sold at a profit. At least, I think so. I've never met such a person.'

Both young people were impressed by Alma Franklin. Before this day and this conversation they had looked on her as a bird of paradise, making an easy living looking after Harold, and who had, for all they knew, a wider objective: to marry her employer or at least inherit something substantial from his fortune. She had seemed crafty, slightly grubby in a moral sense, hiding her aims under the disguise of an over-dressed, powder-daubed madam with nothing to recommend her beyond sexual attraction of a rough, youngish-middle-aged kind. This Alma was thoughtful, even educated; she impressed Jon by a slightly derogatory remark about Eliot's first quartet, which showed she had at least read it closely. She said she'd been to adult education classes.

They walked round the house together after dinner, and she pointed out not only architectural curiosities or beauties, but also the places where she would make alterations, were she in charge. She would have completely redecorated one of the studies, but otherwise her suggestions seemed minor; she'd alter the placing of furniture in the dining-room, move pictures around, though not wildly, a mere shift of one or two, a connoisseur's delicate adjustment. Jon couldn't see that these changes had much advantage. As he told Emma afterwards, they could have let Alma loose on her improvements, and he wouldn't have noticed any difference.

'Did you not turn things around when you were here?' Emma asked Alma. They were interrupted by the telephone. Jon dashed away to answer.

'He moves quickly for a big man,' Alma said admiringly. 'No, I wasn't allowed to touch pictures, except to clean them, and only to shift furniture from one room to another. I suggested alterations sometimes, but he wouldn't have it. Those things had been chosen and placed by Sheila, Jon's mother, and what she had done was sacrosanct.'

'Even when she was alive?'

'I expect she changed things about. She'd good taste. Knew her mind. And that meant she'd always be trying things out. Especially when she made new acquisitions. But that was all right; she was the mistress of the house; she could do and, I guess, spend as she liked.' Alma straightened a water-colour, stepping back to test her eye. 'I'm not saying I didn't just adjust this, or vary something a bit here and there. But I had to be careful. He'd have noticed if, let's say, I'd swapped the picture over the mantelpiece in the dining-room for the one in the large drawing-room.'

'Did he mind, for himself? Had he any view?' Emma asked.

'He'd no idea. He could live in a prison cell with white-washed walls as long as there was plenty of light and a comfortable settee. When I'd suggest that some room needed a picture or two more, he'd look serious, and say, "we'll go to the next exhibition. That's what Sheila and I did", and he'd be as good as his word. But when we got there, he'd not the slightest notion. "Look at that," he'd say. "Look at the colours. They're real." And it would be some daub of red sails in the sunset. He hadn't the faintest. But he'd leave it to me.'

'How do you know?' Emma asked.

'Both my parents were artists.'

'Did you paint?'

101

'Yes, I did. Not a great deal. There was too much competition at home. That's why I did my training as a nurse. But we were always talking about art at home.'

'And wasn't there competition between your parents?'

'Wasn't *there*?' Alma laughed with a coarse relish.

'And who was the better?' Emma asked mischievously.

'My mother did big canvases. Circuses, fairs, flamboyant historical sea battles, crowds at public events, and my father painted smallish portraits, grey ladies, pale poets or one lilac bush in the wind, that sort of thing.'

'And who . . . ?'

'No doubt of it. My father. He went out of fashion in his own lifetime. Not that he was ever really in. But now people buy him. He's mentioned and illustrated in books about twentieth century English art. They borrow his stuff now for exhibitions in prestigious places. Especially in the USA.'

'From you?'

'I own about a dozen.'

'Where are they?'

'Some on loan, five in my house on Stockfield Road, and one, two, three,' quickly, moistening her lips with her tongue, 'four, five. Five. No, six. One, two, three, four, five, six. That's right. In my rooms.'

'And have you a favourite?'

'Yes. It's a small nude. A woman sitting on a bed, back to us, at an angle, hair up, looking slightly to her right. The wall in front is dove-grey and light spreads in from over her nearer shoulder.'

'Is she beautiful?'

'Yes. Slim. Well shaped in what's really a modern way. Good profile. You can't see her breasts. But her skin is pearly, that's not the word I want, and her shoulders and arms are lovely. Her bottom is slightly splayed because she's sitting down, otherwise it would be boyish.'

'Who was she?'

'I don't know. A professional model. My mother, who had a great deal more contemporary success than he did, but knew his quality, used to say to me "Just draw the outline of that woman, copy it, and you'll learn".'

'And did you?'

'Yes. And I thought I copied it exactly, but my mother used to shake her head.' Alma rubbed her face in present puzzlement. 'When I asked my Dad, he just used to say something like: "not quite fluent enough" or "wrong place on the paper." '

Jon returned, face excited.

'Well?' Emma ironically turned her attention to her husband.

'Father. From America. New York.'

'Is he all right?'

'Enjoying himself, he says.'

'And is he?'

'As far as I could hear. He sounded cheerful enough. Everybody is very hospitable. He rang to see that we had settled in.'

'And have we?' Emma asked.

'I think so. I said so. I told him that Alma was here for dinner. He said that was sensible because she could tell us all about the house, and where things are kept.'

'What things?'

'I've no idea. I didn't ask.' Jon looked questioningly at Alma.

'Neither have I,' she said, bluntly.

'He sounded pleased enough. It's early afternoon, and he's due at some big legal function tonight.'

'Will he come back with some fancy American wife?' Emma suddenly asked Alma.

'You never know with him.'

'Is it likely?'

'I honestly don't know. I wouldn't think so, but he often does the unexpected. I've told you that.'

'Was he always capricious?' Emma asked her husband.

'I pretty well left home at eighteen. He always seemed the know-all provincial solicitor to me. Except that my mother had twigged how to handle him. Very quietly. She never appeared miffed, whereas he could sometimes lose his temper. About politics. Or a partner. Or a client. Or me. Once or twice. But I saw him as so utterly predictable.'

'Even when he was cross with you?'

'Yes. I knew what would rile him.'

'And sometimes you tried it on with him?' Emma asked.

'It's my recollection that at that age one hasn't much choice. Your glands take over. From your brains. Even if you argue with the appearance of reason.'

'We're learning something,' Emma said to Alma.

'I'm sure Jonathan's always been amenable to reason.'

'How did you come to know the family?'

'We, that is Sheila and I, attended a WEA class on philosophy, of all things. And we used to have a cup of coffee before or after. And then we began to visit each other. My husband had not long died. That's why I started the class.' She laughed. 'The consolation of philosophy. When Sheila started to be ill, Harold asked me if I'd look after her. So I came to live in.'

'Did you mind that?'

'I just wasn't sure. My husband was a surgeon. I was his second wife. He'd only just retired when he was killed. He'd gone back to the hospital for a conference, and he fell into some sort of excavation for a new building. It wasn't very deep. He could easily have got away with a graze or bruise or two, but it both broke his neck and fractured his skull. He was dead by the time they got him out of the trench.'

'It must have been awful,' Emma murmured.

'He set off at nine, full of life, pleased to be going back to the hospital. He'd specially cleaned his car the day before. Apparently he'd parked it and was just asking his way over to the conference room when he fell into this hole.'

'Wasn't it marked off?'

'Not as well as it might have been. They think he slipped on a plank which was greasy. It had rained the night before. That was why he was walking on this plank alongside the trench, because the ground was all ploughed up and muddy. And he was meticulous about his shoes. Always kept them polished. The workmen had left things lying about, both in and out of the excavation. A couple saw him go over. They rushed across. Paramedics, I think; they were used to accidents, but they couldn't do anything for him.'

'It must have been a tremendous shock.'

'Well, yes. He was there. Himself as I'd always known him. And then suddenly wiped out. I came to the hospital. They let me see him. It left me at a loose end. Harry was an energetic man, even at sixty-seven.' She looked about her, as if for strength. 'When I come to think of it, it might have been for the best, if you could say such a thing. He'd no outside interests. He played golf at one time, but he'd given it up. Nothing existed outside his work. He had private patients as well as NHS. He kept up with all the latest developments, and there were a good many. He wrote papers for *The Lancet*. And the job gave him status. He might have complained, but he loved the ward-rounds, haranguing his students. It gave him a place. He was respected. And above all he never lost his interest in the operating theatre. You would have thought he'd seen it all, done it all, that he was ready for his young men to take over. But it wasn't so. He loved it.'

'Retirement didn't suit him.'

'Not one bit. He was asked to give a lecture or two when he first retired, but, as he said, they wanted to hear from performers, not has-beens. He did a day a week for an insurance company. But it wasn't money he wanted. You understand me?'

' "Othello's occupation's gone",' Jon quoted. Alma looked affronted.

'In a year or two, unless something had drastically changed,' Alma continued, 'he would have been lost. I could see it coming. I dreaded it.'

'How long ago's this?' Emma asked.

'Very nearly ten years. Harry would have been seventy-seven next October.'

'He was much older than you?'

'Thirty-eight years.'

She smiled almost brightly.

'He was a good man. Respected for his work. And this accident cut him off before he'd had time to become depressed. It didn't seem like that at the time, I can tell you. I thought I'd never get over it. But you do. You do.'

'Did you go back to work?'

'No. He left me pretty well off. I'd no dependants. There was no need.'

'So you have no necessity to work for my father?'

'Financially, no.'

'Otherwise?'

Alma shrugged, histrionically, smiled broadly but did not answer.

'You and the old man seem to get on pretty well,' Jon ventured.

'Well, Harold's another who's immersed in his work. When Sheila was first sick, he'd no idea how to manage. You were away at university, and didn't always come home for the holidays. They knew, both of them, how seriously ill she was, and what the chances were of survival. I don't know if they told you at the time, or how much?'

'They said it was cancer, and serious.' Jon answered. 'I think, at first, Harold hoped for a miracle, that my mother would prove an exception.'

'Yes. Your mother was a remarkable woman. Religious, in a way. She put up with the pain and discomfort and humiliation like a saint, never made a song and dance about it. Nor assumed a holy face with it. I loved her. "I'm a nuisance to you, Alma," she'd say. I felt like crying sometimes. It was so unfair. She wasn't very much older than I was. Six or seven years. In her forties. And there she was marked down to die. She'd persuaded Harold to buy this house, and she decorated, furnished and organised it. Jon was doing really well at university. She and her

106

husband had engaged in all sorts of charitable work together. And she wouldn't see the end of any of it. She had looked forward to attending Jon's degree ceremony, for instance, and having photographs of it. But it wasn't to be. He was only in his second year when she died. It knocked Harold sideways.'

'Um?' Emma murmured her interest.

'Harold's father was a man who had worked his way upwards by his own efforts. Harold followed him into the law, but by way of the university. I think, I didn't know him, that William, his father, was surprised that he didn't want to be a barrister but "only a solicitor". In William's view, Harold started life with many advantages over most people. And Harold thought the same. But they both had this idea that if you worked hard, gave value for money, all would be well. And in Harold's case he put a lot back into society with his charitable enterprises. I often think with such affairs that people become presidents or secretaries or committee chairmen because they like to throw their weight about, feel the power, give orders to all and sundry, organize this scheme or inaugurate that campaign for the sake of their own ego. But in Harold's case I don't honestly think that this was so. Or at least not the primary cause. He wanted to put back something into the society that had been so good to him.'

'And?' Emma harried the woman.

'He did all this and what happens? His wife, whom he adored, is struck down, is doomed to die on him. It seemed unjust. And it was. There was no justice in it. That's often the case. Harold didn't believe in God or the after-life. We had our span here, long or short. I remember seeing him on a beautiful spring morning in the garden not long after Sheila died, and he pointed to a little, featherless, new-born bird lying there dead. It must have fallen out of the nest. And I remember the church bells ringing, not that he cared much for that, so it must have been Sunday. And he said, "Well, that poor creature's few hours of life can't have changed the universe much." '

'And what did you say?' Emma asked.

'I told him that when most of us have had our full seventy or eighty years it wouldn't have altered the universe by all that much. And then he said something that really surprised me. "If we believed in divine providence then the few minutes that the fledgling lived would be accounted for, be an integral part of the pattern." He'd never said anything like that before. Well, it was religious in a way. And I thought his wife's death had affected him. He asked me later what I was thinking of doing, whether I intended to go back to nursing, and if I'd consider staying on and looking after him.'

'Was he ill, then?' Emma asked.

'No. In no way. But he wanted continuity. I certainly hadn't thought of it. I'd let my house, but once Sheila had died I expected to move back there. The tenants were going in August, but suddenly asked the agent at the last minute if they could have it for a further two years. I suppose that helped me make my mind up. So I stayed. It's eight years now.'

'You get on with my father?'

'Yes. Though I have less and less to do with him. Just after your mother died, we were very close, helping to support each other. But he grew out of his grief, and found more and more things to do. And that's as it should be. I thought he'd perhaps marry again, and I should have to go, but it never happened. But you never know, he's not sixty yet.'

'Is he happy, d'you think?' Emma asked.

'You should ask Jon. He knew him when he was young, and was successful for the first time in his own right, and had a wife, and something of a large future.'

'Well?' Emma asked Jon.

'Contented, I'd guess,' he answered. 'He does what he wants to do. He's successful at his office. He has influential contacts. Why do you ask? Do you think he isn't?'

'It was the giving away of this house. I wondered if he was quite as settled or satisfied as you think. I wondered if he wasn't trying to change something. I mean, radically change. Make something happen in his life. Giving away his house seems so unusual.'

'He can be very generous,' Alma said. 'And I'm sure he's very fond of you both.'

At dinner Alma talked freely of the hospital training, of her life with her husband. She ate and drank with relish but sparingly, described the holiday, a cruise, she intended to take to Scandinavia.

'Will Harold be all right?' Emma inquired.

'He doesn't need me.'

Alma had come by car because she said she feared walking the streets at night. She drove off into the half-darkness, smartly, like a chauffeur.

'More there than meets the eye?' Jon said, back in the house.

'What makes you say that?'

'She thinks about things. I didn't expect that. I'd written her off as an overdressed feather-head. The old man could do worse than marry her.'

'Just because she attends WEA classes on philosophy or literature doesn't make her perfect.'

'Really? But I liked her. And I didn't expect to, even though I thought I knew her quite well.'

'Has she been your father's mistress?'

'I'd never even considered it.'

'Do so now,' Emma said.

'It's quite possible. He's not as old as all that. On the other hand I guess he'd be very wary about entering a relationship he couldn't exactly weigh up or see the end of.'

'He married your mother?'

'He was younger. And in love. Like his son.'

'We don't know how our marriage will end,' Emma said.

'Do we want to?' he asked.

Hand in hand they made their way up the wide staircase. Emma hummed loudly.

'What's that?' he asked.

' "Prepare thyself, Zion, with tender affection." '

'Um,' he said. 'It seems appropriate.'

11

By the third week in August Jon Winter had completed his final draft of the book on George Eliot. Emma spent any leisure she had from the garden reading it. Jon attempted to elicit her views, but she seemed reluctant to be drawn.

'I'm quite enjoying it,' she said. 'And I'm learning a great deal.'

'What's wrong with it, then?'

'I haven't said there's anything wrong with it.'

'But you think so. Don't you?'

'No, I don't. Not at all.'

'What is it you don't like about it?'

'I've just told you I enjoyed it.'

'What are your reservations?'

Emma looked at him. She wore half-moon glasses to read and they seemed inappropriate to the beauty of her face, though they by no means spoilt it.

'Sometimes I don't quite understand the language you use. And you seem to refer to theories I don't understand.'

'Publishers want that sort of stuff these days.'

'But, in my case, and I'm ignorant, I admit, it gets between you and me.'

'Isn't that exactly the case,' he objected, 'with legal jargon. Ordinary people don't understand it, but it's there in that form for other lawyers so that they know exactly what was intended. They're sometimes unsuccessful. And they don't altogether mind about this, because it means argument and that will make them rich. But the principle is the same. Because nowadays literature's in the hands of academics; they are writing to enlighten or impress their fellow practitioners rather than the man in the street.'

'And you approve?'

'No. I'm like old Gormley. I'd like to write for the well-educated historian or scientist or lawyer rather than the closed circuit of university conferences and common-rooms.'

'Why don't you then?' she asked.

'I shouldn't get published.'

'But Gormley did.'

'To the amazement of the prof, for example. He wouldn't have recommended it to a publisher, even though it's to his advantage to have plenty of books coming out from his department.'

'How did it get accepted, then?'

'Nobody knows. We all begin to think that Gormley must have friends in high or, at least, the right places.'

The argument continued, easy-going and sprightly enough, enlivened with gin and sex, but it was from this evening that Emma dated a change in her husband. He made no attempt to send his typescript off, but spent much time gloomily checking it through, making alterations. He complained that he was dissatisfied, but would not say why.

'Everybody feels like that,' Emma argued, 'at the end of a long, tricky piece of work. You can never be sure that you've said exactly what you meant.'

'That's why I'm reading it.'

'Show it to the prof.'

'His view's of no importance. It's outside his period. In any case I wouldn't trust his judgement.'

'You don't seem to trust your own.'

A few days later, on an evening of humid heat, over the light meal he had prepared Jon said, 'I've lost confidence in myself. Over this book.'

'What's wrong with it?'

'That's what I can't say. I read it through and it seems I've said nothing that hasn't been said before, and better. It's not original; I'm not even sure that what I put down is anywhere near the truth.'

Emma, eating hard for she was hungry after a whole day without meals dashing between a dusty office and court-house, paused, cleared her mouth with wine and lectured him, as though talking to a valued, decent, but rather obtuse client.

'First, the people who read and profit from your book won't have read one twentieth of what you've read. So these truisms you come out with, and I don't doubt you've acknowledged your sources, will be new to them. And it's your arrangement of them that counts.'

'You're an expert, then?'

She recognized the exasperation of fear in his voice, and smiled, continuing to eat, appearing to cogitate. Clearing her mouth, she continued. 'Not on George Eliot, no.'

'On what, then?'

'Just stop interrupting and listen to me, will you? I don't doubt that it is in your arrangement of the researches and insights of other people that your originality, or strength, lies. If you've done your work properly, and I expect you have, you've ordered the conclusions of others, adjudicated on them, laid emphasis on those you think are important. Originality doesn't much apply to lit. crit. It's like law. You look at the work of your predecessors, and use it. It's not original, but if you and they have done it properly it's useful. You point out what's wrong with your predecessors and why they haven't got it right. You clear the ground so that your students, intelligent young people without a great deal of time, can read George Eliot properly. You help them to see what's there, and what their ignorance prevents them from grasping. As to origin-ality, well, you might discover in one case in ten thou-sand something that nobody knew or suspected before: that George Eliot was a lesbian or practised levitation and wrote her novels ten feet off the ground.' He soured his mouth at this. 'The other sort of originality is when you interpret an old book by modern standards, make Shakespeare our contemporary, make what a writer said about his time seem specially applicable to our period.

That could be useful. I don't think your book does that but you do explain why you think George Eliot is worth reading. You don't chase hares: saying why Eliot is better than Dickens and Thackeray. You say why in your view what she says is worth listening to, and that should make your pupils think and re-read. And that's what you're there for.'

They argued thus through the meal and afterwards. Emma did the majority of the talking; he grudgingly offered a few contrary opinions, but without enthusiasm. The argument continued over the next few days, without conclusion. Jon set off for his office at the university to prepare or realign his lectures for the new term, but his pile of typescript remained. His life sagged.

On the following Saturday Emma made her move.

'We'll pack your book up and send it off.'

'To whom?'

'Same lot as last time. Routledge, was it?'

'They won't be interested.'

'We'll try it. You don't know.' She set her face, ready for opposition, but none came. She wondered if he needed her to bully him into action. 'You write them a letter, quick, and tell them they can have it on computer disk if they want it. Otherwise, three sentences explaining what the book's about.'

'They'll know that.'

'Run along, and do as auntie tells you.'

She walked to the post office and sent the packet off, registered delivery. He argued that if they left it until Monday the university would pay the postage. She replied that she wasn't altogether poor. He accompanied her to the front gate saying nothing, not quite hangdog; she feared he'd tag along with her the whole half-mile, but he did not. He stood, one hand on the front gate, like a man without bones.

On her return he seemed slightly more cheerful, and went out for a preliminary training session with the rugby club. When he returned he claimed that it had been far too hot

114

for anything too energetic, and that in any case he was quite unfit, that he would have done better to do a stint in the garden. He seemed suspicious of the world, taciturn, not surly but not interested. When she failed after a day or two to persuade him to let Professor Towers or Ian Gormley read the typescript, she tried a different tack.

'I tell you what. Let my father read it. He's the sort of non-expert we need. He's sharp on the uptake.'

'Wouldn't it be like his asking me to comment on the Psalms with no knowledge of Hebrew?'

'Most readers of the Psalms don't know the original language.'

'Most people don't read the Psalms.'

'Nor George Eliot for that matter.'

She delivered the work to her father, who seemed flattered.

'I'll need to read George Eliot's novels again.'

'Fair enough. Do you have copies?'

It appeared that he had. He reported that he read *Silas Marner* out loud for an hour each evening to his wife.

'I've not enjoyed anything so much for years,' Barbara confessed.

Ashley did not report very quickly on Jon's book, but Barbara said he was reading it carefully, making a meal of it.

Jon continued with his preparation for the new term, began training with the City rugby club, prepared meals in time for Emma's return from her office, but though he worked a full day he did it without zest.

'I'm perfectly all right,' he told Emma. 'I'm resting.'

He wrote an article commissioned by the *TLS* on the influence of philosophers on novel writing. He groaned, but the editor expressed satisfaction. They had heard nothing, as expected, from the publishers about the George Eliot book.

In the end, at the beginning of September, Lionel Ashley wrote a long letter, seventeen pages, expressing his views. He had greatly enjoyed the book, which had enlivened him,

and sent him back time and again to the novels. Occasionally he had been put off by, and failed to understand, the
theoretical jargon, but he presumed this was included for
the satisfaction of fellow academics.

Jon had visited his father-in-law on his own, and had
spent a couple of hours with him. Ashley had said that the
book would be useful to students because it pointed
out time and again matters they would have missed.
'Pretty well every time you drew attention to something I
hadn't noticed I had to admit that you were right, and
that I ought to have spotted it for myself.' Ashley
said, tentatively at first, then more strongly under Jon's
encouragement, that he resented the authorial interventions in *Middlemarch*. He saw the power, the liveli-
ness of the novelist's mind, but she interfered with his
reading.

'That's the idea. You wouldn't object to a bit of authorial guidance in a sermon.'

'A novel's not a sermon.'

'George Eliot was concerned with its moral aspects.'

'A novel should entertain.'

'So should a sermon.'

'To some extent,' Ashley admitted, 'but that's by no
means its first endeavour. I'm not sure that it was Eliot's
first aim.'

'Why did Jesus do his teaching by parables?'

'Presumably because his sort of society found that sort of
teaching not only palatable but powerful. The audiences
remembered the story, and then the doctrine associated
with it.'

'If they understood.'

'True. Even the disciples were a bit baffled sometimes.
But a parable's a very short, oral, self-contained story, as
opposed to the complicated length of a novel. The text
there is much more diffuse, aiming at more targets, acting
over a wider field, and often more subtly. That's what my
critical, theoretical jargon is trying to do, to make an
exploration of these facets. I know the cynical suggest that

116

I'm just showing that I know and can handle the terms and modes of thought of modern, post-modern critical theory, but I think they throw some light on areas that we've tended to neglect.'

Jon talked to his father-in-law for an hour and a half to the delight of Barbara who reported that Lionel was like a dog with two tails, pleased as punch that this dialogue had taken place; Lionel had been down in the mouth, but was ready now for his duties. The afternoon had done him more good than their fortnight's holiday in Bournemouth.

Emma saw no such improvement in her husband.

Jon reported that clearly Lionel had read Eliot and at least some parts of his book. His father-in-law was clever enough, had a literary background of sorts, but tended to cut corners or concentrate only on the bits that he understood or which caught his fancy.

'Like all of us,' Emma objected.

'Yes. But it invalidates his criticism of, his pleasure in the whole book.'

'It's the way your fellow academics will review you. They'll write about what interests them, and spend time on bits of niggling correction where they think they've caught you out.' Emma watched her husband. 'There wasn't much point in letting him read it?'

'Not really.'

'Did he say anything that made you regret having written the book or which pleased and encouraged you.'

'No.'

Emma persisted. 'What was the best thing he said?'

'Best? Thing? Said?' He stupidly repeated her words.

'Exactly. Go on.' She would not let him escape.

'He said that it sent him back to the originals.' Jon spoke with a drawling flatness of voice that frightened her. 'But anybody could say that. He didn't tie it up tightly enough to specific points either in my book or in George Eliot's novels.'

'So you wasted your time?'

'I knew I'd do that. But I could question him to find out what he had read, and I did that.'

'My mother said he enjoyed every minute.'

'Good.'

'I think he was flattered that his learned son-in-law had condescended to bandy ideas with him.'

But Emma could not provoke him.

In September he played his first game of rugger for the season, a practice match, and came home with a black eye and swollen cheek-bone, apart from the usual bruises. Next day he moved stiffly, and complained he was not nearly as fit as he had thought. Emma said next to nothing, because she had little sympathy. Not that he asked for pity, even though his closed eye was bloodshot and his face unpleasantly disfigured.

She had spent the last few days in Derbyshire, helping out a cousin of her principal, himself a solicitor, and now engaged defending a doctor accused of neglect. Tom Crowder, the cousin, ran a one-man office, busy with what he called 'bread-and-butter' work, and in his own view incapable of defending the medico adequately. She thoroughly enjoyed the task, which was equally new to her, studied unfamiliar corners of the law, quizzed witnesses, discussed it all thoroughly with Crowder, who said that he did not think he'd take on such a case again; it cost too much 'sweat and money'. In a small 'one-horse concern' like his, of many years' standing, he made quite enough for his requirements. His son and daughter, both married, lived away; neither was a lawyer. He ought, he admitted, to take on a young solicitor, and settle him in, but his own retirement was ten years away at least, so there seemed no hurry. He did, however, offer the place to Emma, outlining the advantages of living in a town like Matlock. She, with no thought of taking up the offer, asked what the disadvantages were.

'Dullness. Every day much the same. An interesting case like this I'd tend to refuse, recommend somebody better qualified.'

'Why did you take this one on?'

'My wife pressed me. She was a friend of Walker's wife. And there was no real evidence against the man. He seemed a damn sight more conscientious, never mind considerate, than my own quack for instance. And I met Toby, my cousin, and asked him about it. He knows it all. Well, he runs a large office as you know.' This was Tobias Wharton-Renton, Emma's principal. 'And he told me he'd got a bright girl. "She'll bone up on the law inside a week and run rings round the medical tribunal and the other side. But she'll need you for the local considerations." That's why I discuss the case with you. I'm learning a good deal. It's quite livened me up. I'd never look at a law book outside the call of duty. Now I sometimes try to keep up with you. Carol's quite amazed. She says she'll have to keep an eye on the pair of us, though I tell her you're a blissful newly-wed.' Crowder chuckled to himself. But on each of the days she was at his office he gave her half an hour on 'local colour'. When, months later, they easily won their hearing, he offered her a partnership again.

'No, thanks. I've enjoyed my time with you. But it wouldn't be wise.'

'Why, may I ask?'

'My husband may have to move about. I may have children. It's all too uncertain for you to base future plans on.'

'I shall miss you. I really looked forward to the days you spent here.'

'Thank you.'

'So I would take the risk.'

'No, Mr Crowder, no.' He'd asked her to call him Tom, which she sometimes did. 'You'll soon get used to the old ways.'

He looked as if he was about to make some more personal appeal, but he rose, clamping his lips, pulling down hard on the bottom of his clerical-grey jacket. His eyes glistened wet. When she spoke to Renton, her principal, he pulled legalistic faces and told her she could do

119

worse. 'Tom's not without brains, you know. And he's a fine sportsman like your husband. Still plays from seven at his age. He's something of a lady's man, but I suppose you noticed that. Or I shouldn't ask. That doctor you defended, now. Tom was having it away with his wife at one time. We're a curious lot.'

'His behaviour to me was impeccable.'

'Yes. I suppose old age is creeping up on him.'

During this Derbyshire interlude Jon seemed inconsolable, moving about the house like a zombie, smiling to order, grimacing, efficient but caught up elsewhere in doubt. She admired the way he worked, prepared her evening meal, struggling against the tide of his spirit, his despondency, his sense that nothing would ever right itself again. This husband of hers was a good man.

At the end of September, again the weather had turned bright, he received a letter from his publisher. The editor, a woman, wrote a dull note to tell him that she was pleased to say that they would take the George Eliot book and announced her proposed terms. She envisaged, her words, that they'd both want to make one or two alterations, and suggested that they met to discuss these, either in London or at his home. She enclosed readers' reports.

The effect was electric. That so flat a missive could so change a man's life interested Emma strangely. Certainly an illiterate note rescuing a man from the hangman's or the posse's noose would so alter the intended victim's view of the world, but that her husband's whole attitude could be so transformed seemed almost incredible. He sang about the house; he looked forward to the beginning of term; he scored a brilliant try against Bedford. Of course he complained at length, but cheerfully, about the 'envisaged' changes. He mocked the verb, but mowed the lawn at twice the speed. He went out and bought Emma a small, exquisite necklace to her intense delight. Nothing could go wrong. Harold Winter and Alma came over to dinner; high spirits reigned. Jon's explanation of the theses of the new book to Mrs Franklin seemed a perfect piece of teaching, uncondescending, humorous, intelligent, and directed exactly at catching and holding the listener's attention. Father sipped his coffee, and beamed at Emma. The world displayed for them a buoyant, cheering reflection of their life.

'I've never had such a good evening,' Harold said, in the warm dark of the pavement, lime leaves stirring overhead. 'You young people know how to entertain.'

'Yes,' Alma said. 'I think that's what heaven will be like.'

'You and I'll never get *there*.'

'Speak for yourself.'

Hand in hand, Emma and Jon went indoors. Though it was nearly one in the morning they sat for a few minutes together on the settee, almost in silence, before they crept upstairs for bed and love-making and sleep's content.

12

The university term opened with two or three long meetings, and then steadied to the round of lectures, tutorials, social affairs. Jon had a great deal of work, and Sunday was the only day he spent completely at home. In October he and Emma were invited in to their neighbours' house for Saturday lunch. The neighbour, Tom Street, who acted as host, owned a factory which made drinking straws; he was a tall, laconic man with an engineering degree and an interest in racing-cycles. It was said he had invested money in a new model on which someone had broken the world record and was likely to destroy all opposition. To Jon, this seemed nearly impossible; the design of a cycle was so basic, two wheels and a frame, that it seemed unlikely that it could be so radically altered to leave opponents behind. Was it the bike or the powerful legs of the man riding it which had worked the miracle?

The neighbour from the other side was a very smart, youngish consultant from the university hospital. He and his pretty wife were said to be keen gardeners, and they flashed Latin botanical names about without apparent intention to impress. They fell into small technical arguments about delphiniums or spire-cherries and quizzed their host about an artificial stream they were planning to build in their grounds.

'Use a spade,' he'd advised. 'It's slow, but it allows for late alteration.' There were two barristers, both unknown to Emma, and their wives; the headmistress of a huge comprehensive school serving half a dozen dormitory villages and her husband, a handsome businessman in up-to-date gear; the professor of geology from the university, whom Jon had never clapped eyes on before, or his insignificant, shy spouse; three or four well-to-do couples whose names were never announced or learnt; and, finally, a bishop, a small, dark man, not unlike Lionel Ashley, and his smaller, darker, lurking wife.

All were friendly, but with nobody of the age of Jon and Emma. Many asked after Harold. One lady suggested that the old man was much influenced by Alma.

'And is that good?' Emma asked.

'I guess so. Harold would only let her have her way when it was to his advantage.'

'Harold invariably knows what he's doing,' her husband said. 'More than somewhat.'

Another man identified Jon as the county rugby player and began a long disquisition on violence in the game, and laid it down that no amount of legislation or alteration of laws by official bodies would improve matters.

'It depends on the common sense and judgement of the players. They harm their opponents, bruise them, but draw the line at gouging their eyes out or scraping skin loose with their boots. But the dividing line between acceptable violence and criminal behaviour is so narrow that we're beginning to suffer from a great number of cripplings, serious injuries and even deaths. I'm not saying deliberately inflicted; a player did not mean to kill, but . . .'

'And what's the answer?' Emma asked.

'Application of the criminal law. As in ordinary life. You are allowed to protect yourself against a burglar or aggressor, but you're not allowed to blow his head off as your first move.'

'So every game should have a referee, two touch-judges and a policeman or a lawyer,' Jon mocked.

'That day's not far off,' the man said, gloomily, but he turned cheerfully enough to quiz Jon about the City's chances of promotion this year.

The young couple were parted. The host led Emma round his three acre garden, while Jon remained with a woman whose idea of conversation was to sling at him a hypothetical question or two.

123

'What would you do if you inherited a great deal of money? Enough for you to give up work?'

'I'd carry on as I am now,' Jon answered.

'It wouldn't make any difference, then?'

'I'm not saying that. I'd look about. If my work became too boring or annoying I could easily consider giving it up.'

'You're Harold Winter's son, aren't you? Or George Garrard's nephew?'

'Winter's the name.'

'So you'll be a lawyer, like your father?'

'No.'

'What are you then?' Her voice took on a small squeak of anger.

'Guess.' He'd play at her own game.

'A school teacher.'

'Nearly right. I teach English at the university.'

'Does that need any teaching?'

'It would seem so.'

The woman suddenly sidled away and approached a trio of middle-aged men. She put an end to their conversation and pointed animatedly at the French windows. Jon could not hear what she said, but imagined it for himself. 'What would you do if a man walked in from the garden and pointed a shotgun at us?' The men looked at her with feigned interest.

Nobody in the room smoked. In the far distance he could see the host, with a grey-haired woman and Emma, standing by a large philadelphus. All three were looking upwards, as if at an aeroplane, and the senior two gesticulated, vigorously, but conveyed nothing to the observer.

'Are you all on your own?' a female voice inquired.

'It would seem so.'

'I'm Jenny Smom.'

'I beg your pardon. Jenny?'

'Snowdon. Like the mountain.'

'I'm Jonathan Winter, and I live next door.'

'You teach at the university, don't you? You'll know my father?'

'Who is that?'

She was in no hurry, but stood there lightly dressed in a silk blouse of squared, intersecting blotches, red, blue and green, and a long dark-green skirt.

'Ian Gormley. Like you, in the English department.'

The woman seemed in her thirties, smoothly tanned as though she'd returned the day before from the Greek Islands or North Africa. Her blue eyes searched his face.

'Yes,' he said, brooding. 'Yes.'

'I'm Jenny. Jennifer Snowdon now. That's my husband.' She pointed vaguely. 'He's a physician. We came with the McKinnons, your other neighbours. We all went together to Rhodes. Ian didn't like it much. It was too hot. He barely went out. He read, and dozed, and swam, and drank jugs full of barley-water.'

'And you?'

'It suited me. Swimming pool, light diet, people to talk to. And I get on well with Janet McKinnon. She knows her way round the corners of the world.'

'Don't you?' he asked, not understanding her.

'Not always. I sometimes wonder if I know who I am. But Janet's a Scots nurrrse.' She comically rolled the r. 'She'll tell you what you think.'

'It must be very satisfactory to be as confident as that.'

Jennifer informed him that she had two children, aged nine and eight, and that she had known her husband, the boy from across the road, most of her life.

'You both hail from Beechnall?'

'Yes. We went away to university, I to Liverpool and John to Leeds. He's older than I am. And I taught in Leeds while he was working in hospitals there, and then in Norwich, and two years ago we came back when he got his first consultancy here.'

'And will you stay?'

'That depends what's going for him. He's started a new piece of research. Slightly different from his M.D. On cancer, still.'

'And are you glad to be back?'

'I don't mind. This is quite a pleasant city. And John's doing what he wants, for the time being, at any rate.'

'And you have friends here?'

'One or two. But we've made new ones. In the medical world. There's plenty going on. As much as I want.'

'Do you live near your parents?'

'Five to ten minutes away by car. Depends on the traffic.' She nodded, wryly. 'We don't see each other as much as we ought. Daddy's always busy, or says he is . . . '

'He's just written a book on Shakespeare's obsessions.'

'Has he? I didn't know. He's always writing something or other. But he doesn't waste the finished articles on me.'

'And your mother?'

'Ah, my mother. Yes. Well, she lives in a world of her own. With her painting and piano playing and embroidery.'

'Does she do these well?'

'Yes. Moderately. That's unfair. She's quite talented. But she makes such a fuss. And makes them an excuse for doing just as she likes.'

'Does she play at concerts?'

'It's been known. And she's had one or two of her paintings framed and hung. She did one for me. And she gave me a pair of elaborate cushions. My father seems serious about his scholarship, is always pursuing some topic, or looking something up to correct somebody, so I suppose my mother thinks she must have something of equivalent importance on hand.'

'Are you an only child?'

'Now I wonder why you ask that. But no, I'm not. I've two sisters, both married, both away, one in London, one in Pittsburg.'

'Not married to doctors like you?'

'The American one is. You ask plenty of questions, don't you? It's a real inquisition.'

'I'm sorry,' Jon answered. 'I think people enjoy talking about themselves, and so I encourage them.'

126

'If you don't ask questions, you don't get people talking?' Jennifer sounded superior. 'I wonder. I often have difficulty stopping them.'

'Though I worked with your father every day, or at least near him, attended meetings and lunched sometimes with him, it was a year at least before I found out that he was married. I thought he was a typical bachelor.'

'I can understand,' Jennifer said, 'that he never spoke about me and my sisters, but I think he admires my mother. In his selfish way. They're two of a kind. They do as they like. My mother brought us up, but that's not unusual. She had help. Both my parents inherited money, so they could partially shelve their responsibility as far as we were concerned.'

'Did they send you to boarding schools?'

'No. Daddy was unhappy at his school, so we were sent to the High School here.' She looked at her polished fingernails. 'I quite liked it. That's your wife over there, isn't it, with Tom Street? She's a pretty girl. And well dressed.' Jon bowed his head at these compliments. 'Does she work?'

'She's a solicitor?'

'With your father's firm?'

'No. Timms and Renton.'

The names obviously meant nothing.

'You live next door, don't you? It's a lovely house.'

'My father gave it to us as a wedding present. Otherwise we wouldn't be able to afford a place of that size.'

They talked on. Jennifer often touched him, laying a hand on his arm to make some point. She had little in common with her father's formal, old-fashioned manner. She had read economics at the university, and had begun work in London on *The Times* after training at the Institute of Education as a teacher. When she became engaged to her husband she had moved to Leeds to be near him, and had taught in an infants' school, which she'd thoroughly enjoyed.

'And you didn't regret the end of your journalistic career?'

'Not really. I'm glad I did it, but it wasn't very exciting. And I didn't like living in London. I had to waste too much time travelling, and too much money on accommodation. But as I say, I'm not sorry about my couple of years there. I learnt to look after myself.'

'You don't work now?'

'Not for money, if that's what you mean.'

Jennifer moved away saying that she hoped they'd meet again. Emma asked who the striking woman was to whom he'd been talking.

'Ian Gormley's daughter.'

'She's not much like him. Does she take after her mother?'

'I've never met her. According to Jennifer here, she spends her time in artistic pursuits, and can't be bothered with social life.'

'Artistic pursuits?'

'Painting. Playing the piano. Embroidery. Quite well, all of them, if I read her daughter's comment aright.'

Just before the Snowdons left Jennifer led her husband across to introduce him. John had the thin, well-shaven, sharp face of a man who knew his position in society. He frequently touched the receding hair over an already high forehead with long, well-kept fingers. His spectacles sparkled, and he smiled to himself as if he knew something to the disadvantage of his auditors. He spoke in a clipped voice, without much emphasis, as if his thoughts were occupied elsewhere. He lacked his wife's gorgeous tan, but he looked healthy enough, carrying no spare weight. He was no taller than his wife, and the backs of his hands were heavily covered with black hair. His clothes were admirable, but unshowy. He seemed genuinely glad to meet the young couple.

'You must come to visit us.'

Back at home Emma and Jon could see the last guest or two in Tom Street's garden.

'I wonder why Tom invited us,' Jon asked.

'His wife's a bit of a social being, and she'd like to know who her neighbours were. She wasn't much in evidence.'

'She spoke three times to me.'

'Perhaps she only notices the men. How did you like Tom?'

'Very quiet,' Jon answered. 'Shy. I understand from my father that he's pretty well-to-do. I quite took to him. What did he talk to you about?'

'The garden. Whether we'd settled in. How he'd taken another place over in Derby. A factory. He grumbled because he said people didn't go out of their way to help him. "I'm bringing jobs in, but they don't want to know." He didn't make a song and dance about it. He doesn't shout ever. I imagined tycoons to be a lot more emphatic.'

'It's possibly what they choose to do not what they say that counts. We belong to the oral professions.'

'I'm told he works about eighteen hours a day,' Emma added.

'Not good for his wife.'

'I expect she's used to it.'

Jon came across Ian Gormley on the corridor outside his room. Gormley made as if to pass with a nod.

'I met your daughter on Saturday,' Jon said.

'Oh.'

'At Tom Street's.'

'Oh, yes.' The name obviously meant nothing.

'Jennifer.'

'I know my daughters' names. And it would be either Jennifer or Catherine. Patricia lives in America. Catherine doesn't spend her Sunday socialising. She plays a church organ. I take it it wasn't in church you met her.'

'No. Saturday. not Sunday.'

'No? Oh.'

'Tom Street's a business man who lives next door to me.'

'Lucky for him.' This schoolboy repartee was delivered from lips almost closed. By now Gormley held his head back, as if the conversation suddenly interested him, and he was ready for the next snippet. Jon made no answer. His colleague would have to work for information. Two could play awkward. 'And what had she to say for herself?' Man to man, with joviality.

'The usual garden party guff. Weather. Entertainment. Where she'd lived before. She worked for *The Times*.'

'In some small menial capacity.'

'And taught in Leeds.'

'She'd be not without merit in the classroom. She has, one can assume, what they call a personality. She can make a listener feel that she is somebody of interest with something important to say.' Gormley sniffed. 'My students hint that you have the gift. I'm afraid I haven't. I tell them what I think they should know, but I don't go out of my way to make it palatable.' Jon was surprised that Gormley appeared to discuss colleagues with his students. 'She's married to a doctor, you know. Man called Sampson, no, Snowdon. That's it, Snowdon.'

'Is he good at his job?'

'Presumably. He manages research as well as patients. She says he's in line for a professorship, if not here, then at some other teaching hospital.'

'Your daughter is ambitious for him?'

Gormley jerked his head back, as if they were approaching taboo subjects. 'I wouldn't be surprised. But he will be ambitious for himself. I understand that in his field he's quite highly regarded. Oncology. Thank God I've had no relationship with him as a patient.'

'He seemed very quiet.'

'I imagine that in his line there is no need for histrionics. The news is more often than not bad enough, without needing Gielgud or Olivier to deliver it. And if it's a good prognosis, that'll speak for itself.'

'Yes.'

'Yes. I must press on. It's good to talk to you, now and then.'

'Have they given you a date for your book?'

'They have. It's November now. The seventeenth? I forget. I hardly believe them. There'll be some other snag before long. Curse them.' He hissed out his last words like

130

some pantomime villain, quite out of character, and then stumbled off to his room.

As Jon opened his door, the professor passed.

'What's the news?' he called.

'Gormley seems very pleased with himself.'

'Oh. That will be a change. I wonder why.'

'The Senate hasn't decided to give him a personal chair, has it?'

'Young man, young man. This cynicism, this levity ill becomes you.' The professor looked over his half-moon spectacles, mimicking some Victorian patriarch.

'Is this department rehearsing for a play?' Jon asked.

'It does little else.'

Professor Towers resumed his care-worn expression to hurry on, but first thing in the afternoon he called in on Jon in his office. He seemed quite unembarrassed by his first question.

'You weren't serious this morning, were you, about a personal chair for Gormley?'

'No.'

'There's no talk in the department about such a thing, is there?'

'No.'

'I don't like to hear of such suggestions, even in jest. I know you'll think that's ridiculous, but the headship of a department comes with a good many snags. Many of them, like this, I suppose, trivial. You make your little joke, and somebody takes it seriously, and before we know where we are there are threats, and solicitors' letters, and nervous breakdowns. Gormley's not altogether steady, you know.'

'How old is he?' John asked.

'Sixty-one, two. Thereabouts.'

'You haven't long to put up with him.'

'Three years is long enough. An undergraduate's complete time with us.' Towers locked his fingers together behind his head as if to start some gymnastic exercise. 'This term has begun extremely easily. Everybody seems settled.

Gormley's waiting for the appearance of his book. Of course, when it appears and the critics set about it, or ignore it, then he'll be annoyed. But by that time, he'll have enough mundane work on hand to stop him from concentrating on his wrongs.'

'Do you think so?'

'You're suggesting they'll make his sorrows worse? It's a possibility with Gormley. He's unpredictable.'

'I was talking to him about his daughter.'

'What about her?' Towers snapped the question.

'I met her at a party. She seemed slightly unusual. She'd worked on *The Times* as well as in an infant school.'

'What does she do now?'

'She's married to a doctor, a cancer specialist.'

'Christ.'

'What's wrong?' Jon asked, surprised at the violent delivery of the word.

'Wrong? Nothing's bloody wrong. What's his name?'

'Snowdon. Gormley made out he had difficulty in remembering it.'

'That doesn't surprise me. No. Just keep us all on an even keel, Jon. Not too many of your little quips.'

'Are you warning me?'

'Oh, come now.'

The two men stared each other straight in the eyes. The professor tapped the thumb-nail of his right hand on his front teeth.

'I'm more concerned these days with public relations than with scholarship,' he said, and turned. 'It doesn't suit me.'

Towers's visit had not gone unnoticed. Gormley stopped by Jon's table at afternoon tea.

'What did tin-arse want, then?' The epithet surprised.

'A social visit. A public relations exercise.'

'Sometimes I think you're as bad as he is.'

Gormley shuffled to the far end of the room without another word.

13

Jon found the term thoroughly absorbing, not only with his teaching but with a new piece of work on Samuel Butler. 'Nobody lectures on Butler,' he told his wife. 'No questions are set on the examination papers. Why do you think that is?'

'Because he isn't interesting enough,' Emma answered, challenging him.

'But he is. People slip through the academic net. Since the feminists have been publishing women novelists, then we've had to deal with them. In my view Harriet Martineau's not in the same street as Butler.'

'Does anybody at your university lecture on Shaw?' she asked.

'We have courses on drama and I'm certain he'll have his place there.'

'If I know your little lot,' Emma answered, 'your students will know more about Terence and Plautus than Shaw. Or Tom Stoppard and Howard Brenton.'

'And what do you know about those ancients?' He laughed.

'Nothing. They were a couple of fancy names we palmed about in A Level English. And Seneca. That's learning for you.'

'Did you read them?'

'Certainly not. Neither did our teachers.'

Emma spoke in a lively way. Her Derbyshire doctor had faced his medical council and emerged without a stain. A week or two later her principal had come into her office one morning and set himself down.

'I've heard from Tom Crowder again. He's bandying your name about.'

Emma sat, not giving her senior the satisfaction of an interested question. She smiled, arranged herself neatly at her desk, and waited.

'Another doctor. In trouble.' Renton spoke with impressive slowness and weight.

'He knows now how to handle such a case.'

'Yes. But this is different. This doctor is called Goach, and the police suspect that he's murdered his wife. You may have seen references in the newspapers.' He put down on her desk an envelope on which three cuttings were clipped together. 'Tom sent these. Read them at your leisure. Now this Dr Goach is a colleague of your Walker, and he strongly recommends you as leaving no stone unturned in the pursuit of justice.' Renton wagged his eyebrows. 'So the pair of them went to Tom, when the police started to be awkward. No charges have been laid, but the woman's friends, the locals, have been kicking up about her disappearance. So I suppose Goach was sensible to see a solicitor to find out how he stood legally.'

'What impression did Tom form of the man?'

'You know him. Goach's a well-respected, rather quiet, middle-aged man. His wife was not unlike him in many ways. She's an ex-nurse. Helps out in the practice. Both conscientious, but rather dull. Nondescript.'

'Did Tom . . . ?'

' . . . think he was guilty? I don't know if it even crossed his mind. You can't tell in my experience until you've met them a few times. But Tom doesn't want a case of murder on his books. That's nearly as bad to him as committing it. I don't blame him. He doesn't need time-wasting court work either. He has enough of his own lines to keep him occupied. So when Walker raised your name at every verse end, Tom suggested passing the case over to us. Not only have we this brilliant young woman on tap, but we're a largish concern, likely to know which barristers to call if the worst comes to the worst.'

'But he'd be better to use a local man.'

'Except he lives in the country, about halfway between them and us.'

'And what do you think?'

'Ah,' Renton spoke like a cello tuning. 'There's the nub of it. Indeed. The heart of the matter.' Emma knew he was giving her time to consider the proposition. 'What do I think? Not that that's of any importance. Well, now. You're shaping exceptionally favourably here. You're conscientious. And if we left you doing nothing but conveyancing, which is what I took you on for, there'd be no errors. I can't guess whether you'd be bored in time. You would, I think. That's why I put you on to the law books. You're quick and you're thorough. Not all clever people are. They're too impatient. You'd have made a good academic lawyer. I tell you, Emma, if anything tricky comes up, I think, no, I'm glad that I have you about. And I've been at it thirty-odd years.'

'Thank you.'

'Of course, you know that practising law doesn't depend entirely on law books. I wish to God it did, but we're human beings. You may think we have a watertight case, and some failure in court, or some preciosity on the part of a judge, even a change in the weather,' Renton waved a well-kept hand, 'may sink us.' Again he moved, this time to hop like an organist with his feet. His shoes, she noticed, were light, polished, dancing pumps, not his usual leather solid black footwear. These were both in and out of character, she thought. 'But this Goach business, now. We shan't make a fortune out of it. But it will be different. It will widen your experience, and if you handle it well, it will do no harm, like our Dr Robert Walker case. We're not short of work. We needn't take this case. But I leave it with you. It's your choice. Now, what do you say?'

'Are there any snags?'

'It won't be easy. Especially as we don't know what's what. The police were obviously impressed enough by the villagers' tale to make inquiries. And went away unsatisfied from the doctor.'

'I'll talk to Tom Crowder about it.'

'Right. I don't think you'll regret it, even if it comes to nothing. I did a couple of murder cases when I was a young solicitor and I've never regretted it. I didn't learn much law. But I learnt something about courts. And about one barrister. He's retired now.'

'Were you defending?'

'Yes, and we lost both cases, or both our clients were found guilty. But we made as strong a case as could be made, and it stood our clients in good stead. Even, as I say, with one of her barristers so weak that I wouldn't employ him to push my wheelbarrow. But enough.'

'I'll ring Tom.'

'Yes, but not today. He's out. First thing tomorrow morning. It'll give you time to have second thoughts. I expect the village where Goach has his surgery is buzzing with talk.'

'What will the drill be?'

'If the police haven't moved, then I guess it will be an unofficial interview with Goach. To hear his side, and to see what sort of impression he makes on you.'

'Might Dr Goach not object to being represented by a young woman?'

'The initial suggestion came from them. But we shall see.'

Emma talked it over with her husband.

'Are you interested?' he asked.

'Oh, yes.'

'And what are the snags? Well, it's not much connected with research into the law. It's as if the *Mirror* or the *Sun* asked me to pick a short poem out every day for their readers for a year. I'd be better paid than for any academic work, but it might stand in the way of promotion later, you never know. And I'd be worried to death that nobody would bother to read my choice. But I'd do it.'

'Why?'

'The money. And the half-chance that somebody would read the poems. And the challenge of choosing pieces that might just appeal to people with no experience of such matters.' Jon bit his lower lip. 'The snag with a murder inquiry is that you're dealing face to face with a man, or woman, who has gone so far as to kill somebody.'

'That might be where the whole interest lies.'

'I know we're all inquisitive. But these are human beings you're expected to get to know, to understand.'

'Divorce cases are similar.'

'Except they haven't effected their own final divorce settlement. With a gun or a knife.'

'What do you think?'

'Oh, that's easy. You're going to do it.' They both laughed at his certainty. 'Just as I'd pick out my three hundred poems. It's an opportunity that no self-respecting teacher could turn down. And so with your case. You're sensible. You know more about the law than most. But I reckon you'll be capable of finding out the ins-and-outs, the motivation, the background, and then applying common sense.'

'That's not always appreciated in lawcourts.'

'No, I suppose it isn't. But you can't prepare your case in the expectation of a batty judge and a jury of lunatics. If this turns out to be so, then you'll change tack, surely.'

'Guided by my famed common sense,' she said.

Next morning she rang Tom Crowder. He arranged for her to see Dr Goach in his office the following afternoon. She was to arrive half an hour early to give him the chance to put her in the picture. Whether this was wise she felt unsure, but she accepted with good grace.

The half hour told her little that she hadn't learnt from the newspaper cuttings. Some seven weeks before, Louise Goach, the doctor's wife, had disappeared. Goach had given the impression, when asked, that she had gone on holiday with her mother. When she did not return, talk spread in the village. The receptionists, the second nurse, the cleaning women all began to talk. There was a report of midnight shouts, and blows, a car driving off at much the time Mrs Goach was supposed to go on holiday. It was generally understood that the Goachs quarrelled,

137

frequently, and that Mrs Goach ruled the roost, had been known to strike her husband.

Crowder gave his account of this, a look of prurient delight on his wooden face.

'Did you know Mrs Goach?' Emma asked.

'Hardly. They live some distance away.'

'This is basically Goach's account, then?'

'Yes. You said "did" as if you believed her to be dead.' Crowder giggled at his own percipience. 'Did you notice?'

'Not really. Now tell me what you think of Goach.'

'Not very clear. Slightly favourable. He seems a quiet sort of man. A bit lost.'

At this moment Goach's arrival was announced by Crowder's secretary, who then ushered him into the office. He was taller than Emma expected, well-shaven with thick, black hair, cut fashionably short and well pomaded. He wore an open-necked check shirt, grey flannels, a thin black pullover and muddied brogues. He shook hands shyly with both solicitors, and Tom made introductions. When Crowder had left the room, Dr Goach sat, knees together, on the chair square to the rather small, new desk where Emma presided. He began.

'I don't know how much Mr Crowder has told you, Mrs Winter. I don't even know whether I need a solicitor. My wife has disappeared. She drove off one night after a prolonged quarrel. To the station. At least that's what was reported.'

'Has she done this before?'

'She's visited her mother often enough. But not in circumstances like this. She knew it was inconvenient in this holiday period, when people go away. I've had quite a job getting a temporary nurse in.'

'Have you heard from your wife?'

'No. This was not surprising given the circumstances of her departure. So I was not unduly worried. But after a fortnight I rang her mother who lives on the Northumbrian coast. Louise had not been there. Neither had her mother heard from her.'

138

'Did this surprise you?'

'Yes.'

'What I meant was: does your wife often make these unusual moves without saying anything to you?'

Dr Goach appeared momentarily embarrassed, nonplussed. 'Well, yes. She's apt to do things on the spur of the moment. Yes. She's headstrong. But she's never disappeared for a long period before.'

'A short period?'

'Once or twice.'

'Was your quarrel so intense that it warranted, however slightly, this untoward behaviour?'

'I wouldn't have said so. We bawl at each other. But we're well away from other people. We have no family to consider. The old lady next door is deaf. So we are noisy.'

'Do you shout?' Emma asked.

'I'm afraid so.' Goach spoke in a whisper.

'And was the subject of your quarrel unusual?'

'No. Money. As ever. She thinks I am mean, that I keep her short. It's not so. When she went away she had something like fifteen thousand pounds in her own name in a building society account.'

'That won't last for ever.'

'She'll find a job. She's a well-qualified nurse. She took her references with her.'

In a subdued way, though he looked Emma straight in the eyes, and his were washed-out blue, he explained how he had contacted the police. They had been both sensible and sympathetic, explaining that there was little they could do. Adults were allowed to take off and vanish, and, as long as there were no signs of foul play, that was that. Discreet inquiries would be made to other forces, but . . . In the same unemphatic voice Goach outlined his own feelings. He had been annoyed with his wife, as she with him, but he had not remotely considered complete disappearance. She had left her car at the station, and had bought a ticket for London.

139

There had been talk, amongst the surgery staff, in the village and through the practice. He had received anonymous letters taxing him with the murder of his wife. The police had mentioned similar anonymous accusations, on the surface from three or four different sources. The guard on the train, who had sold her the ticket to London, now began to be unsure of his story. The police had twice visited Goach, had been open and above board about their inquiries, and had shown him some of the letters asking if he could help identify the writers. He could not.

'You have no enemies?'

'No. There are people I don't get on with, but enemies, no.'

'Have you made your own inquiries?'

'In these last few days, yes. She'd left her telephone list, and I rang up friends and a couple of relatives. They'd heard nothing. I felt a bit of a fool. I mean, they asked questions. It's seven weeks or thereabouts now.'

'And these anonymous letters?'

'In the last fortnight.'

'That means she'd only been away five weeks. They were fairly quick off the mark.'

'Yes. It surprised me. I admit that Lou and I used to exchange words in front of the receptionists and nurses. Not very wise. But I expected them to be more discreet than we were.'

'So they are the source, however innocently, of the rumours?'

'I suppose so. People love to talk.'

' "What great ones do the less will prattle of." ' Goach's face registered mild puzzlement. 'That's a quotation from *Twelfth Night*. Shakespeare?'

Emma felt at home with Goach. He was clearly embarrassed by his wife's disappearance, which in itself was bad enough, but the subsequent scandalous accusations had shaken him, reshaped his view of the world. She liked the man, or perhaps her first impressions were favourable. He made no great claims for himself. She was suspicious of his account of the discord between his wife and himself. They shouted at each other, even in public, and the cause of dissension was money. It sounded likely enough as he told the tale. But Louise had upped sticks, had run away. This suggested that his wife was less stable than he described her. As he sat there patiently enough waiting for Emma's next burst of questions, she considered him as a potential murderer. He did not suit the part. He was a dull man, grey and quiet, and yet by his own admission he had shouted at his wife. Most murders were the result, she had read, of domestic altercations, a blow struck too violently, an immediately regretted lunge with a knife, or jerk on the trigger of a shotgun. We were all capable of a temporary, short loss of control. But how would we act then, as we saw the slumped and bloody corpse? She examined the pale face, the bloodless fingers hovering by his chin.

'I have to ask you,' she said at the end of her inquisition, 'if there is anything you have failed to tell me.'

'Are you asking me if I killed Louise?' Sharpness crackled in his voice; here was the doctor with an awkward, disingenuous patient.

'That question is there amongst others.'

'I didn't. You believe that, don't you?'

'It doesn't matter what I believe.'

'Do I look like a murderer?'

'No,' she answered. 'But my experience is limited.' She would give him no easy way out. 'I shall work on the assumption that you didn't kill your wife, until it is proved otherwise.' She wanted to put it clearly, demonstrate the seriousness of his position, if that were possible.

'I am at a loss to account for Louise's behaviour. Disappearance is the last thing I expected. Before I came here today I rang the police inspector, told him what I was about to do, and invited him and his team to search my place, surgery as well as house, especially if they could do it tactfully and not raise further suspicions.'

'What was his reaction?'

'He said it was wise to talk it over with a lawyer. He'd not heard of you, but that's not surprising. He thanked me for my offer, said they probably would come in, but they'd give me notice. "We can't ignore these letters absolutely," he said, "but you'd be surprised how many nutters there are about even in quiet country villages".'

'You're quite sure that you haven't enemies? Somebody you have crossed in some way, however small? Or Louise, for that matter?'

'No. I sometimes have to speak bluntly to patients, and I suppose that could upset a twisted mind. But no. Nor Louise. She could speak plainly, but was, well, much more at ease socially than I was. No. These letters have been an eye-opener.'

Goach arranged to let her know developments, about the police visit, and said he'd go over in his mind all they'd talked about in case he remembered something or 'put two and two together and made five'.

He left cheerfully enough, exchanging a parting word with Tom Crowder, who hung about waiting for the doctor to leave, and drove off in a large Volvo estate, new in August.

'You'd get a corpse into that,' Crowder said.

Emma gave him a brief account of the interview, and left for home. Not a mile away she saw Dr Goach's car parked in a side-street.

For the next week or two Emma discussed the Goach affair with her husband. It fascinated both as the Alf Perkins' rugby selection had a few months before. Both felt that there was some motive lying hidden that would explain the oddity of behaviour. They dismissed the obvious: Perkins' wish to choose his son or Goach's murder of his wife. And yet they felt both puzzled and frustrated that they could not spot some crucial obvious clue. Such discussions delighted, and were carried on in a kind of formal, even adversarial, convention, each challenging the other to present some new face to the truth.

'Have you heard from our friend?' Jon would open the conversation once they had sat down to dinner. Over preparation the subject had been unbroached, left as an accompanying spice to their eating.

'Not a word.'

'Have the police made their visit?' He knew they had.

'Yes, but it seemed all very cursory.'

'Did he expect them to dig the cellar floors up?'

'You don't get any idea of his expectations from him. A plain description that I have to excavate word by word.'

Neither knew Goach's first name. Typically in this case. Jon looked it up in the *Medical Directory*.

'Robert Goach,' he announced. 'Robert Anthony Petersfield Goach.'

'That sounds very proper,' she answered.

'There was one question I wanted to ask you. Did you get the impression that Goach loved his wife. Or that he was genuinely upset by her disappearance?'

'I formed no impression,' Emma answered after thought. 'He's used to interviewing people, and I suppose he assumes the persona of the detached scientist. He said he couldn't understand Louise's disappearance. If he showed any signs of emotion, and it was precious little, it was over the anonymous letters.'

'Do you think there was more in that than meets the eye?'

'I'd no means of judging. Whether his patients are more cracked than is usual I don't know. He's a cold fish, and that may not suit. He'd have difficulty in appearing sympathetic.'

'I thought you were on the whole on his side?'

'I am. But it's like trying to deduce a story from a rather wooden picture.'

Jon told her a children's joke about the doctor who asked his patient calling in for the result of tests whether he'd have the good news first or the bad. 'The good. "The good news is that you'll die tomorrow." "Good?" asked the staggered patient. "What's the bad, then?" "I should have told you this yesterday." '

'That's a bit like him,' Emma conceded.

143

Goach rang to tell her that the inspector and two CID subordinates had searched his house and grounds. They had turned up discreetly in plain clothes, but had been exceptionally thorough, going through the drawers of his wife's belongings, looking through his papers, letters and safe, asking all sorts of questions about the contents of the refrigerator where he kept his drugs. The men had held muttered conferences, and had sometimes gone back to repeat an operation after one of these colloquies. They'd turned over the contents of the outhouses and the garage. The constables had been surly, but in the end the inspector, apologizing for the length of the proceedings, said they had found nothing incriminating. 'It's as well though to do the job properly as you've invited us in, as regret it later. And these two constables are trained and versed in searches of this sort.'

'What are you looking for?' the doctor had asked.

'Anything slightly out of the way.'

'And did you find anything?'

'Not really. But she's left behind a large amount of clothes and underclothes for somebody who'd intended a fortnight away.'

'She'd a great variety,' the doctor had said. 'I used to think her occupation in life was buying new wearing apparel. That was one of the things we rowed about.' The inspector had expressed his satisfaction.

'Have there been any more letters?'

'I asked him that, and he said "No", neither to him nor the police. He gave me the impression that the police were pretty sure who'd written them.'

'This inspector seems a real expert.'

Emma shrugged. A day or two later Goach reported that the same three policemen had searched his premises again. This time all three said little, but Goach thought they had something in mind.

'Such as?'

'He'd no idea. They just did their search, thorough again, behind furniture and so forth, as if they'd given him a day

144

or two to stew over the first, and had then offered him time to conceal something.'

'Had he? Concealed anything?'

'He didn't say so. He asked the inspector what would have happened if he had refused the request. "We've a warrant ready, sir." '

'It sounds serious.'

'He didn't think so. "They couldn't have found anything," he said, "because there was nothing there." '

Jennifer Snowdon, Gormley's daughter, invited them over to dinner in what appeared from the street as rather a dull house. The passages and rooms were full of pictures, many attractive. One rather small seascape, the main almost purple and breaking in squiggles of foam along a beach, with pale cliffs in the distance under a cloud-streaked sky, caught Jon's attention.

'My father did that,' Jennifer said.

'I didn't know he painted.'

'He doesn't much. Not these days.'

'It's very good.'

'I sometimes think he's capable of anything, that man.'

There were three other couples, about the age of the Snowdons, two medical. The third pair sat painfully quiet, gripping sherry glasses almost desperately. The young woman had been at school with Jennifer, and her husband worked in a bank. Emma talked to them and they came to life when they mentioned their family, an eight-year-old boy, a girl of five and a baby, another girl, of fifteen months. They became no less dull, worked on the principle that everybody was as interested in their children as they were, but their waxy, set faces seemed to light up, not change exactly, in fact Jon would have had difficulty in describing exactly where the difference lay, but there was a spark of attention, a slight sharpening of the voices of both. They seemed grateful to Emma for introducing a topic they knew something about. Jon marvelled, not for the first time, at his wife's social gifts. She dropped her sharp intelligence and listened, and intervened exactly to encourage. Perhaps she'd learnt the art from her mother, the parson's wife.

The doctors talked about golf. The youngest, a GP, had apparently done two scratch rounds in the last four days. Emma questioned him on how he maintained this high standard in the limited time at his disposal. He was only too delighted to explain. Two competitive foursomes every week kept him up to the limit. His wife seemed just as interested or excited, although she did not play herself, saying that in the summer he'd be on the course to play a hole or two before his morning surgery. And his holidays were spent entirely on golf courses. His wife said she did not mind, but expressed her preference for links so that she could spend her time on the shore or the cliffs.

'Don't you want to learn to play yourself?' the banking-man asked.

'No. I wouldn't be any good. And so I'd be a drag on Geoffrey. And if it turned out, and it's utterly unlikely, that I had some talent, Geoff wouldn't like it if I got anywhere near his standard.'

'Could you, if you had practice, get anywhere near the standard of these professional golfers we see on the telly?' Jon asked the husband.

'No. If I played all day and every day I'd improve slightly, a stroke or two. I'd be able to give a better account of myself on any course and whatever the weather. But after that it would be a matter of temperament. You see some of the finest players in the world missing a short putt that you think you could hole with an umbrella handle.'

That led Dr Snowdon to describe the pressures of the professional. A gust of wind, a slight unevenness in the ground could alter a perfect stroke into an imperfect one. 'That's bad enough in itself, but when tens of thousands of pounds depend on these slight differences, you can see how stresses mounted. Then, as Geoffrey says, it's a matter of character. You can blow a small fortune away with a tantrum.'

146

'They all seem to have coaches,' the banker said.

'That's right. The competition is so cut-throat that some slight eccentricity of swing can put you out of the top twenty in no time.'

'Would this be the same with surgeons?' Emma innocently asked Francis Snowdon.

'We're all physicians here. Why do you ask?'

'Aren't they in much the same situation? They're dealing with a different problem that, in spite of scans and so on, they don't exactly know how to handle until they actually come to do so.'

'There are all sorts of medical conferences where new ideas are mooted, and new techniques demonstrated.'

'The essential difference between medicine and golf,' Jennifer interrupted, 'is that golf is at bottom trivial. Knocking a ball into a hole. You can spin a yarn about its beauty and difficulty, about the enormous pleasure it gives to a great number of people, about the vast fortunes to be made, but what a medico does is to take some action to save, to prolong life.'

'Mayn't golf in some way prolong life, by exercise or by providing aesthetic pleasure,' her husband objected.

'They're on the edge of its advantages, as opposed to being its primary aim,' Jennifer answered. She sounded slightly like her father to Jon, putting the world to rights, dismissing spurious arguments. 'And the fact that the experts spend so much time on it, and that such millions can be made by it doesn't alter its ultimate triviality.'

'Could the same argument be raised against writing a sonnet?' Jon asked.

'Yes. And rightly. Though a sonnet is written down, and so lasts. The element of ephemerality that exists in games is taken away.'

'We have television recordings of games now,' her husband said.

'Do you rate a great round of golf above a fine performance of *King Lear*?' Jennifer asked.

'Personally, no,' her husband answered, smiling slightly. 'But it is only a personal preference. And I'd guess I am one of a small minority.'

They questioned Jon about his rugby-playing. One of the doctors seemed to know a fair amount about his playing record, spent some of his Saturday afternoon watching the County club.

'When you get older will you regret the time you spent practising and playing games?' Jennifer asked.

'I expect so. Especially as I'm nowhere near the top of my class. And even then . . . On the other hand my main job is to introduce clever young people to the classics of their language.'

'And is that useful?' one of the doctors asked, very diffidently.

'Yes. Even at the level of entertainment. I would consider watching, let's say, *Twelfth Night* on television preferable to watching a football match on the small screen.' His voice expressed scorn as did the choice of words.

'Why?'

'Because it's telling us more about ourselves, in a wider sense, than watching a match can. And I think, in my old-fashioned, puritanical way, that considering why we're here, how we handle our lives, our relationships with each other, never mind time, eternity or death is important. Here, by following literary tradition, we are listening to great experts offering us their views.'

'Would the same reasoning hold,' Jennifer asked, above the battle, judicially, 'if the work to be read or seen was Terence Rattigan not William Shakespeare?'

'I think so. Rattigan may not be the peak of our literature, but at least he deals with human problems deliberately as a football match does not. That's why I pitched my argument low and chose a Shakespeare comedy, *Twelfth Night*, and not *Lear* or *Hamlet*.'

'Why not,' the diffident doctor asked, 'deal with the problems at first hand instead of by means of literature?'

'Like a philosopher or a psychologist or a social worker? Well, I think this word "entertainment" now makes its appearance. As long as you interpret it widely. A psychiatrist explains to his students what the characteristics of a certain mental disease are, and then of course has to continue by applying these to the case in hand. What he aims at is clarity. So he probably employs what I should call "jargon". But a writer, by his choice of words, by his choice of situations, deliberately plays on the emotions of his audience. They may, in the first place, have no interest, but by his skill the writer draws them in.'

'And what's your part?' Jennifer asked. 'Where do you come in?'

'I have to make sure that they understand what's said. I help them to interpret the, let's call it, the code. It's necessary, very much so, when the work under consideration is three or four hundred years old, like a Shakespeare play. Young people have no knowledge or sense of history.'

As the Winters left the house, Jennifer Snowdon accompanied Jon to the gate.

'You livened them up,' she said. 'These are really intelligent people, but they delight in being dull.'

'You mean they talk about matters which don't interest you.'

Jennifer took his arm and squeezed it.

14

Jon was surprised to receive a telephone call from Jennifer Snowdon as he sat in his office at the university. She thanked him again for visiting her house, saying how much both her husband and she had enjoyed the company. He told her that he and Emma had found themselves much at home, and had discussed only last night an invitation to the Snowdons to return the visit.

'There is one thing more,' Jennifer said, very deliberately, after a further exchange of politeness. She waited for his reply.

'Yes?'

'I would like to speak to you on my own. Is that possible?'

'Yes. About what?'

'Basically I suppose it's about my father.'

'Is there something wrong with him?'

'I prefer not to talk about confidential matters on the telephone. Look, could I come to the university, because there we could walk about the park and talk? Are you free on Wednesdays at any time?' He said he was. 'I choose that day because my father is never in there on a Wednesday.'

Puzzled, he offered her lunch, but she refused saying she would meet him by the south gate at two o'clock.

'And if the weather's bad?'

'I will ring and cancel before midday. If it's a slight drizzle, we'll wear appropriate clothes and carry umbrellas.' She sounded almost too sane, as if organizing a WI outing or a Guides' rally.

When that evening he told Emma about the assignation, she laughed, asking why Jennifer had insisted on a walk

150

rather than a phone-call to discuss her father. 'It's like MI5 or the NKVD. Does she think her old Dad's bugged your room?'

'Gormley wouldn't know the use of the word "bug".'

'Why does she want to see you about him?'

'I've no idea. My influence in the university is exactly nil. So if she wanted something doing for her father, she'd do better to ask the prof, or the Dean of the faculty.'

'Perhaps,' Emma said, 'she thinks she can find out something about the father, something she needs to know, from you.'

'That's unlikely. Gormley keeps himself to himself, doesn't go spouting his guilty secrets, if he has any, to colleagues, especially the younger ones like me.'

'She thinks perhaps that you've noticed something about him. Have you?'

'Plenty.'

Emma waited for him, without reward.

'You don't think,' she asked, 'she's taken a shine to you, and so has trumped up this excuse to spend an hour in your company?'

'No, that was not uppermost in my mind.' She aimed a comical blow at his solar plexus.

He met Jennifer as by arrangement. The weather was fine. She had found somewhere to park the car, and had made a considerable effort to dress herself to advantage.

'Do you want to walk?' he asked.

'Yes. My shoes are sensible. I often take a stroll these days.'

'Isn't it dangerous?'

'I haven't found it so. I don't usually go into out-of-the-way places.' They set off. Her pace was brisk, but unhurried. 'You may wonder why I have asked to see you.'

'Yes.'

'It's my father. Have you noticed any changes in him recently? Physically, mentally, emotionally?'

'No. I can't say that I have. Nothing radical. I thought he was glad to bring his Shakespeare book out, but his

151

pleasure was modified by fears of its reception. But that's par for the course with academics.'

'My father is sixty-two,' she said. 'I think he looks older.'

'I don't know.'

'Why do you say that?'

'He has a good skin, not too many wrinkles. Strong voice. Can argue a case.'

'He's nearly bald; he's stout; he walks badly. He's short of breath. He has to take tablets for high blood pressure. He thinks his heart's dicky. He's more like a man of seventy-odd than sixty.'

They walked in silence until she pointed to a wooden park bench. She touched his elbow to guide him towards it, and there they sat in the late October sunshine. Jennifer raised her hands chest-high, palms facing inwards, like a fisherman indicating the size of the one that got away. Jon took it that it meant she was to make an important statement, and that he was forbidden to intervene while she held her hands up. He was disappointed when she spoke and asked a question she had put to him in some form at both their previous meetings.

'Do you know my father well?'

'I've been here for four years and I've known him all that time. We've attended meetings together, have passed the time of day. That's about all. Your father's more than twice my age. He'll have little regard for my qualifications as a scholar. He'll think I've spent my time following the demands of the literary theorists, instead of acquiring, as he did, a knowledge of three or four other languages and cultures; this isn't absolutely true, but that will be roughly his view of me as a critic of literature, and my value. He won't hold it exactly against me; it's not precisely my fault, but I've nothing to say to him because I haven't sufficient knowledge. On the other hand, he did surprise me by asking me to look through the proofs of his book on Shakespeare's obsessions. Presumably he'd decided that I'd a sufficiently firm grasp of the difference between a comma and a full stop.'

'Is the book any good?'

'Yes, in an old-fashioned way. It won't set the Isis or the Cam or the Charles on fire. Here's a well-read man giving his conclusions as to why, let's take a very small point, Shakespeare the poet, however unseriously, makes out that poets are liars.'

'I see.'

She stared across at the main block of the university buildings, now occupied by administrators. In the end it was she who broke the not unpleasant silence.

'So it won't make him famous?'

'Literary critics are rarely famous these days, unless they perform on the television screen. And there they'll not be able to do their job at all seriously, at least in the view of other practitioners who do not make such appearances. There's another sort of fame, that of performers at conferences where they lecture other lecturers. But your father won't want to be included in either category.'

'So it won't in any way alter his lifestyle?'

'No. A few people, like me, will read it with pleasure, and learn from it. I don't even know how many university libraries will buy it. I expect it will go into paperback in time, but it won't make him either a fortune or a household name.'

'And will this worry him?'

'Not if other matters are level. He'll remember when Eliot or Leavis were great figures. What they said filtered down to the sixth forms of the public and grammar schools and the literary societies. I don't think such influential critics exist today. We're not a reading society, for one thing. And secondly, well, Leavis was a deeply unhappy man towards the end of his life for all his influence. And Edmund Wilson.' She stared ahead. 'I've never heard your father complain about not getting a chair. I don't know whether he applied earlier in his career, but certainly not in my time.'

'Would he have been a strong candidate?'

'Hard to say. It depends on circumstances. Luck, if you like. He's not been prolific with his publications, and I guess he's always seen as a bit out-of-date, excellent for the generation before. I'm only guessing.'

'He doesn't think very highly of Professor Towers.'

'No. They are, well, a bit incompatible.' Jon drew in breath between his teeth. 'I don't know whether your father's failure to get a chair rankles with him, or even if he considers it a failure.'

'Would you say that Towers has deserved promotion rather than my father?'

'He's published more. He's done the rounds of conferences. He's bothered to get noticed by the right people. He'll go out of his way to do himself a bit of good. So, I suppose the answer to your question is "yes".'

'You'll be wondering why I'm asking these questions?' He did not answer. 'My father's behaviour at home has shown marked changes. He never regarded my mother as his intellectual equal, but as long as she did her part satisfactorily, that was as it should be. She looked after the house and the children. She saw to it that he was properly fed. On the rare occasions he invited people to the house she provided for them, and looked decorative. Now she has outlived the majority of her uses. They entertain no guests; the children are out of the way; they are not very interested in elaborate meals, and four days a week he has a substantial lunch at the staff club. She has help about the house. So.' Jennifer stressed the last word, so that it sounded foreign. Still Jon made no reply. She waited then asked briskly. 'You realize that what I shall say to you . . . is confidential?' He nodded. 'I don't want it discussed. Anywhere. But especially not here.'

'I understand that.'

'Not even with your wife.'

'Yes.'

'My father, in the last six to ten months, has taken to violence against my mother.'

'What sort of violence?' Jon asked.

'Violent violence.' Her voice burst stinging out. 'He hits her with his fists. On the face. On the breasts.'

154

'This is, to the best of your knowledge, recent?'

'Yes. In the last year.'

'What does your mother say?'

'She's frightened.'

Jon rubbed his face with the fingertips of his left hand. 'I don't think I have ever met your mother. Is she physically frail? Easily scared?'

'No. She's a normal woman, I should have thought. She was a student at Oxford when he was there. He was some years ahead of her.'

'Has she told you about these attacks?'

'I forced it out of her. I noticed her injuries. A black eye, a bruised cheek. Marks on her arms and shoulders. She talked about falls, accidents at first. I pressed her. I thought that if she was falling about she should see her doctor. In the end, she confessed. "There's nothing wrong with me. It's your father." I didn't quite get it. The penny didn't drop immediately. I didn't expect it.'

'He wasn't a violent man, then?' Jon asked.

'He's bad tempered, and he'd slap us girls when we were small. But nothing out of the ordinary. I expect we deserved it.'

'There's a story in the department that he once threw a pile of books at a student, a man. But it happened before my time. And it must have been unusual or it would have been forgotten.' He thought for a moment. 'I've seen no signs of violence recently, nor of any changed behaviour.'

'I thought we, that is I, ought to do something about these attacks on my mother. They can't be allowed to continue unchecked. But there might be some reason for them, here, with his work, that could be cleared up.'

'I haven't noticed it, even if it exists.'

'No.' She sounded disapproving.

'And your mother? Has she changed? In respect of attitude to your father, I mean?'

'No. I don't think so. Not until he began to sling his fists about.'

'She's not talking about leaving him?'

'She isn't. I am.' Jennifer's face was set. 'I shall face him with it, but I first of all had to find out if he was in any sort of trouble here. That's why I'm questioning you.'

'Will your mother want to leave him?'

'She's in a state of shock. One, that it's happened and, two, that I've found out. My mother was a scientist; she read chemistry at Oxford. But there's nothing scientific about her attitude now. She had her children, three girls, early in her married life, and I guess the lady-like existence she's had, child- and home-based, has suited her admirably. How she'd shape if she left my father I don't know. She'd be fine looking after herself, but the loss of status, the little meetings of university wives and all the rest she'd miss. She'd be better able to look after herself than he is, but whether she'd want to, whether she'd consider it worth the effort is another matter.'

'So you'll have to tread carefully?'

He felt her pick his right hand up from the seat. She intertwined her fingers in his. Her flesh was firm, cool.

'I shall tread carefully. Yes, that's so. I don't want my mother settling in on us. It would drive Frank spare. But he can't go on like this, slinging his fists about.'

'You'll face him with it?'

'After I've learnt what my mother wants.'

She stood, dragging his hand up with hers. She shook it, like an inanimate thing, patted it with her right, then laughingly let it drop.

'Thanks very much,' she called out, over-loud.

'For nothing.'

'One never knows. Let's walk.' They marched for twenty minutes under the avenues of trees and huge hedges of rhododendron. She warned him once again about confidentiality, and then questioned him about rugby football, saying that she'd get her husband, or Luke Fielding, one of the other medicos at the party, to take her to see him play.

'Not worth the money,' he warned. 'I'm on the wing for my sins this season and so most of the game I just hover about on the edge of the battle.'

156

'I'll just admire your legs in that case,' she said, and slapped him fiercely hard and noisily across the buttocks. A passing female student backed off in grinning alarm. From her car Jennifer thanked him again, did a smart three-point turn and drove off.

In spite of his promises he discussed the matter with his wife. Emma said, 'As you tell the tale, she doesn't seem quite stable.'

This surprised him, but he did not argue.

'Once she'd established that you'd noticed no change in Dr Gormley, then your usefulness was done. But, from what you say, she was in no hurry to put her question to you, and when you'd answered it, she didn't just thank you and clear off. Why was that?'

'Perhaps she was trying to establish what sort of witness I was.'

'Good. Perhaps not. Did she seem excited by this?'

'Not particularly. If I had to categorize her attitude at all it would be as one slightly put out, perhaps amused, by the vagaries of human behaviour.'

'Did she seem fond of her parents?'

'Difficult to judge.'

'Did she prefer one to the other?'

'She felt sorry for her mother, but her father seemed the dominant personality, but that's not surprising in view of her story and that Gormley was the one I knew.'

Emma said that she looked forward to the outcome.

Her doctor, Goach, had seen her again, at her Beechnall office, to report on developments, very few, in the police investigations. He'd talked again to the inspector, who'd had two more anonymous letters, but after a fairly strenuous interview with a woman, he named neither names nor places, there was silence. The doctor, oddly, gave his own views about the identity of the writer, and said, perhaps not seriously, that he had considered bombarding her with a malicious missive or three.

Four days after the Winters' first discussion about Jennifer Snowdon and her father, Goach rang in the middle of

157

dinner to tell Emma that he had received a card from his wife. It was postmarked Blackpool, and was of the old-fashioned comic variety, on which a huge wife guided her hen-pecked, half-sized, meek husband, in blazer, collar and tie, trilby hat, weighed down with bags, along a beach littered with nubile blondes in bathing costumes laid out lasciviously tempting in the sunshine. The wife is, according to the caption, enjoining him to make the most of the beauty of the scene. Mrs Goach's message read: 'I am well, and I hope you are. I am also busy. You are never anything else. Regards. Louise.' First-class stamp. Posted the day before. Had arrived by the early delivery. Yes, he was absolutely sure that the card was in her handwriting. Yes, he had told the police, who had not seemed too excited.

'Now tell me what you think,' Emma pressed.

'She's still alive.'

'Yes. Yes. And the message?'

'What do you mean?'

'Why is it expressed as it is?'

'I haven't thought about it. Are you suggesting that she's heard from somebody about the rumours?'

'Is that possible?' Emma asked. 'Likely? Has she been in touch with somebody, some close friend who lives locally?'

'Not to my knowledge.'

'You don't find it odd?'

'No. Louise is by and large a decent woman, and she'd know I'd be worried over her whereabouts. So she sends this. It came to the surgery. She has a mischievous streak in her, and she'd know the receptionists would read the card, and giggle over the picture. She wouldn't mind my being embarrassed.'

Goach seemed in no way elated by his news.

Emma, by chance, met the inspector in the case, who interviewed her on another matter concerning one of his constables. As he was leaving the man said, 'Your appearance isn't quite as formidable as your reputation. You have

158

quite a name in our neck of the woods. "Don't go in against Miss Ashley with half a case." ' Not what he'd told Goach.

'I've hardly made an appearance in your part of the world.'

The policeman named two. She had won both times, and obviously against police expectations. He mentioned another, it had been widely reported in the city. He suddenly jerked his head upright.

'You're representing the egregious Goach, I understand,' he said. 'I know you won't discuss your clients with me, but . . . There's more in that little story than meets the eye.'

'Is there?' Emma tried to sound cold, unencouraging.

'That card from Blackpool from his wife. Have you seen it?'

Emma explained that she had not, but that Goach had given a full description.

'There are two things,' the policeman said. 'It was sent to the surgery. Now, why? Well, witnesses. Two or three chattering women would read it. Moreover, Goach went off, unusually, two days before, after his morning round. No evening surgery. In his car, nobody knows where. He could easily have gone to Blackpool.'

'Are you suggesting that he forged the card and posted it himself?'

'I am not. I've seen the card, and I had no means of judging whether the message was in his wife's handwriting. The police band was playing last Saturday in Blackpool, and three of my DCs are in it, or connected with it. I asked them when they took a stroll on the prom to see if that particular card can be bought in Blackpool. It can.'

Emma brightly acknowledged his thoroughness, and asked, 'And what conclusion do you draw?'

'Nothing suspicious. Local run-of-the-mill bobbies like me generally have to take things at face value. Sensibly. Because that's the way they usually are. But I keep my mind open.'

'You don't seem to like Goach?' she asked.

159

'Neither one way nor the other. He's a bit too sure of himself. But perhaps that's the result of laying down the law all day and every day to his patients. Doctors are the nearest thing we have to God these days.'

'And you're an atheist?'

'I'm a Methodist local preacher, when I have the time.'

Inspector French grinned companionably at her as he waved goodbye, slipping round the door even as he quietly closed it.

15

Jon Winter broke his leg and dislocated his shoulder playing rugby for the county team. He had been heavily, if fairly, tackled into the crowd and a hidden, carelessly placed iron-legged trestle table. He hobbled about, leg in plaster, arm in a sling, attempting stoicism.

'He's quite a good patient,' Emma admitted. She drove him to work each morning, and if it were feasible picked him up. When she was not available he used taxis. After a week or two he had become skilful with his stick and his stiff leg, but the pain and inconvenience troubled him.

'I'm amazed,' he confessed, 'how much my sort of work, sitting at a desk reading and writing and talking, depends on fitness.'

'You've got into the habit of rude health,' his wife argued. 'And now because of your awkwardness and creaks of pain your mind tends to flit away from literary thoughts.'

'And that places a low value on literature?'

'I didn't draw that conclusion.'

'Didn't I.A. Richards say how easily we were moved by literary passages, even poor ones, when we were recovering from flu?'

'Are poems written for invalids, then?'

'In the sense that one is most likely to read 'em with the greatest interest when one's sensibility is especially heightened. That may be the result of recovery from influenza viruses or falling in love or being frightened to death and so on.'

'Do you explain this to your students?'

'No. Apart, perhaps, for a mention, en passant, in a seminar. My job is to explain what I think is important

161

about the poem, in subject matter, in form, in choice of vocabulary, rhythms, devices, background and all the rest.'

'It sounds all very clinical.'

'I don't mind letting my students see that I am moved by something we're reading.'

'Your tears fall onto your book?'

'No, not these days, but there are recorded historical periods, and not so long ago, when this would have been the case. In Dickens's day, for instance. But I'm speaking of exhilaration, joy, even something nasty like aggression as well as sorrow.'

'Religious ecstasy? Lunacy? Tipsiness?'

'All these will affect the reading, but it's not my business, except by way of mild warnings, to talk about the states of mind, the emotional balance or lack of it in the reader. Each reader must see to his own.'

'But these attitudes, if that's what I can call them, will be part of modern critical theory?'

'Well, yes. I always say that criticism is very like psychology. I've found that people are attracted to, driven towards literary works that in some way reflect their own lives.'

'That's not surprising, is it?' she asked. He lifted his injured leg and placed it more comfortably.

'No. Not any more than some lawyer taking up a cause that has similarities to his own troubles. He'll need all his skills, his coolness, his experience of juries, but his emotional drive may well keep him in pursuit of his aim when his common sense or intelligence or that of friends he trusts show him it's time to give up.'

Jon became used to disability, and though he disliked it he soon realized what he could and could not do. The banter was over inside a week. The sympathy; people became used to seeing him on crutches, or with a stick. One of his girl students cheekily said that it suited his style.

'In what way?' he demanded.

'Gives you a Byronic glamour.'

He shook his stick at her and limped away.

One evening his father-in-law rang to say that Barbara Ashley was shortly to go into hospital. Jon had not heard that she was even ill.

'Is it serious?' he asked.

'Well, comparatively so, or they wouldn't admit her as quickly as all this.'

'Has she been ill long?'

'A month or two. The doctor was treating her for this and that. She's very sensible and does as she's told, but in the end he sent her to the consultant. She had to wait a week or two, but it was moderately quick.'

'Who is it?'

'Professor Rhys-Jones.'

'Does Emma know anything about all this? She's out at the moment.'

'No. She knows her mother's been feeling a bit off, but that's all. It'll be a shock to her, as it is to us.'

'It's cancer, I take it.'

'Yes.' The pronunciation of the monosyllable seemed to breathe relief at Jon's frankness. 'And the surgeon said after he'd seen the X-rays and so on that he hoped he'd be able to remove it all.'

'How does she seem?'

'She doesn't make much fuss, but I guess she's afraid. I am, certainly.'

Jon said he'd get Emma to telephone as soon as she was back. He broke the news carefully to her, watched her wince.

'I wish they'd said something to me.'

'They wouldn't want to worry you,' Jon answered.

'Yes. Typical. They think I'm still a child.'

Emma spoke to her father, instructed him to keep her posted, said she would do the required driving. In any case the hospital was only a few minutes' car ride from the Winters' house. She spoke easily but firmly, as to a client, showing no signs of emotion or stress. When she came away from the telephone her face looked white and drawn and her hair mussed.

'God,' she said, drawing air through her teeth.

'Your father seemed to speak optimistically about what the surgeon said.'

'He always talks on the bright side, even when he thinks the opposite way. And my mother is likely to have put up with pain for long enough not breathing a word to him, or to anybody else. She's been saying this past month or two that she's not been feeling exactly herself, and I've been pressing her to see the doctor.'

'Your father says she's been regularly.'

'Yes, but when she gets there she'll underplay it all. Bit of discomfort; not feeling ever so well. That sort of thing.'

'Is the doctor up-to-date?'

'He's not young. But he's all right. But if somebody comes in with some uncomplaining account of her symptoms, what's he to do? If he sent every patient with indigestion or diarrhoea or constipation to the hospital the waiting lists would be even longer than they are now. They don't expect the worst as soon as a patient appears.'

'Probably rightly,' Jon answered.

'As you say. But he ought to know my mother after all this time, that she'd understate her symptoms. Then he would have sent her for hospital tests straight off.'

'Would it have made any difference?'

'It must have. The cancer would have been less advanced.'

Jon kept her talking, realizing she needed to complain in order to come to terms with the new situation. She considered how her father would shape if he had to look after her sick mother, saying that he'd fail.

'He depends entirely on her. What he's managed to do has depended entirely on her freeing his hands. He doesn't have to think about food or clothes or living conditions. Nothing but his studying and sermons and going round praying with old women.'

'Your mother would approve of that. She'd look on what you say as a deserved compliment. She might not quite like your form of expression – "praying with old women" – but properly paraphrased it would be a true description of her work for the Lord.'

'And if you hadn't broken your leg I'd give it a hell of a kick.'

He knew then he was on the right course, and winning, and encouraged her to telephone her sister about her mother's illness while he prepared supper.

It was all of half an hour before she returned from the phone, and she was blazing again.

'She's a selfish bitch,' she stormed.

'Did she know about your mother?'

'Yes. Daddy had given her a ring.'

'And what did she think or say?'

'Oh, "wait and see. Marvellous what they can do these days. Daddy's pretty well able to look after himself". And then it was all her aches and pains, and the children and the expense and education. And what the Reverend Venerable bloody Archdeacon was up to, and the trouble with priesting women, and what a dim creature the bishop was. She never stops her tongue wagging. But she hadn't much time, I can tell you, for all the discomfort Mummy was in, and the chance of her dying.'

'Yes,' he said, slowly, drawing it out.

'Oh, I know what you're going to say. But . . . '

' "If a way to the Better there be, it exacts a long look at the worst".'

'Who wrote that?'

'Thomas Hardy. *In Tenebris.*'

'What's that about?'

'In the darkness, the shadows. There are three poems, and that particular one is about Hardy himself, I guess, saying that anybody who describes things as they are won't be popular, will be told to clear off, because everything's as right as could be. It's a meditation on a psalm, quoted in Latin. My edition gives the wrong number to the psalms in all three poems. I don't know why.'

'You're a bit of an old pedant,' Emma said.

165

Jon took her in his arms to hug her, and they stood together in front of the hearth, still or swaying, clinging tight.

When they broke away he took her hand.

'That's what your sister needs, a squeeze from the Venerable bloody Archdeacon.'

'I expect she gets it,' Emma said, stirring the malted drink he had made. 'I quite like Tony. It's Diana who's such a pain in the neck. He's very reasonable.'

'And handsome,' Jon said.

'Oh, yes. And popular with the clergymen he's in charge of, if we're to believe Diana. She's lucky to have found a husband as good as he is.' Emma laughed. 'She expects him to be made a bishop, and then she'll be insufferable.'

'Does he want it?'

'I shouldn't be surprised. He's quite ambitious. And he also likes to please Diana. I don't know why he doesn't see through her.'

'Perhaps he does.'

'And?'

'He forgives her like the good Christian he is.'

They talked for half an hour over their late snack, laughed a good deal, criticised the world, but their mood was febrile, uncertain, fear-based. The next evening they drove over to her parents' home. Emma's father sat stiffly in his armchair; he had spent the whole day at some useless conference in Derby called by the Chairman of his District. He had not arrived home until almost six-thirty, and had only just finished his tea when the Winters appeared. He wore his long-suffering face, martyred in a poor cause.

'Tea or coffee?' Barbara Ashley asked.

'You sit down,' her daughter ordered. 'We'll get that.'

'I'm capable of boiling a kettle.'

Mrs Ashley seemed normal, perhaps slightly slower to their suspicious eyes, but more concerned about her husband's weariness than with any mortal illness of her own. She did as she was ordered, and allowed the young people to brew and serve. She gave a thorough, utterly clear account of her visits to the consultant surgeon, her tests, and said cheerfully enough that she had already packed her bag for her stay in hospital, and was cooking and baking, filling the freezer so that her husband would be able to feed himself. She was not exactly cheerful, but genuinely stoical, ready to smile, down to earth. Her husband, more silent than usual, sat uncomfortably not in control of himself, nervously feeling with his left forefinger inside his dog-collar. He answered questions, but uncertainly, as if nine-tenths of his attention was concentrated elsewhere.

When Emma eventually, if tactfully, raised the matter of her mother's having said nothing about her illness, as Jon knew she would, Barbara answered readily enough.

'You have quite enough on your plate, having to drive Jonathan about, and do your own job, and look after that great house and garden. You would have been running up here at every verse-end making yourself ill.'

'How old do you think I am?'

'Twenty-six.' Delivered as if Emma sought information.

'Not six.'

'I wasn't open with you, and perhaps I was wrong, but it won't do any good raising it now and quarrelling over it, will it?'

'You might act differently in the future.'

'If there is any future?'

Barbara Ashley's answer fell leadenly. Her expression, her body movements did not change; a woman in late middle-age, she had set her sense and vigour aside for a moment to allow herself, out of character, to express what should have been kept hidden, to bare her naked fear. Emma turned her back on the company so that they could not see her face.

'We've been invited out for both lunch and tea on Sunday,' Barbara said. 'People are very good.'

'Daddy has two services?' Emma asked.

'Yes. And he's prepared two different sermons.'

167

'It keeps me occupied. I sit in my study with my books, and then I can just manage to keep a hold on myself.'

The Winters stayed only until nine so that the parents could go early to bed. Just before they left Diana rang. Even from a distance they could hear her voice rattling away.

'Good advice?' Ashley said ironically when Barbara returned.

'You know Diana,' his wife answered. 'She means well. Don't do this, don't do that. They're very good these days in hospitals.'

Mother and father accompanied them outside to the street where it was dark. Barbara joshed Jon about his awkwardness dragging his injured leg into the car.

'It has a mind of its own,' Jon said.

'Like the trolleys in the supermarket,' Ashley added.

They all laughed, louder than necessary, as they had kissed and hugged beyond normality. The Winters had barely done a hundred yards down the road when Emma, driving, burst out, 'That Diana. She's like a bloody duck.'

'I could hear her quacking.'

'She knows it all.'

'Your mother didn't seem to mind.'

'She's a saint.'

'They kept very cheerful. At least while we were there. They must be worried, but they were very stoical.' As Emma did not answer Jon continued, voice low, earnest, determined to sort it out. 'They didn't want to talk about it religiously.'

'They know I don't go much for that, and the last thing Daddy would want would be an argument. He's very protective of my mother. Especially now.'

'She would be thinking about dying?'

'I expect so. She's no great hankerer after change. And so even if she believed that the next life would be a great improvement on this, she'd be in no sort of hurry to try it. She'll hold Christian views . . . '

'Strongly?'

'I guess so. My mother's clever, but not argumentative. "In my Father's house are many mansions" is good enough for her. She wouldn't want scientific proof. My father's a different kettle of fish. He'd have doubts, I guess.'

'And won't the prospect of, of cancer . . . '

'You mean dying.'

'Yes, of dying, then, alter your mother's views?'

'No, she enjoys her life and wouldn't want to change. It's like you when they offer you tickets for an international match, you're not mad keen to go. You can see it all on the telly, with no journey there, no journey back, no hanging about. Once it's over and you know the result you can get on with something else. So that's what you do. Even though you know that the atmosphere of the match, and the drinks and the friendship will all be better than a solitary seat in front of the box.'

'I see.' He loved explanatory Emma.

'It's not death she fears, it's dying. The lack of dignity and the pain, incontinence, squalor. And she wouldn't want to leave Daddy behind. She thinks he's not really capable of looking after himself, and thinks he won't do his work so well if she's not there to provide him with meals and clean shirts and a warm bed.'

Emma drove with a patient speed.

'There's no saying, either, that she's going to die,' Jon ventured.

'No. And they can do marvels. And that's the way we must think. But it's our usual long look at the worst.'

'Your parents seem to come from a different world,' he said. 'They're older.'

'It's not altogether that. I mean, they're not a bit like your father, for instance. He thinks as we do, in essentials, and as they don't. I've heard my father talk about his childhood. The chapel-going three times on Sunday, the interminable meetings, prayer-meetings, class-meetings, Guild meetings, outings, concerts. You could spend a good deal of your leisure time there in matters connected with religion.'

169

'That would be in the Thirties, wouldn't it?'

'Yes. My father started grammar school in 1942.'

'But, then, in Huddersfield, was it, his family would be only a small minority? Church attendance was the exception rather than the rule.'

'Yes,' Emma answered. 'But it seemed natural to him. His family and their friends went regularly. And a very large number of children were sent to Sunday School whatever the beliefs of their parents. And there'd be Bible readings and hymns in day school. Religion was alive to him.'

'And he never grew out of it?'

'By and large.'

'And do you think it's a comfort in times like this?'

'In one way, but not in another. I've never heard my father say, in private or in public, that Christians get preferential treatment, or were shielded from tragedy or adversity. They'll suffer just like anybody else. Their strength is that they believe God will be with them in their troubles, helping them to bear them, and behind all this is Providence, a divine plan, so that in the end all will eventually turn out for the best at the final reckoning in the next world if not in this.'

' "All manner of thing shall be well". Dame Julian of Norwich,' he said. Emma changed down, halted at a large traffic island. 'You listened to your father pretty carefully by the sound of it,' Jon continued.

'He's always worth listening to.'

'But not convincing? To you?'

'No. But I don't think it's because he argued the case badly. I couldn't in the end believe in God. That's the top and bottom. Or in the God my parents believed in. I don't doubt that Jesus existed, and, to judge from what he's reported to have said and done, he was an outstandingly good and wise man, but the Son of God, of the same essence as God and all the rest of it . . . '

'It's poetically very powerful. God Himself coming to earth to die. God being crucified. It's very bold. Magnificently so.'

'I'm sure it is. But it cuts no ice with me. It's a wonderful parable, but that doesn't make it true.'

She turned smoothly up the hill and then left to their house. Jon struggled out of the car, attempting a limping speed, to open the gates.

'You're getting more spry,' she called out cheerfully as she drove past him.

Some days later Jon drove for the first time the short distance to the hospital where Mrs Ashley had been operated on earlier that morning. The mother still appeared dazed, though sometimes she spoke coherently, smiling in a distant way, knowing them but now no longer responsible for them or even for her answers to their questions. It was frightening to see the woman they knew so unlike herself, and yet basically unchanged. 'Where were the shared memories? Held in abeyance? How could the prick of a needle so radically change a character built up over years?' Emma wondered. 'Where were the relationships her mother held so dear? Where the revealed truths?' Emma looked at the face, still pale, still beautiful without glasses or teeth. The useful hands outside the sheet seemed clean, and still, without garden dirt or flour to mar the surfaces. The nails, cut square, had been scrubbed. Skin was white, bloodless, not dead but shamming life. The sheets, pillows, bedhead, drips, all were solid, all part of the scene, the background to the white figure whose eyes opened from time to time on a world that was partly unrecognisable.

Ashley had been driven down by one of his congregation, a retired schoolmaster, who had insisted that his minister would need company on the way back. This friend had now taken a subservient seat, behind the family, poking at his moustache, appearing as one who did not listen to the intimate, attempted exchanges. Older than Ashley, broader, with polished black shoes and a suit, he seemed to Emma, shaken beyond rationality, to sit there in judgement on them all.

Jon and Emma slipped out for a few minutes to make enquiries from the ward sister. She reported that the operation had been successful, that the prognosis was good. The information was offered with a kind of friendly authority, reassuring in one way, but too certain to settle the minds of the suspicious young people. They wanted to hear good news, but hardly dared believe it, realizing that they had no access to the code these hospitals used. 'She's doing really well,' the sister said. 'And how do you know?' Emma wanted to ask. She steadied herself. This young woman in her archaic headdress must have seen hundreds of hysterectomies in her time, could compare and contrast the mother's with scores of post-operational conditions. They thanked her as she settled down again to her desk. 'And the cancer?' Emma threw in, from her distress. 'We shall have to wait and see. But Professor Rhys-Jones is hopeful.' Again the broad smile of sympathy, an advertisement for dental hygiene, and they were left to dismiss themselves.

They spent another ten minutes at the bedside. Mrs Ashley fell asleep, and, as they rose to go, the schoolmaster suddenly said, 'Sleep is good. I saw wounded men in the war make marvellous recoveries once they could get off to sleep.' He looked suddenly stricken, as if he'd spoken out of turn. Ashley, Emma, then Jon went to kiss Barbara. The father, fiddling, straightened the edge of the sheet, putting off the moment when they had to leave. At the door of the ward Ashley, then Emma, looked back. The mother had not moved.

Out in the car park Emma made sure that her father had her office telephone number.

'I shall be in the office all day. Until five-thirty, six. Do you want a lift down to the hospital tomorrow?'

'I'll see to that,' the ex-schoolmaster said. 'I'll act as his chauffeur. It gives me something to do.'

'Doris'll find something for you,' Ashley said, suddenly social.

'If I didn't drive you down here I shouldn't half get the length of her tongue.'

'And Ted's car is very large, and warm, and comfortable.'

'Good. It's very kind of Mr Broadley.'

Back at home, Emma sat down and cried, with paltry
tears. Jon, hopping, prepared drinks, and made his wife
smile with his fancy, clock-face arrangement of biscuits on
a plate.

'Are you busy?' Jon asked.

'Not really. There's always some day to day stuff. I'll be
on with that. She looked so ill, Jon, didn't she?'

16

Three days later, Mrs Ashley was still in hospital, Dr Goach rang Emma at her office.

'I'm speaking from a telephone box,' he said. 'I'm on my rounds. I don't like to ring from the surgery; there are too many listening in.'

'Home?'

'I don't put it past the police to check on that.'

Emma let it pass. Certainly Goach seemed strained.

'I had another visit from Inspector French.'

The doctor waited for her comment.

'Is there any more news of your wife?' Emma asked.

'No.'

'What did he want, then?'

'To question me. He went all over the events of that first evening again.'

'Did he say why? Were there any developments?'

'No. He just wanted to make sure, he said. Quite often people remembered things when they thought back. I didn't believe him.'

'Why not?'

'Police inspectors don't come round on the off-chance. He must have had something in mind.'

'And you didn't remember anything helpful?'

'No. I've been over it all so many times.'

'I see. Is there anything you'd like me to look into for you?'

'No. I don't think so,' Goach answered, steadily again. 'But I thought I should report to you that French had been round. I don't think he's satisfied.'

'In what way?'

'He's not convinced I didn't murder Louise.'

'What makes you say that?'

'He didn't come straight out with it.' Dr Goach sounded hot under the collar again. 'But that was the impression.'

They talked on for another ten minutes. Emma learnt nothing more, except that Goach was now nervous. When she had first interviewed him he had given the appearance of a cool customer, but he seemed jumpy, in need of reassurance. She asked if he was over-working but he said, 'No more than usual.' He thanked her, claiming she had set his mind at rest. She advised him to ring if there were any developments.

When she discussed the matter with Jon he said that Goach's behaviour did not surprise him.

'His Louise has been snatched away from him. He thinks people are talking all the time behind his back. He feels his status is impugned. Even if she's just upped sticks and left him, without much blame attaching to him, he'll feel uncomfortable.'

'How do you know all this?' she asked.

'I don't. But it's how I'd feel.'

Ian Gormley had knocked at the door of his office. He had brought in an early copy of *Shakespeare's Obsessions*.

'I haven't signed it for you yet. I would like to put in your wife's name as well as yours, but I've forgotten it, that is if I ever knew it.'

'Emma. She'll enjoy that.' Jon spoke with a forked tongue.

'Do you think she will read it?'

'Possible. She doesn't usually read literary criticism, but, but in this case . . . '

'What is her line? Her training? Was she a teacher of some sort?'

'The law. She's a solicitor.'

'It might be interesting then. Shakespeare had some knowledge of the law, some interest.'

'Do you think he'd worked, say, for a lawyer?'

175

'No.' Gormley drew in breath through pursed lips in a ghostly whistle. 'It's impossible to say. One with Shakespeare's quickness of mind could pick up the terms from his conversation with lawyers. The knowledge would be superficial, but so would it be in a play written by a lawyer. He was involved in various legal proceedings himself. But you knew that.'

Gormley signed the book, very neatly, but ended with a flourish. He waved the inscription in the air, then held it out to show Jonathan.

'Thank you,' he replied. 'From us both.'

'Tell me what your wife says.' Gormley made for the door, but halfway there turned and marched back. 'You know my daughter, I understand? Jennifer Snowdon?' Jon nodded agreement. 'How did she seem to you?'

'Seem?'

'Yes, seem. Is she normal? In her right mind?'

Jon laughed in Gormley's face at the questions, but the older man did not alter his expression. He sweated, and dabbed at his forehead with a silk handkerchief.

'I've met her only a few times, but, yes, she gave me the impression of being perfectly sane.'

'You'd say you knew her well?'

'No. We've talked together three or four times.'

'She did not seem worried?' Jon shook his head. 'About me, for instance?'

'No.' Jon lied easily.

'Are you quite sure?'

'I don't know her well enough to make judgements of the sort you seem to want. Why do you ask me?'

'You were seen with her walking in the park. Only last week. My informant was Dr Irene Lonsdale of the philosophy department.'

'Yes. We met in the park. Took a stroll together. Very pleasant.'

'There's no sort of affair, affaire between you?'

'No. Is that what you're afraid of? Is that the trouble? You can put it out of your mind.'

176

'Isn't that what they all would say? Adulterers?'

'I suppose so. In my case it's the truth. I get on quite well with Jennifer. And her husband.'

'I'm pleased to hear that.' Gormley paused, put his fingers on Jon's desk and leaned low towards him. 'That is not what I had in mind when I spoke to you. But I thought I should clear the air. It came as a shock when Dr Lonsdale said she had seen the pair of you together.'

'Behaving improperly?' Jon could not resist.

'No. As far as I can tell, and I questioned Lonsdale closely because she is not always to be trusted as an informant. How she came to specialize in philosophy I don't know. But she said you were walking along in perfect propriety. I was a little suspicious because I've never known Jennifer walk in the university grounds before.'

'She doesn't live too far away.'

'With cars no one lives too far away these days.' Again Gormley stopped. 'I wished to check with you on her state of mind, because she came to see me, rather unusually, and made accusations against me in what I considered a wild way. She shouted. Kept hitting her chair.'

Both men waited.

'These accusations were untrue?' Jon said.

'Largely.' Gormley repeated the word, with unction. 'Largely. But I don't think it will be necessary to dwell on the nature of her accusations.'

'No.'

'It came as a surprise. Both the accusation and the violent manner in which it was made.'

Jon nodded. He had never seen Gormley look so uncomfortable. The man had now straightened up, and was pulling at the flesh of his face with his left hand.

'Thanks very much. Perhaps you will be so kind as to keep an eye on her, open to her behaviour.'

'I don't know when I shall see her again.'

'No. No. You will not mention this conversation to her, I hope. It is confidential. Especially when I wonder if perhaps I have made an error. Of judgement.'

177

'Thanks again for the book.'

Gormley started at the change of tone, but accepted his dismissal and made a small obeisance, a slight inclination from the hips. He then turned and made good, if awkward, speed to the door.

When Jon mentioned this to Emma she immediately asked, 'Do you think it's likely that he attacks his wife?'

'I've no idea. How do you know such things? That's one of Shakespeare's obsessions, this inability to read the character from the outward appearance:

> There's no art
> To find the mind's construction in the face.

Duncan in *Macbeth*.'

> 'And though that nature with a beauteous wall
> Doth oft close in corruption, yet of thee
> I will believe thou hadst a mind that suits
> With this thy fair and outward character.'

'Well done,' Jon showed his pleasure, clapped his hands.

'I learnt it for A Level. We had to make a little book of useful quotations, and then get 'em by heart.'

'You'll get along with Gormers's book.'

'And if I don't he'll come and beat me up.'

Barbara Ashley's progress in hospital was slower than expected. They had her out of bed early enough and shuffling around, but infection and high temperature weakened her.

'Perhaps it's as well,' she told Emma. 'I don't want to go home until I'm really fit. I shall be such a drag on Daddy.'

Emma proposed that when her mother was discharged, both she and Lionel should stay with them. 'There'll be three of us to look after you, and Daddy can easily run out in his car to visit and preach and so on. And he'll be free

178

every evening for these everlasting meetings of his; we shall both be at home.'

'He won't want to impose on you. Nor do I.'

Ashley agreed, eyes wide. His wife's illness had shaken him into a kind of stupor. He said he would make preliminary arrangements, and then, unexpectedly, scratching his head, 'It's a good job we haven't any pets.'

At much the same time Jon received a phone call from a man who claimed to be assistant secretary to the Old Morleyans Rugby Club. Neither name nor voice was known to Jon.

'I wonder if you could find the time to attend our committee meeting on Wednesday next. It's very short notice, I know.'

'I'm not even a member of the club now.'

'I realize that. I also realize that the club treated you shabbily, and now we're throwing ourselves, as it were, on your mercy.'

'What is it you want?'

'We want to pick your brains. About coaching. Somebody said that you were a university lecturer, had played rugby at a much higher level than anybody else in our club, were not playing at present on account of injury, and perhaps you'd be willing to give us an outline of coaching and training.'

'Why are they so keen?'

'We're doing quite well so far this season, and some of them think we can do even better if we take it more seriously.'

'Who proposed this?'

'Andy Starr. He spoke well of you.' Starr was a friend of the late Alf Perkins.

'And what was the general consensus?'

'Ted Wareham said you'd just tell us to go jump in the Trent. And some others thought much the same. I imagine some of them were feeling guilty. That's why they picked on me to approach you. You didn't know me, so you'd hear me out. I'm new.'

'I see.'

179

'There have been a lot of changes in the club. We're showing signs of ambition.'

'Why have things changed?'

'Alf Perkins died, for one. That's what they tell me.'

Jon arranged to attend the meeting, but said he needed an exact time, because he did not want to sit through boring minutes of the last meeting, team selection and so forth.

'You might get some idea of the present state of the club.'

'If I understand you properly, you're asking me to coach players not committee members.'

The caller huffily said he would try to organise this, and gave his name again as Bill Burton. He would ring back.

Barbara Ashley came out of hospital, settled into the bedroom which the Winters had arranged on the ground floor. She seemed cheerful, but weak. Ashley moved in with her. Jon spent his free afternoons at home. Emma came back in the lunch hour three working days a week. The mother did not stay in bed all the time, was shown how to work the television sets in drawing and dining rooms, was given free rein in the pantry but was forbidden to cook. They ate their main meal at night. This itself was not altogether satisfactory in that Lionel had to go out for meetings. He spent at least one whole day at the Derbyshire home, and two evenings in his own bed. He best prepared his sermons in his study, he claimed, because he knew exactly where to lay his hands on his books. All four of the family seemed to learn their new responsibilities quickly, and as Barbara Ashley's health gradually improved she began to enjoy having the run of her daughter's 'mansion'.

One morning, between lectures, Jon sipping at his coffee was interrupted by Ian Gormley. The man's face seemed drawn, and he carried a rolled-up newspaper in his hand, slapping it oddly across his leg as he approached.

'Have you seen this?' He held his newspaper up and

opened it out. 'Last week's *TLS*,' Gormley said. 'There's a review of my book.'

Jon offered Gormley coffee which was stonily refused as he straightened the paper on Jon's desk. Jon had already read the article.

'Just read that.'

Jon picked it up, turned first to examine the table of contents before reading about Gormley.

The paper had several page-long reviews of books on Shakespeare, and a large account of two recent productions of *A Comedy of Errors* and *Two Gentlemen of Verona* with photographs. Gormley's book was given two half columns, shuffled into a corner, and headed 'Back to Bradley'. The reviewer, one Timothy Heron, disliked the book, saying it was thoroughly old-fashioned. It paid no attention to the work of any modern critics, neither the Frankfurt School nor the Post-structuralists, nor did it give much credit to the researches on Elizabethan and Jacobean rhetoric or history. The reviewer admitted that Gormley appeared to know his Shakespeare texts well, and had clearly read some of his sources, and had looked at contemporary playwrights and poets, but his conclusions were of the sort that a bright sixth-former or first year undergraduate could draw for himself, and were therefore unnecessary. Heron concluded that it was a pity that a scholar with close knowledge of texts, and not without ingenuity, had not taken his opportunity to use modern procedures to make younger readers aware of the difficulties inherent in the explication of even a leader in a modern newspaper, never mind a play written so far back in time, by a genius of so complex a mind in so esoteric a code.

'Yes,' Jon said, uncertain. 'Who is this Heron?'

'He teaches somewhere, I understand. At Cambridge, I think. All it says here is that his book *Shakespeare's Secrets* will be published next year.'

'He seems to be big on theory.'

'You've read my book. Does this seem to be a fair

account?' Gormley almost ground his teeth, as he jabbed a finger down on the flat of the paper.

'I can only guess. I've never heard of this man before. He's never attended or, at least, drawn attention to himself at any Shakespearean conferences I've attended. Not that that is many. I'd go on to conjecture, perhaps wrongly, from the title of his book that you have anticipated some of his ideas. Not that will concern him much. But . . . '

'Is it fair?'

'No. But fairness isn't an attribute of reviewing, academic or any other sort. This man probably believes that continental theorizing can throw new light on Shakespeare, by a means which is more logical or scientific, whereas the likes of you and me just stand in front of the text giving vent to Oohs and Aahs of admiration because we've always been taught to think that's the right way to react. The fact that we shan't be able to understand what he's saying when his book comes out he'll put down to our idleness, that we won't exert ourselves to think or speak of Shakespeare in any way except that of effete old littérateurs. So, no, to answer your question, the review is not fair. He thinks that you will not pay attention to new and important methods of literary discussion which would make his pupils rediscover new strengths and beauties, though he wouldn't use such words, in these plays.'

'In my view there is not much in these theories to throw light on these texts or on any other. The theories themselves are written in language that is barely intelligible.'

'Yes, but he'll see you as standing there with your glass of port and your cigar and your bow-tie and velvet smoking-jacket murmuring admiration for whatever Shakespeare chooses to do.'

'He wouldn't say that if he'd read my book.'

'No,' Jon answered. 'But he'd regard any adverse criticisms you level at Shakespeare's dramatic method as too small to count, and probably put in merely to demonstrate how clever you were.'

Gormley's face purpled, his jowls shook.

182

'Is that what you think?' he said, in what he would consider a passionless voice.

'Of course it isn't. As well you know.' Jon leaned back in his chair, shifting his injured leg with his hands. 'And, Ian, let's look at the other side of the picture.'

He rarely called Gormley by his first name, and now waited for Gormley to agree to his proposition. All he received was a throaty, pacific grunt of acquiescence.

'Imagine some teacher in a school or university reads this review. He or she'll see that in spite of Heron's unfavourable reception of your views, he admits that you know the texts well. He/she,' he did this to rile Gormley, 'will probably know your *Shakespeare's Comic Masterpieces* as well as *Themes in Restoration Comedy* and so will know the method you use. He/she,' he emphasized the feminine pronoun again, 'will be glad to turn his student on to a book that is written by a man who knows the plays thoroughly, who quotes aptly, and can refer to equivalent passages both in Shakespeare and in other dramatists. It will save him/her, a great deal of time and donkey-work. Even if he/she considers it elementary, they'll add their bits of theory later for the enlightenment of their pupils. So. They'll buy the book for their libraries. It will appear on reading lists. It might even be understood by a fair proportion of readers. And what more can you want?'

Gormley spluttered, to himself.

'Once the book is there,' Jon continued, 'on the library shelves, it must take its chance. It would be very fine if influential professors pronounced it of crucial importance to the understanding of Shakespeare, but they won't. It would be magnificent if journalists took it up as throwing light on the way human beings live today, or in Shakespeare's period. It would be fine if the Prime Minister quoted some masterly sentence from it to floor his opponents in the House of Commons. It would be marvellous if the book became a campus cult, so that not only students of English, but scientists and sociologists all made reverent reference to it. But you don't expect it. You don't think it's that kind of book.'

'No, but . . . '

'Never mind the buts. You can name books less well-thought out, less well-illustrated or well-written which for one reason or another have made a considerable impact in their time. They happen to be published at a period when people are particularly receptive to their sort of notions, be they sound or crack-brained. I don't think your book is of that sort. And though you'd like it to be widely read, and not disparaged by young fly-by-nights like Heron, you would, I think, in the end be embarrassed by the book if it took off in the way I've outlined. You might laugh all the way to the bank, but you'd know that it was praised in the press and talked about in the common-rooms for the wrong reasons.'

Gormley stroked his chin. He seemed calmer. 'What do you think of it, then?' he asked.

'I enjoyed it. As my wife is doing now. I learned a great deal from it, some of which, *pace* Dr Timothy Heron, I would not have found out for myself. It's a book by a scholar, somebody who has read Shakespeare through and through, who has read Plautus in the original, and Plutarch in Greek and in North, and Holinshed and the Geneva Bible and Montaigne and the rest, and knows how to use his knowledge. The book is there, and printed. It may well be that it won't be as widely read as it ought to be because of unfavourable notices by the egregious Heron . . . '

'Including Towers.'

'Has he written about it, then?'

'No. But he'll be drawing the attention of all and sundry to the bad reviews.'

'I doubt it. You and Towers may not see eye to eye, but unlike Heron he has no fish to fry in this corner of the literary vineyard.' Jon giggled at his mixed metaphors. 'And he knows enough to recognize the strengths of your book. So, you will have to be satisfied. Or make up your mind who it is you're going to believe. Me or Heron?'

'Heron gets his views into print.'

'Pretty well by chance. He knows the editor, or some friend of the editor has recommended him. But, and I'll repeat this till I'm black in the face, your book has been published, and will be read.'

Jon very neatly folded the *TLS*, handing it over.

Gormley nodded, thanked Jon, marched off. As he reached the door he turned, said, ' "Go, little book".'

'Exactly.'

Jon felt pleased with himself. Later that day he ran across the professor, brushing crumbs from a fancy waistcoat.

'I've just seen Gormley,' Towers said. 'He seemed at ease with the world. Did you see that his book was reviewed last week or the week before last in the *TLS*? I don't know whether he's read it.'

'Yes. He showed it to me.'

'Wasn't he angry about it? I wouldn't mention it to him. He seems very touchy these days.'

'He'll get over it. Who's this man Heron who did it?'

'I've never heard of him.'

'Have you read Gormley's book?'

'No. Not really. Is it good?'

'Of its kind. Yes.'

Professor Towers grinned to himself and did one or two elaborate dance steps before marching off, humming to himself. King Irony.

Later that week Jon attended a specially-called meeting of the Old Morleyans R.F.C., arranged for his convenience, where he lectured them, modestly, on the steps they should take to improve their record. He was listened to carefully and politely, and they invited him to act as coach, but did not seem too disappointed when he turned the offer down.

'I've too many other things to do at present. Family and work. It also looks to me as if my connection with rugby is going to finish. I shall be very lucky to play again this season, and certainly not in the first team. So I'm inclined to give it up altogether.'

'All the more reason for you to take up coaching,' the assistant secretary interjected.

'No. I've enjoyed my rugby. But what you need is a near-fanatic. That is if you're serious about raising standards.'

He named the man they wanted, a schoolmaster, who lived the game twenty-four hours a day. Jon pointed out the snags. They needed thirty dedicated players for whom the club came first, who were prepared to train hard and fight for their places. 'And when you begin to make a name you'll attract others who'll displace those who've sweated to make you what you are. And when you're really successful the big clubs will poach; they'll entice your players away. It's not easy. It will cause trouble. I know. I was taken away from this club, and it did me no good with some of your committee. I didn't blame them. But once you begin to be competitive this is the sort of thing that happens. You'll have to be prepared for it. And lay on all the administrative groups behind the players, to attract sponsors, organize events. It needs time and money and enormous dedication.'

'You don't think it's worth it?' a sharp-eyed committeeman asked.

'I'm not saying that. But it's a hard grind. I'm the wrong man. Dai Morris will do you proud, if your players can stand him, and are as mad as he is. And he's in touch with the schools. He'll bring good young players in. But be prepared for upsets. You don't do what you say you want to do without blood.'

They questioned and thanked him. He drank a half-pint of beer with them in the quarter of an hour before he left He had the impression that they thought he exaggerated.

Jon explained all this to the family over dinner one evening. He enjoyed these meals, which he helped Emma to prepare. Barbara Ashley seemed sprightly, and though her consultant had prescribed radiotherapy, ('it's usual, the safeguard, you know, just in case I haven't quite cleared it all up'), laughed and talked as if she was completely cured.

'Do you like to be called in as an expert like this?' Ashley asked his son-in-law.

'I quite enjoy it, but I'm surprised. It doesn't happen often. I know so little about it all.'

'I bet you lay down the law all the same,' Emma chaffed him.

'I do. But I feel so ignorant. I'm talking from my small knowledge, and think all the time that they're asking themselves. "What does he know about it?" '

' "Who made thee a prince and judge over us?" '

'Who said that?' Emma asked.

'One of the two fighting Hebrews to Moses in Egypt. Book of Exodus.'

'But will they pay any attention to you?' Barbara demanded. She was beginning to relish these evening meals when three people entertained her with their day's thoughts.

'Vaguely. I made some suggestions to them, and named some names. But it boils down to how much work the players are willing to put in. If there are twenty or thirty in the club who are willing to put rugby very high in their lives they'll begin to do well. But there are so many snags. Injuries. Jealousies. Bad luck. One can't guarantee anything. It's the only way to get on, but it may not work. Too many lifestyles to be changed.'

'It must be difficult for the committee,' Barbara said.

'For everybody.'

'And then you say it may not work out?'

Lionel Ashley sat up straight now at the table, and laid down his knife and fork. They knew he intended to make an announcement. Emma giggled, but covered her face with a flat hand. Ashley frowned, rolled his head. The others went on eating, not attempting to interrupt these preliminaries. He now shook his napkin.

'I've been a minister now for thirty-seven years. And when I look back what do I see? What appears as important?'

Nobody answered. All gave the appearance of eating steadily.

187

'I will tell you,' Ashley said. 'I have spent my time closing churches. Only yesterday I passed an old chapel where I'd served. Main Street, Wensley,' he said to his wife. 'It had been for some years a repository for furniture, but now it's plastered with "For Sale" notices again. I remember great services in that shabby, empty place.' He shook his head. 'What should I say in excuse for that?'

They waited. Jon, recognizing the necessity of rescue said, 'Matthew Arnold felt the same in his poem, 'Dover Beach'.'

'Go on,' Emma said. 'Blaze away.'

' "The Sea of Faith
Was once, too, at the full and round earth's shore
Lay like the folds of a bright girdle furl'd.
But now I only hear
Its melancholy, long, withdrawing roar." '

'Ah,' Mrs Ashley said. It was an odd, beautiful, unexpected sound.

'The rum thing is that Arnold thought Sophocles had the same sadness about life. "The turbid ebb and flow / Of human misery".'

'Presumably,' Emma said, the lawyer bringing them nearer reality, 'Daddy feels a sense of disappointment about all these closures. How would you cheer him up, Jon?'

'Well, it would have to be with talk of quality rather than quantity. All the excellent sermons. Those people introduced to religious depths and heights. Those comforted. That's the quality. And for all I know, though figures for church attendance are falling here, that's incontrovertible; in Africa or China or somewhere more and more are turning to western religion. Change will take place.'

'Will that do, Daddy?' Emma asked.

'I don't regret my thirty-seven years. I might not have been as good in a period of expansion. I don't want to boast.'

188

' "Joy shall be in heaven over one sinner that repenteth",'
Emma said, ' "more than over ninety and nine just persons,
that need no repentance." '

'Not quite ninety and nine in the fold these days,' said
Barbara, smiling.

'True, times change,' Ashley said. 'And we must expect it.
Nor do we know what's to come. Moses never reached the
Promised Land. We must be like your rugby club. Consult
the experts. Put more work in. Change our priorities.'

'Yes,' Emma answered. 'But it may not always work out.
I took Jon to Gunthorpe Hall earlier this year, before we
were married, to see a rehearsal of Purcell's *Fairy Queen*.
They'd gone to enormous trouble. Spent at least two years
gathering sponsors and money. And then getting together,
with dates, that was important, a first rate body of singers
and players. We went to a rehearsal, the first big gathering
of everybody concerned, and it seemed to be shaping
wonderfully well. But then from that time it began to crack.'

'Why was that?' Lionel Ashley.

'Singers withdrew. Illness in two cases. The conductor
quarrelled with everybody. The ticket agency failed. Sponsors drew their horns in, wouldn't face the rising costs.
They'd some really first-rate people who'd given months of
their time, but once the rot set in there was no chance of
recovery. It's such a shame.'

'Wasn't there any chance of putting it on,' Jon asked, 'in
some less lavish form?' He and Emma had often discussed
this.

'They seriously considered that, once the top players and
singers began to pull out. And it was possible, they said,
without losing much of the musical quality of the work.
But then the accountants weighed in. They'd all finish up
to their ears in debt. If there had been some big leading
figure about to rally the troops they might still have done
it. But the producer, the head of admin, the secretary and
the replacement conductor were nowhere. All away for one
reason or another. Just by pure ill-luck when they were
needed, and the whole thing collapsed like a card-house.'

189

'Weren't people disappointed?' Barbara asked.

'Yes, they were. Dozens of people who'd invested time and talent and money felt let down. But it's as Jon told his rugby people: it's no use feeling sorry or disillusioned or disgruntled, you need some fanatic, some near-madman to pick the bits up and rebuild, and drive, and scourge it all back into life. But there was nobody there to do it. Most of us, in whatever it is concerns us, are willing to go so far, but after that we back away.'

'And so the battle's lost,' Jon said lugubriously.

'It would have been a marvellous week,' Emma answered. 'It would never have been forgotten. And it started so well. That's what's so maddening. All the initial apathy was overcome. I could weep. I would have taken all four of us together. Oh. It makes me despair. If only luck had run our way. Just slightly. But it didn't. It was as if fate had marked it out for tragedy.'

'It was only an opera,' Lionel said.

'Only.' Emma's voice spilt bitterness.

'Is there no chance,' Barbara asked, 'of it being done again in the future?'

Emma shook her head. 'There is some suggestion, but people have lost confidence. When so much has been invested it seems all the worse. If it had been a Gilbert and Sullivan it could have stood up to trouble, but people had aimed too high.'

'Are they in debt still?' Barbara asked.

'I don't think so. Helpers have been generous. Salving their consciences, the producer says. I don't know. It's wound up now. Financially.'

Barbara leaned over Emma, put a hand on her arm, kissed her daughter on the cheek.

Emma smiled, shook her head. 'And I was only very vaguely attached.' She hung her head.

190

17

While Barbara Ashley was undergoing radiotherapy Emma did not allow her mother to return home. Mrs Ashley, who seemed not too adversely affected by the treatment, now occasionally cooked meals for them all, and was allowed out on Sunday to one service with her husband. She clearly enjoyed the company in the evening, and vied with the cleaning woman, who came in two mornings a week, to talk the hind leg off a donkey. If the weather was fine she took steady, short walks along the tree-lined streets or round the garden, and now and then accompanied Emma into the city centre for shopping expeditions. 'I've not had such a lady-like existence ever before in my life.' When the doctors spoke optimistically of her chances of complete recovery all seemed to blossom. Even Ashley expressed, out of character, his pleasure to his son-in-law.

'I can't tell you how grateful we are to you and Emma for all you've done for us.'

'It's Emma you must thank.'

'Well, yes. But you have to agree to it. It's done us both a power of good. I've been able to continue with my work as I couldn't have done if your mother had had her convalescence at home, and she's revelled in it all. She really is resting.'

'It's called "comfort",' Jon answered. 'Something you puritans don't much appreciate.'

'We do now we've tried it.'

'We're ruining your moral character.'

'No. You're both living examples of the protestant work ethic.'

Ashley had taken up reading Milton, and Jon raided the university library for books for his father-in-law.

'I read the first two books of *Paradise Lost* at school, and thought I enjoyed them. The language at least. I don't suppose your students read Milton much these days, do they?'

'You'd be surprised. I marked an outstanding essay on *Lycidas* the other day from a girl. She seemed quite caught up with Milton's cleverness and his preoccupations, or at least the one about living on to complete a life's work as opposed to dying young with promise unfulfilled, and her grasp of the marvellous ear, the use of language, of sound, was remarkable. I felt as if she was the teacher and I the student.'

Emma was quite firm with her parents that they were not to return home until after Christmas.

'Go back in January, if you're fit, and then there are only two or three months of winter left to sit out in that damp manse. You build yourself up first.'

Barbara Ashley laughed, but was reassured. 'That Emma of yours,' she told Jon, 'is a proper little dictator.'

'But more often right than wrong.' They both laughed. 'Was she like that when she was a girl?'

'She spoke her mind. But then she always seemed as if she was fighting herself. Now she's so calm. It surprises me. I suppose it's because she's happy here as she wasn't at home. And you must take the credit for that.'

'I let her boss me about,' Jon said, 'as you and her father didn't. Is that it?'

'She's very like her father. And she could be a little firebrand if she was crossed. She used to lecture us on what narrow, circumscribed, impoverished lives we led.'

'Was it true?'

'Yes. Given her premises. She'd argue that we made no attempt to widen our knowledge of great music or great poetry. "There you are with your hymns," she'd say. "You don't try to come to terms with the great Christian poets or musicians. There's no Dante, no Donne, no Milton nor Herbert," I remember her saying, "only Watts and Wesley, and more often than not, not even those two. Adelaide

192

Ann Proctor, Horatius Bonar, Bishop Heber and Ira D Sankey, Anna Laetitia Waring. No Bach only John Bacchus Dykes." She really used to get hot under the collar. And Daddy would make it worse.'

'In what way?'

'Well, he'd say that the greatness of God was so far above humanity, that the master works of Bach or Handel or Beethoven were barely distinguishable to Him from the latest pop-hit. All were of equal smallness compared with his great creations.

"You mean God's got no critical faculty," she'd shout. "You haven't followed my argument," he'd say. "Yes, I have. And it's just an excuse for your singing and reciting low-grade productions." '

Barbara's face was alight.

'Did her father get angry with her?'

'Oh, yes. He was furious sometimes. He used to try to keep cool, because he felt that the strength of the argument was on his side. But he came away sometimes absolutely fuming. She was very good at putting her case. Of course he's more, well, composed these days.'

'It's only eight or ten years ago.'

'Yes. I suppose it is. But he's calmed down. Perhaps Emma even taught him a thing or two.'

'Wasn't Diana like that?'

'No. She was a great talker. But a smoothie.' Barbara smirked at her word. 'Sly, even. Diplomatic. Not like any of the rest of us.'

Two weeks before Christmas the Ashleys spent three days with Diana. They said when they returned that they were glad to be back. They had been made most welcome, but Diana had treated her mother like a piece of valuable china, not to be moved. They'd eaten well, the children had been marvellous, energetic and the Archdeacon a distant, calming influence. There had been some sort of financial scandal amongst the clergy that Tony was working day and night. He never spoke about it, and what bit they learnt was from Diana, who herself seemed by no means clear, as if her husband had not confided in her. Tony looked strained, but he had sat and chatted with them on both evenings until they went to bed, when he went up to his study to prepare for the next day's work. At breakfast he looked cheerful, chaffed the children, drove the two younger ones to school. First thing in the morning Diana had barely a pleasant word to throw to anybody.

'I washed up, and then got out of her way until coffee time when she was more human,' Ashley said.

'I don't know how Tony puts up with her,' Emma said.

'She has her points,' Barbara answered. 'And she made us very welcome. It did me good to see how they live, and how the children are growing up.'

On Saturday afternoon, unannounced, Jon drove himself down to the Old Morleyans' ground to watch the First XV. He had asked his father-in-law to accompany him and had watched the surprise and fright on Ashley's face. He refused, of course, and had taken his wife out to visit some friends from a former circuit who had now settled in Beechnall.

Members of the Old Morleyans seemed equally caught out by his presence. They spoke to him, cheerful and suspicious. The team lacked the club captain and a power-ful newly-signed back-row forward, but played with vigour, sweating and swearing. At half-time they were leading by a penalty goal; play had been ragged.

The assistant secretary sidled up to Jon. 'What do you think, then?' he asked.

'Enthusiastic.'

'Not skilful?'

'Not really. The other lot are just as bad, thank God.'

'We've three of our best men missing.'

'And they would restore discipline?' Jon asked sarcast-ically.

Burton grinned. He was a non-player; he'd done some serious damage to a leg in his school team, but he kept up his interest by doing the paperwork. He was a chartered secretary by profession. Jon looked at the peaky face, the sandy eyelashes, the pale hair, and liked the man.

'Did the committee approach Dai Morris?'

'They discussed it at length.'

'And?'

'They told me to make a preliminary inquiry.'

'That was big of them. What did Dai say?'

'He was very cagey. I think if I'd have gone with a straightforward proposition he might have been more forthcoming. I mentioned your name as the one who'd recommended him.'

'And he wasn't impressed?'

'Led off about Oxbridge amateurs.'

'Of course.'

Jon's insouciance seemed to worry Burton. The secretary shuffled, stared at his muddy shoes. 'The club's had bad luck this year. Injuries and so on. I don't think we've had a full first team out more than twice. And Alf Perkins's death. I know he crossed you, but he put an enormous amount of effort in. And now Ted Wareham, another old stalwart, he's been taken into hospital.'

'Serious?'

'Nobody seems to know. It's all very sudden.'

'How did the players react to the suggestion of Dai Morris as coach?'

'Not much said, but on the other hand they seemed willing to try it. The only view against it was somebody who took me into a corner, I'll name no names, and growled, "As long as he realizes we're not schoolkids . . . That's his trouble." '

The second half was as uncouth as the first, with both sides committed, angry and voluble. A penalty near the end of the game to the opponents made the result a draw. Hands were roughly shaken. The O.M.s' fly-half, passing Jon on his way to the pavilion, said, 'You didn't learn much about the finer points of the game this afternoon from that little exhibition.' He trotted on, steaming.

'Did you enjoy it?' some stranger asked Jon.

'Not the word I'd choose.'

The sky was overcast so that daylight seemed almost dead by the end of the game. Jon looked at the empty pitch over which the players were trampling ten minutes before. Lights shone from the bar, but no one invited him to join them. Cold, small winds swooped. The opponents' bus, a large vehicle, rather high-seated with space for luggage underneath, and designated along its coffee coloured flank as 'Executive Coach', exhibited modernity in the raw twilight. Jon made his way across muddy grass to the next field where his car was parked. The stranger was already there, dangling keys. He nodded again to Jon.

'I don't know why I come out here,' he said. 'I hated rugby at school. I wasn't built for it.'

'Have you played since you left school?'

'Good God, no. I tell myself that I'm getting some fresh air, but all I do is soak my shoes through and catch cold. I think my wife likes to be rid of me for an hour or two.' Jon, who had judged the man homosexual, was surprised. 'I teach at the Morley School.'

'It's an open club now, isn't it?'

'Yes. But I think they'd like to keep the connection. Or so some say. I've not been here long. Are you a native?'

'I was born here. I wasn't at the school.'

The stranger looked up at the cold skies where patches of shredded black cloud moved over grey. It began to rain, not fast, but drizzling icily.

'The air's too fresh for me,' the man said. He unlocked his car. Jon bounced into his, and drove off into the rutted lane without hurry. The stranger was leaning back in his seat, the engine not yet turned on.

On the following Wednesday he received a letter from Bob Burton thanking him for his presence and encouragement on the previous Saturday. The committee, who were responsible for this note, thought he would be interested to hear that they had arranged to hold a discussion with Mr Dai Morris on Thursday evening.

196

On the same morning Emma received a short communication from Dr Goach, informing her that though there had been no further developments he thought that he ought to make a report of some kind to her. He'd heard nothing more from his wife, and the excitement had to some extent died down amongst patients and neighbours. He would let her know if anything else happened.

Emma passed this information on to Inspector French, whom she came across by chance in the corridors of the Guild Hall next morning.

'I don't know why he needs to write to tell me this,' she ventured.

'One, he's lonely. Worried, perhaps. And, two, you're the great outsider, the unbiased observer, the legal eagle mind who can tell him whether he's acting sensibly.'

'I haven't even replied.'

'It's rumoured, with what truth I don't know, that he's making rather a fuss of a Mrs Bull, a secretary-receptionist.'

'Is this new? Since his wife disappeared?'

'That I don't know. My information is second, third-hand. I know Sandra Bull, slightly. Her husband had his car stolen. We found it inside a couple of days. Burnt out. Miles away. He's a jobbing builder of some sort. Self-employed. A good workman, I've employed him. Early thirties. Wife's a very quiet woman. One child. Girl of six. Nothing against them.'

'Pretty?'

'I only saw her the once when she came into the station with her husband. She'll pass. Yes. Pretty. Yes. But quietly dressed. Didn't draw attention to herself.'

'Do bits of gossip like this add up to anything?' Emma asked the inspector.

'You never know. On the whole I'd think not. But occasionally. Knowledge is power, they say. Even in my little province.'

The inspector, moving off, asked how her mother was. Emma did not know how he had connected her with the

197

Ashleys, or how he'd known her mother was ill. He was a Methodist, and they had connections and talked like anyone else. She'd ask her father if he knew the inspector.

She rang Goach, told him she had met French and that the police had made no more progress. Goach thanked her, then added, 'I don't trust French. He's a secretive devil. And thinks he's clever.'

'Is that bad?'

'I don't know what makes a good police inspector. I've not had enough to do with them.' He spoke huffily, rang off rather abruptly.

Ian Gormley also telephoned to invite the Winters round for coffee. He sounded pleased, confessed his book had been favourably reviewed, if shortly, in the *London Review* and at length in some magazine published by the English Association. Jon told him that they'd find it difficult to fit in with the invitation as Emma was working and her parents were still with them. He offered some small explanation.

'Radiotherapy?' Gormley said. 'I take it it's cancer.'

'Yes.'

'How does she seem?'

'Quite well in herself. Cheerful.'

'Optimistic?'

'Yes. Very much so.'

'Will she ever get back to home and normal life?'

'We hope so. In the new year.'

'I think,' Gormley spoke slowly, 'if it was diagnosed that,' spaces opened between the words, 'I had cancer,' he made a curious humming sound as if tuning his voice, rousing his energy, 'I would give everything up. I could not countenance the idea.'

He rang off, dispirited, forgetting the praise.

They all drove out to attend the Christmas Day service at Ashley's chapel, shook hands with many, enjoying the carols and the watery sunshine which flattered the plain, freshly painted high walls, and thin gothic windows. Ashley preached a bare ten minutes on the paradoxes of

198

Christmas; Jon judged the sermon a little work of art, and said so in the car on the way home. His wife raised her eyebrows. The hearty singing, the extempore prayers, the hand-shaking joviality were new to Jon, seemed to belong to an earlier era. These people did not need alcohol; a drink or two would have stimulated them to lift the roof off, to ascend the heavens. Sociability and spirituality were as one to them. Inspector French was not amongst the congregation, though Ashley had claimed to know him. People had dressed for public appearance, especially the two or three black families there; most men had ties; the West Indian ladies wore brightly-ribboned hats. Nobody played the guitar; the organist, a woman, in spite of a wall-full of pipes, made no attempt to match the exuberance of the singing, but played with a modest accuracy, much below the singers' level of volume. They did not seem either to care or to notice, but blasted on.

Outside in the porch one old man, red-faced with exertion, asked Emma if she had enjoyed the service. He went on to tell her that in his youth they had gone 'Christmas singing' round the district, starting at ten on Christmas Eve and completing the circuit by three in the morning. 'But we'd be here for the service, and they preached a lot longer than yer Dad in them days.'

'Did you nod off in the sermon?' Emma asked.

'No,' the man answered, 'no fear. I were young then. Missin' a few hours' sleep did me no harm.' He beamed, teeth large and yellow, hands gnarled and ingrained with rough dirt.

These, Jon thought, are the lively oracles of God, and then he wondered what the old chap had had for Christmas presents, and what his wife would provide for dinner and at what time.

Back at the house the Winters and the Ashleys sat, ate temperately, and read. Mrs Ashley seemed subdued as if the fleeting visit to their home had reminded her of life outside this large, warm, comfortable room. Her husband, almost hidden in a gigantic armchair, skimmed a book, a

199

present, on the Bible as literature. Emma said that he invariably was laid low by Sunday or festival services, and having performed in the pulpit needed to recover, crouching at home in dumb humility. The Winters pressed chocolates, fancy biscuits, crystallized fruit, grapes, figs, dates upon the older couple, and they were at a loss as to how to refuse. Jon's father and Alma Franklin, both dressed for a visit to the Lord Lieutenant's, dropped in in the evening to eat thin slabs of Christmas cake. Harold Winter explained to Barbara and Lionel that it was one of the greatest pleasures of his dull life to sit with a slice of iced, marzi-panned fruit cake and a china cup, preferably wide and shallow, of Earl Grey. He and Alma were off in two days' time for a skiing holiday in Kitzbühel, where the news-papers had reported the snowfall ideal.

'Aren't you afraid of accidents?' blunt Barbara asked.

'No. We practise regularly, and do preparatory exercises, and then when we get there I remember my age and infirmities and go steadily.'

'Don't you believe him,' Alma said. 'He flies at it like a lunatic.'

They drank gracefully, three and three; the Winters enjoyed whisky or vodka, while Alma, who was driving, and the Ashleys raised glasses of orange and lemon. It seemed not only decorous but out of the world. Jon chose the word 'supernal' in his mind; it saved him from sorting out exactly what he did mean. The Ashleys retired early, before ten. Harold and Alma stayed another hour, much relaxed. The old man recalled his life as a solicitor for Emma's benefit; to judge from his anecdotes most of his clients were either stark raving mad, eccentric, stupid or miserly in the extreme. The four laughed a great deal, were laughing still when they went outside to the front garden. The Winters climbed tipsily to bed, delighted with themselves, and much in love.

On the twenty-seventh the four drove over to Diana Gregg's for lunch. The meal was ample, and Diana ruled her roost with pride. The children seemed delighted to

200

welcome their grandparents, and the host saw to it that adult conversation was suitably serious for an archdeacon's house. When her husband quizzed Jon about rugby football, Diana allowed them two minutes before deliberately cutting them short and shunting the talk to something more weighty. It would have been difficult for an observer to decide who was more amused by this ploy – Anthony or Jon.

A matter was raised about which neither of the Winters had heard before, but on which Diana seemed to be thoroughly informed. It appeared that Lionel Ashley, a superintendent minister now for many years, was being pressed to become, or to be considered as, the chairman of a district, the Methodist equivalent of a bishopric. Diana, vociferously, argued the rightness of the decision, the suitability of her father for the position, the lateness of authorities in recognizing his merits. Emma eyed her sister as she would a yobbo in a magistrates' court, and asked her father his opinion.

'I'm a bit old, I think.'

'What's the ideal age?'

'Fifty. A fair amount of energy still. Family responsibilities nearly out of the way. A moderate length of experience.'

'Does it matter much at that level?' Jon intervened. 'Does a chairman make much difference?'

'You'd say not until you saw somebody who was really good at it. I agree we would be quite a long way off from the front-line troops.'

'You'd travel round and talk and preach to them?' Jon asked.

'Yes. And pray with them,' Ashley gently corrected.

' "I pray for fashion's word is out

And prayer comes round again. . . . " W. B. Yeats,' Jon mocked.

'And if they pressed you very strongly?' Diana, undeterred.

'I'd have to think about it. Pray about it,' with a mischievous glance at Jon, 'as I haven't. I've always worked on the assumption that if the Lord wanted to call me to some place or post, I should know.'

'And?' Jon worried him.

'I should go.'

'I should know; I should go,' Emma echoed.

'Are you ambitious in that way?' Jon asked.

'Not at all. I don't really want the job. Though that is no argument against taking it.'

'Are you ambitious?' Emma asked the archdeacon.

'Moderately. And I've always been something of an administrator. They're necessary, I think, if not popular these days. Bureaucrats can be a pain. Especially when they concentrate on numbers and names on paper, not faces. I have to deal with human beings most of my time, and I hope that keeps me within the bounds of sense.'

Diana expressed the view that one should be promoted to the top extent of one's talent.

'Until one reaches a job one's incapable of doing?' her husband mocked.

'Then there should be demotion, relegation,' she said, solemnly.

'Are there many potential managing directors left sweeping the floors?' Jon asked.

'Your examples are extremes, of course, but I think there are people working below their level of ability. It's one of the features of our society; machines take over people's jobs, and those forced into unemployment have to do something else, selling hot-dogs or vacuum cleaners, instead of organizing the labour force or planning the future. It's hard.' The archdeacon smiled, solemn but not overbearing. 'I think I understand how the Luddites felt.'

During the whole of this sporadic conversation, Jon noticed that Barbara Ashley played no part, but concentrated on her grandchildren. They made a self-contained party at the far end of the table; they laughed often enough and one of Diana's daughters argued with all the volubility and ardour of her aunt. Barbara looked well, untired, flushed, in her element. The youngsters paid some attention

202

to the grown-up conversation at the other end of the table, but dashed back, often in whispers, to their own hilarious topics. Grandma laughed, leading the laughter. The children occasionally touched her, laying on their hands to approve. Ashley watched his wife admiringly, as one watches a conjuror, not knowing how it's done.

After the Winters had delivered the parents back, and allowed them to go straight upstairs to bed, the two young people sat over glasses of malt whisky. Emma seemed annoyed, 'frayed at the edges', by her sister. The points she made were valid, even without malice, but there seemed no possibility of retraction. Even when she praised Diana it stung, as 'I don't know how anybody so blatant could have such nice children'.

'She's taught herself to fight for them and her husband,' said Jon.

'And herself,' Emma answered. 'What did you think about this business of being chairman? Look how it suited Di. It didn't matter whether Daddy wanted it or not. What was important was the kudos it brought her.'

'Don't you think he'd be good at it?' Jon asked craftily.

'Of course he would. He's clever. Can sort things out. And he'd be genuinely humble. It wouldn't turn his head to be top dog.'

'But?'

'First of all, there's my mother. He wouldn't want to leave her alone while he was travelling round. And they'd have to do some entertaining, I guess. Not that I know much about it. He wouldn't want to load her with a lot of work, especially now. And, two . . . '

'Ah.' Jon smacked his lips; his wife did not forget the points in her argument.

'He considers his great strength as a minister is in preaching. He spends the whole of Thursday from nine in the morning until late at night preparing his sermons for Sunday, having thought about them all week. And each sermon is two. First he prepares the homily he'd deliver to the Conference, or to fellow ministers, or at a university

203

service. That'll be learned, rigorous, with references to Greek and Hebrew and the Fathers and modern scholars. Then when that's done he'll reduce it in length and difficulty to the twenty minutes he'll preach to the Methodists of Derbyshire and Nottinghamshire. The point and structure will be the same, but the evidence, the incidental detail, the illustrative material won't be as exotic. He's not afraid to mention Origen, or Savanarola, or Melancthon; he never underestimates his listeners just because they aren't as well-educated as he is, but there'll be homely anecdotes as well as literary and linguistic. He takes preaching seriously.'

'I see.'

'I hope you do,' Emma said, 'because I didn't always. He goes to all this trouble to explain some pretty straightforward religious question and its answer to some thirty or forty people at best. Out of them two or three only will even vaguely understand the high quality of what he's serving to them. The majority would be just as satisfied with a few Sankey choruses and a joke or two and frequent assertions that Jesus loves them and that all is for the best. I'm not saying they don't like Daddy, because they do. They see him as a good man, different from what they are. But he's wasted on them.'

'You're beginning to sound like Diana,' Jon said.

'I know. I often do. We're not unalike. But I try to be, or at least appear, reasonable.'

'Do you think he's wasting his time?'

'It doesn't much matter what I think. He doesn't.'

'How would he justify himself, then?' Jon asked.

'He'll tell you he doesn't know who he's preaching to. One of the children might turn out to be a Luther or a John Wesley or a Pastor Bonhoeffer.'

'And might not.'

'None of your cynicism, my man.'

Jon, seated in an armchair, put his feet together and lifted his legs, observing himself, grimacing in silence as one accustomed to physiotherapy. He pursed his lips and held his glass at arm's length before subsiding into normality and silence.

'Penny for 'em,' Emma pressed, not altogether seriously.

Jon did not answer immediately.

'I'll tell you what it's made me think about. Rugby football.'

'Good God.'

'I don't think I shall play again. I've made my mind up.'

Emma was surprised. He'd not mentioned this before. The broken leg had healed perfectly, and he walked well. She had imagined that as soon as he could he'd be back in full training. She tried to determine from his tone of voice and facial expression why he had reached this decision.

'It's not worth the effort.' He spoke slowly. 'I'd have to put in too much time to get back to where I was.'

'Don't you enjoy it any more?'

'I'm not so sure 'enjoyment' is the word. Macho status. Pride in strength and skill. The admiration of others. At a higher level still it's worse because, for one thing, money and jobs are involved. I never got so far up into the stratosphere.' He waited, but Emma said no word. 'The oddest thing about the whole caboodle,' Emma had never heard the expression before, 'is that the decision has been so easy. You know me; I hesitate and procrastinate, but not with this. It's like a piece going into a jigsaw; once it's in one knows it fits, is right. So.'

'Was your mind made up before you began to speak to me just now?' Emma spoke coolly, letting him get away with nothing.

'That's, as they say, a good question. I knew. My mind was made up. But I'd never chosen the exact words to frame my decision.'

'Does that surprise you? Now, I mean? You're a literary person, a man of words.'

'Not really. I knew. There was no need to explain it to anyone else. So I left this vague precision in my head. To see what else emerged. If anything.'

'And did anything?'

205

'No. When I was pretty sure, I waited to put it to you. I thought that would be fairest to us both, and besides I was interested in what you'd say.' He glanced quizzically at her. 'I thought you might mind.'

'Why should I?'

'I wouldn't quite be the goods as advertised. Ever since I've known you I've been playing the game.'

'I see. No, I don't mind. In fact I shall be quite pleased to have you home Saturday afternoons and evenings. As long as you don't miss it.' She laughed. 'You'll find something else to do.' She now examined the serious face, the small gathering of a frown. 'Come on, then. What's the catch?'

Jon rolled round in his chair, an ugly movement, unathletic. Now the cleft of his frown was deep-dug.

'I'm surprised that I could give it up so easily. And that troubles me.'

'Troubles?' She queried his bland word.

'I played rugby quite well. And at a highish standard. I didn't do badly. And it did me no harm in my job. People seemed appreciative. They didn't often meet a lecturer on literature who played for the county. And it didn't get in the way of my work. I had sufficient energy for both. So, it seemed a large, even an unfair, advantage.'

'Unfair?'

'I had something most others hadn't. But I've given it up without turning a hair.'

'Don't boast,' Emma said. 'It may seem different in a month or two.'

'I don't think so. But it's not that which troubles me. As I've given this up so easily, I wonder if in another fifteen or twenty years I shan't dump English literature in the same way, convinced I've had enough of it. And out of the window it'll go.'

'Not very likely.'

'Why not?'

'For one thing your living depends on it as it doesn't on rugby football. And you'll be able to produce your books.'

'I'm not sure of that,' Jon said. 'Just as muscles deteriorate with age, so do intellects. And one of the reasons in this case is that interest evaporates. You'd be surprised how many well-known men in my line, respected professors, produced their best work in their twenties with their Ph.D. theses and the books which they made out of them. And afterwards, they've written and published because it's expected, but the quality, the enthusiasm, the drive have all gone. They're on automatic pilot. They do their administration, sit on their committees, keep an eye on their departments, but as critics of English literature they're dead.'

'Well, you'd better hurry up and get a chair before you go off the boil.'

'But what shall I do, Emma?'

'First, we're not sure that it's going to happen. Look at Gormley. He's not much real interest in his students. He's not willing to take up new areas of study. He hasn't got a chair and won't now. But he's produced his book on Shakespeare, which you say isn't too bad. And if he can keep going, so can you.'

'We don't know what Gormley was like when he was young.'

'No, but I can guess. And it's quite possible that what keeps him going is hatred, dislike of the prof, of his colleagues. But he produces his book.'

'Once every ten years. It's not much.'

'But it's not nothing. You bear that in mind. You'll be bored sometimes by your work and discouraged. You'll be envious of people who've got on better than you, not because they've produced better research, and taught better than you, but because they've pushed and shoved, always appeared in the right places, made a fuss of those in authority or with influence. But you're you. As my father's himself.'

'What's the point?'

'When your life's over, it'll perhaps be seen that you've concentrated on what you could do best.'

'And if it's noticed, very unlikely, what I've done best won't be very highly regarded.'

'Perhaps not. But perhaps it will. Look at your friend Hopkins. And your students still read him. And people still write books about him, and in an age that's not religious.'

'You're just like your father. You'd make a first-rate preacher.'

'I thought it was Diana I was like.'

'The universal figure,' he said. 'Are you like me?'

'Of course. That's why I married you.'

18

'Did you not hear my lady, go down the garden singing?
Blackbird and thrush were silent, to hear the alleys
ringing . . .'

Jon Winter, another perambulating songster, enjoyed
his voice's echo on the long, ground-floor corridor of the
Arts Faculty building. Once he'd begun to climb the stairs
to his office he'd quicken the pace to test his leg, and
reduce the full throat to a wordless hum. He swung his
arms as he sang, elated. There was no one else about.
He felt that his deep baritone was not exactly right for
this piece of Handel, that a lyric tenor would be more
suitable to an unrequited love of this nature, but it did not
occur to him to change pitch. A door opened, and a young
woman, carrying papers, emerged. Secretaries still seemed
to cart notebooks and loose sheets about even in these days
of a computer on every desk. She smiled up at Jon,
stopping to allow him to pass her. He wished her good
morning.

'You sound pleased, Dr Winter,' she said.

'Not unhappy.'

He strolled on, resuming the song where he'd broken off.
She knew his name; he'd never seen her before in his life.
The formal title showed this; nowadays secretaries referred
to their superiors, both to their faces and behind their
backs, by first names. In a few moments he'd reached his
office and was in no way breathless; he looked down the
well of the stairway, grinning, as the lift disgorged Ian
Gormley, who signalled frantically for his attention. Jon
took the ten necessary steps.

'He's changed his mind,' Gormley said. 'He' would be the

professor. 'You and I are to set the Shakespeare paper in Finals.'

This surprised. A typed copy of each Finals paper had to be submitted to the professor before the last day of December. Jon had presented his Victorian paper, done in consultation with a new young man, bright and full of ideas, well before Christmas. Gormley would have been responsible for the Shakespeare, he thought, and though Jon lectured on the Bard, he felt he did so on sufferance, or to fill in a gap, or make his workload up to the level of others. It was marginal. If he had given this examination any consideration, which he hadn't, he'd have decided that Gormley and Dr Elizabeth Gurney should have been responsible for the questions. They usually were, and even though Gormley despised Gurney as a brainless word-counter, they managed between them to produce something reasonably satisfactory to everybody. Gormley, it was rumoured, had been heard shouting from time to time at Gurney as if at a disobedient dog, and she replying in a vinegary, piano mock-humility, but the partnership was respected. It was slightly old-fashioned, yes, but it demanded knowledge of the set texts, and the average member, say, of the audience at Kenneth Branagh's *Hamlet* at the Theatre Royal would have been able to understand the questions, if not answer them. But now?

'Tell me all.'

Gormley motioned his companion towards Jon's room, though his own was fractionally nearer, as if heresy could not be allowed to contaminate the air of his place.

'He asked me last term whether I minded if Gurney and that new young woman from Oxford did the Shakespeare, while I set the Sixteenth and Seventeenth Century which had not been, in his view, altogether satisfactory for the past two years. I kissed his rear. Bowed to weightier judgement. Agreed and submitted my paper. I was allowed to prepare it on my own.'

Gormley suddenly, at a pace of which Jon would have thought him incapable, walked the whole length of his colleague's room, slapped the window-sill with both hands, and turned, almost militarily about.

'What they offered was unacceptable.'

'Why?'

Gormley did not answer immediately, but rocked about, benignly sniffing the air.

'He sent for them, explained his objections. Or so he says. Asked them to revise the questions. They did so. The second submission was worse. He sent for them again, said it would not do.'

'That's not very like him?' Jon asked.

'No. It is not. But worms turn. Then Gurney upped and told him to set it himself, saying she had never been so insulted etc, etc in her life.' Gormley was grinning openly, like some club comedian. 'Towers said that if Gurney refused his request, he'd have to ask me to set the paper. That would be unfair as I was already doing more than most. And, moreover, he would not forget their attitude. At this Gurney burst into tears, and this new young woman gave it as her considered opinion that Towers did not know how to treat his staff.' Gormley sailed his way through every cliché. 'By this time Towers had had enough, showed them the door, and gave them one day to come up with a paper more acceptable to him. Both now in tears refused.'

'When was all this?'

'First thing yesterday morning.'

'Why didn't he alter the paper himself? And was it so ridiculous?'

'I haven't seen it. He's too crafty to amend it himself, because then they'd have precise points to level against him.'

'We shan't be popular with Gurney.'

'Are we already? And are we troubling our heads about it?' Gormley was as gleeful as a malicious child.

'And what about Libby Twells?' The Oxford girl.

'What about her?' Gormley stood grinning. In the doorway he said, 'Can we meet this afternoon to get all this out of the way?'

Jon agreed. Gormley stepped sprightly out. Something of

211

his spirit entered Jon's. He, deny it or not, enjoyed a rumpus.

Jon expected the professor to call in during the morning with his explanation of the business, but he kept clear away. Over lunch Jon met Elizabeth Gurney who seemed in no way distressed by the professor's unease, and at his request gave him half a dozen questions she and Dr Twells would like included. He promised to do his best.

'What's been getting at Towers?' he asked.

'We oldies are not churning out the requisite number of books to keep the reputation of the department up. So he'll get his own back by being as awkward as possible, make our lives a misery. He's also decided to give more firsts this year.'

'I haven't heard him say so outright.'

'No. It'll be a last minute whisper in the corridor to his special friends.'

'Who are?'

'Gormley and you amongst others.'

Gurney cackled, much in charge of the situation. Jon managed without undue argument to include her questions. Gormley, in the interests of time, accepted them, and the professor congratulated him on a sensible paper, 'wide-ranging, testing, but not impossible'.

On a clear Saturday after the beginning of term the Ashleys returned to their home in Derbyshire. Emma had made them promise that they would come back to Beechnall if there was the slightest sign of ill-health in her mother, who had sworn to take things easily, to live the life of a lady. The four parted in high spirits.

In the middle of the next week Inspector French called in at Emma's office. He was passing, he said. 'We've arrested Goach. We dug in his garden yesterday, on information, I can say no more, and found his wife's body. My superior has started questioning him officially, tape recorders and all.'

'Has he not asked for a solicitor?'

'Yes. But it's not you. That's why I've called in. I

happened to be down here. I owed it to you. I've not mentioned this visit to the Super, or anybody else. But I didn't want you to read about his arrest in the papers. He's legally represented by Harold Sparrow, of Barnes, Duncan and Sparrow.'

'I see.'

'I've no right to say this, but I think he was ashamed to call on you. He's strung you along, protesting his innocence over this quite long period, and he doesn't think that in future you'd believe a word he tells you. He didn't say as much, except that you'd supported him well, but now he'd prefer somebody else.'

'How did he seem?'

'Very quiet. Dazed. Slightly pleased we'd caught up with him. They sometimes are. But I thought I ought to let you know, on the qt, and this seemed an ideal opportunity.' French picked up his smart, rather wide-brimmed trilby, fastened the two buttons he'd undone at the top of his raincoat, and made for the door. 'He was ashamed to meet you again. I'm sure that was it. It's sad, isn't it, that at a crisis in his life like this, a small moral compunctation of this sort should trouble him? But I'm certain that's what it boiled down to.' French raised his hat, perhaps an inch, above his head, and with a quick turn and word of parting was out of the room. Emma sat staring at her closed door.

The whole interview could not have taken more than five minutes. French had spoken quickly, clearly, without hesitation. An hour later she mentioned the matter to her principal who had dropped in.

'Do you feel disappointed?' he asked. That was not the question she expected from Toby Renton, who had listened, stroking his jowls, breathing heavily.

'I wonder if I did something wrong somewhere.'

'I don't think so. Your policeman's right, I guess. The man had been systematically deceiving you, and then suddenly he's shown pretty conclusive evidence against himself. And he can't face you.'

'But if he's done it he'd know that all the time he talked to me.'

'Yes. Of course. But these people live in a wild, topsy-turvy world. He'd murdered his wife, and yet you represented for him sanity and legality, all the things he was entitled to before he'd done this dreadful act. We're an odd lot. That policeman must have thought highly of you to let you know.'

'He had to come into Beechnall.'

'Yes, but it's still unusual. He perhaps thought you'd be upset, or rejected when you duly hear about your doctor's being charged, and you don't represent him. Most policemen I know would think it was not their business.'

'He's a decent, fatherly type.'

'It's matters like this that make our business interesting. You've been with us long enough to know that the majority of our work is cut and dried. It's not very often that we get even an interesting point of law. You'd be good at that, and I'd always get you to check for me because you're clever and thorough. But otherwise. Well, I don't know. We have to decide whether our client wants to spend ninety-three pounds an hour to sort out his, her domestic problems or on rows with the neighbours. I suppose we make enough to be able to afford to turn a few clients away early.'

Renton edged out, muttering to himself, as if he would have liked to stay discussing the vagaries of a lawyer's life.

There was no doubt that Emma felt acute disappointment. She did not look forward to a murder trial, to the briefing of a barrister, to court appearances and all the consequent time-wasting; she could well do without that. But Goach in his hour of acute difficulty and distress had decided not to trust himself to her. She was adequate to receive the lying confidences of that man while he was trying to protect himself, cover his crime, but when it came to real evidence, to matters of life and death in a court of law, he'd turned elsewhere.

By the time she'd explained all this to Jon that evening

214

she had, she thought, come to terms with the situation. Jon took French's line, Renton's, but that was predictable, and she was glad for their support for she knew that when she had convinced herself intellectually that they were right, this residue of self-doubt would remain to mock her confidence. She was like her father, needing the times of supreme testing to ensure that she was not lacking in strength. Into her mind came a sermon of her father's, 'Lead us not into temptation, into the time of trial.' She had been excused this final examination, and did not much appreciate her fortune.

It turned out that Goach collapsed within himself, pleaded guilty, so that it was his defence's job to convince the judge that his provocation had been great. He did not, would not, at first plead not guilty to murder, and guilty to manslaughter, and thereby tied his barrister's hands. It was as if in his hour of trial Goach tried to assert his moral superiority by emphasizing his care for truth in the face of legal enticements to lie his way out of trouble. This baffled Emma who remembered the quiet man who for months had asserted his innocence, his ignorance to her. No mention was made at the trial, months later, of dalliance with his secretaries or money troubles. It appeared, if one could believe newspaper reports, that the Goachs had quarrelled, not an unusual event, that he had lost his temper beyond measure, battered her to death, and then quietly, almost scientifically picked the spot to bury the body. This had involved the moving and replacing of a quite large water-butt, of relaying a piece of the patio outside the garden conservatory. An elderly neighbour had, in fact, observed this labour, but had not put two and two together until her third or fourth interview with Inspector French, saying that the doctor was always making improvements to his garden. French had, in the end, tied her down to the exact date of Mrs Goach's disappearance, because that was the Saturday, marked in the old dear's diary, when her daughter was due to come over for a few days, but had failed to do so because of her husband's flu. The daughter would have been interested in the water-butt, apparently, because she and her husband had been arguing for weeks over the size and style of a water container for their small, dry, London strip of garden. Emma could well imagine the patient cross-examination of the old lady by French, the decision taken after lengthy discussion with superiors, several returns to question the neighbour again, an examination of the cement of the patio, the dig for the body. She never found out what Goach's reaction to the excavation had been. Had he stood outside to watch, or been away on his round, or had he immediately called French in to make a clean breast of it? She never knew, and though she ran across the inspector from time to time they never discussed the case. She never forgot it, but remembered the quiet, apparently sensible interviews with a man who'd lost his temper once too often, and lashed murderously out. From the trial, short as it was, Mrs Goach appeared shadowy, extravagant perhaps, nothing like her husband's equal intellectually.

In the end the plea of manslaughter was accepted, and Goach jailed. He had wasted too much police time. Jon's father argued against a more lenient sentence. 'About right,' Mr Winter had concluded, 'though they said he was a very good doctor.'

It happened shortly afterwards that Emma had to take up another case of extreme physical violence, but this time the accused was a dull, aggressive thug who had waited in a pub yard to beat and stab to death an enemy who had 'insulted' him. During their first conversations Emma had found the man sullen, utterly unintelligent, and resentful of her presence. But he changed, even seemed to enjoy her company, though she made it clear to him that his chances of being found not guilty were slim. He had a long history of assaults. 'GBH is my middle name,' he said, coarsely facetious. Somebody must have said this to him, and he'd remembered it, taking it as a compliment.

Yet though he lied, constantly contradicting himself, during his interviews with Emma he now tried to be polite, even affecting, not very successfully, a more genteel accent. When Jon asked her for an explanation of this, she said that prison life probably suited him. He realized he'd done wrong, or perhaps 'gone too far' in the punishment he'd meted out to another such as himself, and even thought that retribution of sorts was in order. The warders weren't too bad; he had regular meals and exercise, and talked to this young lady whose task was to prepare his defence. When she caught him out in lies, she did not lose her temper, merely asked, mild as milk, which version he wanted her to believe. This was not the behaviour he was used to; police interrogation seemed nearer to the street-corner, tap-room exchanges, not far from the fist.

'Do you like him?' Jon asked Emma.

'Not at all.'

'Why not?'

'His appearance is against him for a start. He's half a dozen front teeth missing and those he has are a nasty yellow. I guess he's cleaner and better shaven in prison than outside, but even so he's no oil painting. And he's nothing interesting to say. He's no sense that he's done something terrible in ending someone's life. It happened. Perhaps he was too heavy-handed with the cosh, the knife, but "Steve 'ad got it comin' to 'im." '

'Would he do the same if you let him free on the streets again?'

'I'm sure he would. Somebody would say something out of place, or cheat him, or "put one on him" and he'd lash out. The knife was unusual. He'd only bought it that day.'

'To set about this Steve?'

'I can't make it out. He doesn't know. He can't explain why he should be carrying this great, dangerous weapon about, just hours after he'd bought it. He says it wasn't deliberate.'

'Is he married?'

'He has been,' Emma answered, 'but he hasn't lived with her for some time. The two daughters are grown up. There have been casual women, but the police don't seem to think they played any part in this.'

Jon watched her. She enjoyed careful exegesis.

'And if it were a choice between Goach and this fellow Riley, who would you have?'

'Goach.'

'Why's that?'

'He's much more like me. The way he talks or thinks is similar. Riley can barely put a coherent sentence together.'

'But is he less crafty than Goach?'

'I suppose so. At least verbally. And violence is much more acceptable in their sort of circle than in Goach's. In fact it's more than acceptable; it's even laudable. Do you remember those yobs who tried to attack you in the street? If I felt inclined to set about somebody it wouldn't be a man of your size.'

'There were four of them. But I get your point. Some of these young knockabouts pick on well-known sportsmen in pubs and clubs. It's macho. Builds their image up. Or they're druggies and don't know what they're doing exactly. Has your Stan Riley a regular job?'

'He's a labourer. And he does a certain amount of leg-work for a club-owner. I don't suppose it's weekly pay-packet stuff.'

'Has he a fixed address?'

'Oh, yes. A room somewhere.'

'So you prefer Dr Goach?' Jon asked.

'It's not my job to like or dislike. Of course I can't help doing that any more than you can. Just as you look round for the best ways to teach so I look round for those to defend my client.'

'I bet you make an even bigger effort when you do dislike them,' Jon said. 'As I don't.'

The pair often discussed the Riley case. Emma claimed it proved to be as dull as conveyancing. 'Once the facts are sorted out, I just have to be careful.' Riley was sent down for life, and she counted him to have received a fair summing-up. The judge said he realized that the victim was

218

a man of bad character, with a police record worse than Riley's, who had himself resorted to violence with weapons, but went on to assert that he was not going to allow such characters to use places of public resort for 'duels'. They and their like must realize that such behaviour would often end in tragic circumstances, murder, as in this case.

'You did well there,' Renton told her, 'legally speaking. In my view the best result would have been if they had killed each other that night in the pub-yard. The only person who's learnt any lessons from this is you. You know, Emma, I don't think I'd be much bothered if the Rileys of this world got locked away in dictators' prisons without any lawyers to defend them. I know that's heresy, but I don't much appreciate an able, sensitive woman like you trying to put the best face on a crime committed by a criminal on a criminal, and admitted by him, without whom our society would be better off. But you made a good job of it, and I congratulate you.' He grinned, wickedly. She had no idea whether Renton spoke his real views, or merely used this method to straighten himself out after a bad night at the bridge-table.

When the Old Morleyans learnt that Jon was no longer on the books of the City team, they wrote flatteringly, and telephoned four times, trying to have him back in some capacity into their ranks. In the bleak months of January and February, with an east-wind holding the frost in the ground and the thin crust of dirty snow on top, Jon answered politely, but without difficulty. His mind was made up, and that was that. He would not play, coach, or administer. That part of his life was done.

He told Towers this over lunch.

'You're not going to play, then, again at any level?'

'No.'

'Would this have happened if you hadn't broken your leg?'

'I don't suppose so. It made me think about it all. And I realized my best days were over, and I might just as well accept it, get on with the next stage.'

'Was that absolutely certain? In your mind?'

'No. Perhaps not. But pretty close.'

Towers bit the end of the middle finger of his left hand. 'That's how I feel about my job here. And I've another eleven years to go if I work on to sixty-five.' He held up the left hand now, first finger pointing at Jon's face, precluding him from interruption. 'It's all heavy going now. I have to press myself to stay exactly where I am.'

'I don't know.' Jon felt vaguely embarrassed, attempting to talk to his professor like a Dutch uncle. 'The department's pretty efficient. And the outside reports are amongst the best in the place. The newspapers have done us well. And you keep your end up with publications.'

'Yes,' said Towers, 'but what? Primers for first year students. Small lives of the poets. I haven't written a big, well-thought-out, influential work for ten years. I've got a name now amongst publishers. If they want a new edition of a classic with a plain introduction, call for Towers. Or a pamphlet on Ben Jonson or Dryden, or Gray, or Collins or Matthew Arnold, then Towers is your man. It will be reliable, uncontroversial, thorough, judicious, and will save even graduate students a lot of spade-work. That's not what I want to do.'

'What do you want?'

'I don't know. If I did, I'd do it, but I don't. I haven't the nerve to spend four or five years on a major work of criticism. I might have the energy to start, but would I be able to continue? So it's back to the little books which keep depression at bay.'

'If you did start on a big work, would it be about a man or a period?'

'I'd like to write about Dryden, and in such a way that it would change our attitude to him. The students, the teachers, the common readers. When I look round this department I see nobody reading him. A great poet. The founder of modern English prose. But apart from an odd essay based almost always on that little book I did for Sinclair Stevenson that's all the interest there is. I'd like people to see him differently, to read him for the great man he is.' Again the hand upraised for silence. 'And do you know what I fear? That when I'd done it, spent my blood on it, the six or seven hundred pages, it would be no more influential, or, indeed, even any better,' he paused between each hard-stabbed word, 'than my hundred in the students' primer.'

'You won't know until you've tried.'

'There speaks a young man. I spend my energy crossing Gormley or Gurney. And in a childish way. That Shakespeare paper. Those two women had gone over the top, I admit, in the direction of critical theory and feminism and political correctness. Whether it was the influence of Libby Twells, I don't know. She wouldn't say boo to a goose, I thought, but perhaps I've misjudged her. She's a power, maybe, in the making. But their questions were cock-eyed. They lacked common sense. I said to Gurney that they might well have set a question, say, on 'Shakespeare and fire arms'. If you took that up as a bit of research then you might come up with something interesting, but having it slapped at you out of the blue in a three hour paper, forty-five minutes' writing-time, is not sensible.' Towers leaned low over the table as if a hand round his neck forced him down. He straightened, groaning. 'But if I'd have been more reasonable, they'd have altered the paper without much trouble. I see you've talked to them. Their questions, some of them, appear in an acceptable guise. I knew it would be you. Gormley wouldn't bother. He'd be delighted to see them hanging themselves. But I could have sorted it out. And I didn't.'

'Will it make any difference?'

'Guilt, guilt. But I'll feel better when the next bit of good news comes up. It might even stir Gurney and Twells into activity. Gurney needs a sharp kick from time to time. But so do I. Twells? I don't know enough about her. I don't want to knock the stuffing out of her thus early in her career. It's all a matter of balance. And I'm losing mine.' The professor grinned. 'I don't know why I'm telling you

221

all this, Jonathan. Young Dr Winter, father confessor to the department. You ought to get special responsibility payment for it. The sympathetic ear.' Towers cleared his throat. 'I can't sit here all day. I must be off to scrabble about with my small, inconsequential preoccupations.' He smirked again at his choice of words. He did not mean what he said.

As Jon walked out of the refectory he passed Elizabeth Gurney sitting at a table far removed from the rest on her own. She concentrated furiously on her plate, but looked up as he passed. He nodded and smiled.

'Ah, the professor's blue-eyed boy.'

He stopped, tapped his right forefinger on her table-cloth. 'Watch it,' he growled.

She gasped; her eyes opened wide with fear. She let down her knife and fork clumsily. He was a big man, and she was sitting low.

'Not today, baker,' he said. It was one of his grand-father's sayings, taken from the days when the bread roundsman delivered at the back door. 'I got your questions in on the paper.'

Her hands shook, quite violently. Her lips were thin, bloodless.

'All's well,' he said, not moving. 'One way or another.'

She nodded, stiffly, nervously.

'Don't let me interrupt your lunch,' he said.

Gurney rallied. 'It's the most important thing this university provides,' she said. 'Or I sometimes think so.'

He left, both smiling now.

19

January and February passed cold and wet, with one weekend of snow; March began with small improvement. The Ashleys reported themselves well, and Emma's mother spent three days in Beechnall, idling about, as she put it. University term proved hectic so that Jon found little time for his own research. Libby Twells, 'the girl from Oxford', asked his advice, knocked on his room door, announcing that he was the only human being in the department. She seemed bright to him, self-confident, but in need of somebody to talk to outside the limits of her work. The two new young men in the department were callow, if clever, and had set out to impress her with their knowledge. 'I wish they'd talk about their digs or their clothes or their girlfriends, but they won't,' she complained. Dr Twells described the department like a pagan goddess judging from on high, harshly if unfairly. Her voice never became violent, a velvet contralto.

The professor in her view was a time-server, a nobody, one who'd never been bright, and so couldn't be said to be letting down an earlier self. He also shared with Gurney a quality of volatility. One never knew what they'd do or say next. Whatever it was it wouldn't be interesting, but it was governed by no principles so that one could not guess what they'd decide.

'Doesn't that make it more interesting?' Jon asked.

'No. Especially as I depend on Towers for my continuance here. And it goes against my beliefs. I think fuddy-duddies like Towers should be utterly predictable.'

Jon invited her to his home where she immediately made friends with Emma, describing his colleagues to his wife with some verve.

'What about Ian Gormley?' Emma asked. 'He seems to be the one who most impresses Jon.'

'Selfish or self-absorbed.'

'Learned, Jon says.'

'In his way. But I've just finished his book on Shakespeare. You'd think he'd not read any criticism written in the last fifty years. Or if he has he's completely ignored it.'

'And that's bad?'

'Yes. It means he doesn't take into account sometimes what seems utterly obvious to me, things screaming to be dealt with.'

'And what's he like as a human being?'

'Non-existent as far as I'm concerned. I don't think he's spoken a single word to me in the eighteen months I've been here. Not even "good morning". And some of 'em, Gurney, Lizzie Gurney especially, hate him.'

'He's tricked them or let them down or what?'

'He's told them what he thinks about them. He hasn't let them down, because he wouldn't offer to do anything for them.'

'Why does Jon get on well with him, then?'

'Get on well?' Libby pursed her lips. 'He doesn't, I'd think. But Jon's big, and sensible, and isn't flying too many ambitious kites of his own in Gormley's narrow sky.'

'Would he have made a good professor?'

'Hopeless. He'd be worse than Towers. He wouldn't bother to hide his contempt for his equals or for influential members of Senate or Court or the Vice-Chancellor. So nobody would love us.'

'Will you stop here all your working life?'

'I don't want to. It's quite a good place to start, but I don't want to get bogged down. And that depends on Towers. If he supports me when I begin applying elsewhere then I'll have a chance, but he could easily ruin my chances.'

'That's unfair.'

'So it is. But I'm not thinking about it just yet.'

'Where'd you like to go?'

'Oxford again. But my chances are slim.'

Libby asked Emma about her work, and seemed especially interested in the murderers.

'Why is it that they send you, fairly new to the profession, to deal with such serious cases?'

'I defended a doctor in a professional affair, and that brought me to the attention of Goach and his solicitor once Goach was being watched by the police. Then the swine chose somebody else.'

'Were you disappointed?'

'Yes. If I'm honest I suppose I was. Though they told me that Goach was ashamed to have me representing him after all the lies he'd told me. I don't know. That's quite possible. But I think my principal saw I was a bit down in the mouth about it, and so when this new case came up he put me on to it. I'm not sure. Solicitors don't like hanging round courtrooms. It wastes time and money. Jon says . . . ' Emma paused.

'Yes?'

'Well, Jon says that Toby Renton, my principal, thinks highly of me, and so gives me as many different lines to pursue as he can.'

'That sounds right. When I question you I feel confident that you know what you're talking about. You give that impression without trying. To the manner born. I wish I was. I think if I was in trouble I'd come to you.'

'I'm by no means certain of my mind, though I admit it's easier with the law.'

'Do you want a family?'

'Yes. I suppose we do. We don't talk about it overmuch yet. We've not been married long, and we've the upkeep of this big house to think about. It was a present from Jon's father.'

'It's very beautiful.'

'But expensive. Still, it won't prevent our having children.'

Emma enjoyed the conversation, telling her husband that she could easily make a friend of Dr Twells.

225

Towards the end of the month, with the weather only marginally warmer, they were woken towards eleven after a busy evening at home by a telephone call. Barbara Ashley rang from the hospital.

'I'm sorry to wake you at this time of the night, but it's Daddy. He's in here. We went together to a meeting, and it went on rather long, and we were just coming out into the street when he collapsed. It was a heart attack. They rang for an ambulance, and he's here now.'

'Is it serious?' Emma asked.

'I think so. I believe his heart stopped beating once.'

Emma immediately set about convincing her mother that she should spend the rest of the night with them.

'I can't, Em. Honestly. My place is here with Daddy. How should I be able to justify myself if I went away and he died?'

'We're only ten minutes away by car from the hospital. Jon will come and pick you up. I'll get a bed ready for you. Now you talk to the staff there, and find out from them if it's sensible for you to come. Ask them what good you can do. No, Mum, I'm serious. Jon'll come over in any case.'

They both went.

Barbara Ashley sat whey-faced, wearing her best winter overcoat still in spite of the heat of the hospital. She offered no further argument about going back with them; she had consulted the doctors, they were not too busy, who said it would be a good idea. Lionel's condition was stable, and they expected it to remain so. They even allowed her a brief glimpse of him, stripped and wired and rigidly immobile, eyes fast shut. She could ring first thing in the morning. She spoke flat-voiced, though her hands trembled.

At home they forced her to drink Ovaltine and eat two digestive biscuits. Now she slumped exhausted, unable to talk at length, though keen to inform them of detail. Not until breakfast, at eight the next morning, after a call to the ward had established that her husband was comfortable, did she give them any clear idea of what had happened.

226

He had been off colour for a week or two, had been to the doctor who had arranged for tests, had advised half an aspirin a day as well as other drugs, so he must have suspected heart trouble. Daddy had suffered pains in his arms rather than his chest, and had seemed much better when they set out for their meeting. They had sat together, as the business had been chaired by a younger minister. Lionel had made one or two short but telling interventions, and when it was all over had walked round and talked as ever to various people. It was not until they were outside that he suddenly said he had this fearful, tearing pain in his chest. He looked drawn, and had a grip on the front of his coat as if to contain the agony. She had suggested that they go back inside, so that he could sit down and rest, and he'd agreed and turned and taken a step back along the path to the door when he gave a groan and toppled to the ground. There were one or two people about, and fortunately one had a mobile phone and called the emergency services. They carried him into the church porch, and wrapped blankets round him. He regained consciousness to some extent.

'I think the pain was so violent that he had fainted. The ambulance took about ten minutes, and the paramedics were very good. Once we were on the way he seemed more relaxed, though he said the pain was bad. When we got there they were waiting for us, and whipped him inside, and were dealing with him in no time. Once he was in the ward and connected up to various machines she'd phoned them. The doctor, a young man, had been very kind and informative. It had been a classic case, he'd said, and now they'd do tests to find out the extent of the damage to his heart.

'Will he be able to live normally?' she had asked.

'I don't see why not. We'll have to look at the test results first, of course. But as long as he doesn't overdo it and takes exercise within reason, I don't see why he shouldn't have a very satisfactory life.'

'Will it recur?'

'Well, it is possible. But we'll have to set up the conditions to make it less likely.'

Emma concentrated on her mother's face, which seemed drained. Barbara spoke bravely and normally enough, laughed at their jokes, ate moderately, but the pallor, the sagging, the wrinkles betrayed her condition. Jon promised to come back at lunch-time and run her over to the hospital for afternoon visiting time.

'What if something happens this morning?' the mother asked.

'Ring one or the other of us, not both, then ring a taxi. I'll leave a card with their number, and the money.'

'I've money in my handbag.'

'You don't know what you'll need.' Emma laid down the card, their phone numbers, a ten pound note, and pointed hard at them. 'You know your way about the house. Feed yourself. Use the phone as much as you like. Your friends will want to know about Daddy. Jon'll be back for one thirty, to get you there for two o'clock.'

The day went well. Barbara sat with her husband, held his hand. He did not want to talk, said he felt utterly tired, but had no pain. Everybody was most kind. All three visited in the evening, and afterwards Jon drove Barbara to her home to collect clothes.

'While ever he's in hospital, you're staying with us,' he told her.

'You're a big bully,' she answered, gratefully.

'I'm just carrying out General Emma's orders.'

'Aren't you ashamed to admit it?'

That showed that Barbara had come to terms with the new situation.

At the university friends inquired about his father-in-law. Towers showed particular aptitude for this sort of polite behaviour, had a wealth of small talk about heart attacks. Gormley, on the other hand, said nothing. He had presumably not heard, or it had not registered with him. Libby Twells blossomed, took Barbara one afternoon to the hospital and over to Derbyshire on one day when the

228

Winters were busy. She and Barbara hit it off at once, exchanging confidences like life-long cronies.

'Is Libby clever?' Barbara asked Jon.

'I'd say so. Why?'

'She doesn't give that impression. Or even try to.'

'Do I?' he asked.

'Oh, yes. Often. Daddy would be pleased to talk to her. She seems to have read the New Testament in Greek at school.'

'See if she'll go over with you one afternoon.'

'That's not fair to her. Young women don't want to go hanging round hospital wards.'

'How do you know?'

Ashley made good progress, though there was constant consultation about his drugs, and he was finally sent home to the Winters' at the beginning of April. Emma fetched him; the reception committee consisted of Barbara, Jon and Dr Twells. He sat very quietly, uncertain of himself; he joked that if he were shaken he'd rattle as he was swallowing such handfuls of pills and tablets.

Professor Towers continued to ask after Ashley's health, almost too often, as if he found some perverse attraction in the subject.

'When your father-in-law died, so to speak, did he come back with some, well, revelation of the after-life?'

'He hasn't said so.'

'But he would, wouldn't he, if he remembered anything of the experience?'

'I suppose so.' Jon spoke unenthusiastically.

'You suppose. Where's your curiosity? Here's a Man of God who was technically dead for some short time. He presumably believes in the life-to-come, doesn't he? And here's an opportunity for him to testify. One way or the other. You always claim he's very honest.'

'I'll bring him up here when he's a bit better. He'll enjoy a stint in the library. And you can ask him for yourself. I don't know enough about it, really, but I guess his views of the after-life are rather less cut and dried than you seem to imagine. He'd readily admit that nobody really knows. But if you questioned him further, which I haven't, you might well find that he'd regard the after-life as so utterly different from this, so un-human, so transcendent that we can neither begin to imagine nor describe it, and that it would be a waste of time trying to do so. I once heard him say that human life is about the right length, well, perhaps we could double or treble it, but after that we'd be so bored with ourselves that life wouldn't be worth living. Now if we are going to spend eternity interestingly we shall have to be changed. So I don't think he'd be expecting streets of gold or walls of jasper, or even floating up by the ceiling of the ward looking down at the medics working on his body, or passing along a tunnel on the way to light at the far end. These would be poor metaphors, with strong emphasis on the "poor".' Jon watched his head of department with comical intensity. 'Why are you so interested in all this?'

Towers grimaced, caricaturing thought, enigmas considered. 'It's a continuation, Jon, of our previous conversations. Or an extension.' The professor spoke in his most academic manner, a smile of rationality about his mouth. 'Here's a genuinely religious man, by your account, with a real vocation which he's steadily pursued throughout his adult life. Unlike the majority of us. He has, again by your report, lost neither his faith nor his enthusiasm, though both may have altered, deepened from what they were at the beginning. Now my problem is whether we can achieve anything in this, umh, earthly existence, whether we can, if nothing else, satisfy our own sense of fitness. We'd, as Macbeth says, jump the life to come.'

'I take it,' Jon answered, 'that you feel you have not managed that sense of satisfaction?'

'That's so. I could have done more. That's whence my interest springs, I suppose. But here we have your father-in-law, approaching the end of his working life, a man much admired for his devotion, and scholarship, and judgement. What is his view? Has he satisfied himself?'

'Almost certainly not, I'd guess,' Jon answered. 'But you point out to me, often enough, that the higher our aims, the greater our sense of falling short. Look at your scientific colleagues. Trenchard-Lowe, for example. He's not yet fifty. He's held a university chair for over twenty years. Off to Cambridge next October. FRS. Knighthood. Foreign Honours. Nobel any time now. And he's made discoveries that have benefited mankind. People live longer, more comfortably on account of what went on first inside Lowe's small head. Does he stop and think that he's done well? Which he has, on any account.'

'I don't think he's that sort of man,' Towers answered.

'Expound.'

'He's competitive. And still going strong. He has a team that's still opening the field up. He's too busy to worry about his place *sub specie aeternitatis*. He's the sort of personality who wouldn't wonder about these things until such time that he finds he can't continue with his work. Or perhaps when somebody does better than he's done on a similar or parallel project. He's a fierce competitor, and he'd be asking himself what it meant that a rival mind had sorted it out more efficiently than his had. Or he'd perhaps suspect he'd missed some vital point, and that meant that he was losing his grip because he was getting older. But I don't think he'd ask himself why he was put on earth. He knows. His work's there, and never ending. So!'

'But he's a wife and family?'

'The children are growing up now, have left home. But I guess, though he'd do his best for them, if it came to a choice between family or work, work would take priority. I imagine that might well be so for all ambitious people. Frank Trenchard-Lowe does espouse some good causes, he was strongly against the architectural designs for the new library, but I could never make out why that and not something else.'

'Well, when Emma's father's better I'll bring him up here. I guess you'd probably get a clearer answer from *my* father who's not got an ounce of religion in him.'

231

'Why would that be?'

'Because he wouldn't consider the question of any importance, and so would concentrate on clarity. My father-in-law would see the infinite difficulties inherent in giving any useful answers.'

'But he's a minister of religion. Surely he's pointing his congregation towards heaven.'

'Sure he is. Pointing towards, not describing it. And I guess that he thinks the advantages of serving God are so great, in themselves, that he's not very interested in a palpable reward; he doesn't want a silver cup on the sideboard. He wants to be out there battling away. And there's the difference between football and life. You don't play his sort of game just once or twice a week.'

'You think highly of him, Jon.'

'Yes. He does whatever it is he's doing without respite, and with considerable talent. If it was something I didn't approve of, such as robbing banks or murdering women and children, that would make a difference.'

'So you basically approve of his message?'

'I didn't say so. I don't. But he's addressing himself to serious questions about this life, in a way that does little harm to others. And though he doesn't convince me, well . . . ' Jon shrugged.

Later in the month, during the Easter vacation, Jon drove his father-in-law up to the university where he introduced him to the library. A day or two later they lunched with Professor Towers, who then accompanied Ashley on a short walk in the sunshine. They sat outside, on a sheltered seat, for nearly an hour.

'How did you get on with Towers?' Jon asked as they drove home.

'He was very interesting.'

'In what way?'

'He was explaining why he thought the study of literature was important.'

'Did he convince you?'

'To some extent.'

'You think theology more significant?'

'Of course.' Ashley smiled, thinly.

'He seemed to be justifying, or trying to justify, his job or his way of life?'

'You could say so.' Ashley gave nothing away.

'And did that seem unusual?'

'No. Not at all. I think he guessed I'd be interested in the way he saw himself. We were strangers. Though of the same generation, roughly. I'm probably six or seven years older than he is. So here, on the campus, it seemed only natural that he should try to demonstrate to me what his bit of the university was setting out to do.'

'Did you get the impression that he was satisfied with himself?'

'He didn't say so. In so many words. But he described with some force and enthusiasm his life here. And from his style I gathered he'd made a fair fist of what he was about.'

'And if I told you he was very uncertain about it, what then?' Jon asked, mildly enough as they joined the main road crammed with afternoon traffic.

'We all have our doubts. Even the most self-confident.'

'Did he ask you about being dead for a time?'

'In hospital, you mean? No. He's not interested in that, is he?'

'Shouldn't he be?'

'He seemed to have more sense. When you're so ill that you're unconscious or delirious, then your impressions are not likely to be very clear. I wouldn't expect much. Or trust such reports that I did get. And being dead means several things, doesn't it? I'm no great expert.'

'I think Towers might well think you were the sort of man who'd be granted some experience, or some enlightenment.'

'Well, I wasn't.'

'You don't think God let you down?'

'You're just like those people in the New Testament who were always pestering Jesus for a sign.'

233

'It's natural.'

'Of course. That's why we can't expect God to pander to our wishes. The natural and the supernatural will often, almost always, differ.'

'That's pessimistic.'

One fine morning, with the sun brilliant and great bunches of clouds fluffing over blue sky, Jon walked from the car park with Professor Towers. The professor batted his gloved hands together saying that this was something like it, that he felt that life had something to offer him on mornings like this.

'Such as?' Jon muttered.

'I look on my fellow humans more tolerantly?'

'How did you shape with my father-in-law?'

'I liked him. I liked him very much. But I don't think he was quite open with me.'

'In what way?'

The professor jovially raised his hat, a brown, racecourse trilby, to three passing secretaries. 'He wasn't prepared to argue the superiority of Christian beliefs above all others.'

'And this disappointed you?'

'I expected it.'

'Why didn't he, do you think?'

'I imagine he thought I was something of an agnostic, and so wasn't prepared to waste his time and energy.'

'He's just been seriously ill. As has his wife. And so he's not prepared to offer arguments merely out of politeness. You'd have to show willingness, readiness to believe before he'd start. And he'd regard the whole as a rather long-drawn-out process, not the subject of a happy half-hour's chat.'

'And that puts me in my place,' the professor answered. 'And are you pleased with yourself?'

'No. I'm getting nothing done. It takes me all my time, with these family affairs, to keep up with preparation of lectures and seminars.'

'Do you think that's bad?'

'You'll be quick enough to tell me it is if I don't come out with a book in a year or two.'

'You won't be behind when it comes to publications. You want people to read you.'

Towers turned off to his ground-floor room, waving his hat above his head. Jon's pupils, three of the four, were waiting outside his room. They were to discuss what was meant by 'realism' in the Victorian novel, and decide whether such a concept had any meaning or use. Second year students, they had been introduced to critical theory elsewhere, and grew excited by his questions. At five minutes to the hour they were bandying ideas about, ('Did Dickens think he was describing life as he observed it?'), and growing vehement, when a sharp, almost ferocious knock on the door interrupted them. Professor Towers.

He opened the door without invitation, and stood by it, unsmiling, his face waxen, his mouth working.

'Oh, I thought you would have finished. May I have a word with you?'

Jon dismissed his pupils, slightly unwillingly. Towers could not seem to stand still.

'It's important,' he said.

He extracted a letter from his inside pocket, and threw it on Jon's desk. The young man picked it up, recognized the handwriting, Ian Gormley's. Without hurrying he took out the one sheet of notepaper.

Dear Towers,

I feel, even in my present state of mind, that I owe you this letter. By the time you receive it, I shall be dead.

It forms no part of my intention to explain to you why I have decided on this course of action. Let me say that disappointment, in my home as well as at work, has played the biggest part. I do not expect you to understand this.

Two more letters remain to be written, and then I shall take my life. I am amazed at my calm. I often feel more dread at going on an errand to the supermarket.

My apologies to you and to my colleagues for any inconvenience my action may cause.
Yours sincerely,
Ian Gormley

Jon drew in his breath. The note trembled in his hand. He forced himself to read the missive again, slowly. Slightly nauseated, strength drained from his limbs, he sat down, dumb.

Towers, still moving, but on the spot, said that he had, for one reason or another, been late in opening his post, at twenty to ten perhaps. He had immediately rung the Gormleys' home, to offer his services to the widow, but there had been no answer. In the last quarter of an hour he had phoned three times more, with the same resultant silence.

'You're a sensible man,' he concluded. 'What shall I do next? Your wife is connected with the law.' Jon stared in amazement. 'What shall I try now?'

Jon pointed to the phone. 'Once more.' Feebly.

Towers dialled; Jon could hear the ringing tone. No answer. He pulled his diary from his pocket, and signalled to the professor to put the phone down.

'This is his daughter's number. Mrs Snowdon. Jennifer Snowdon. See if she's at home.'

Towers donned the glasses he had hurriedly pushed into his jacket pocket. He dialled rather clumsily. They both waited. No one answered.

'Now what?' Towers asked.

Jon put his diary away slowly, smoothing the cloth over the pocket.

'We should go down there. I'll come with you, drive you. But I think you should phone the police first, explain what's happened, say what we intend to do, ask their advice.' Towers gaped stupidly at him. 'I'll do it, if you like.'

The professor demurred. Jon found the page for him in the directory. This time Towers, formally at ease, explained who he was, what had happened, what he was about to do.

A question was posed, answered and he was passed on elsewhere. Again, quite clearly, unruffled he repeated his story. He dictated Gormley's address, said how long it would be before he arrived there. He had inquired from Jon before he answered the last. He finally listened to instructions, nodding before recradling the telephone.

'They'll be there in about a quarter of an hour, perhaps sooner. Get your coat. It might be cold if we're kept hanging about. I'll fetch mine. See you in the car park.'

He had recovered.

They set off in Jon's car. Towers asked about Gormley's wife; Jon remembered that she and her husband were at loggerheads according to their daughter. Perhaps she had left home. He did not know. Traffic was thinner than he expected. The journey took seven minutes. Towers murmured to himself, at least thrice, that this day was the one when Gormley did not put in an appearance at the university.

The avenue was short, but wide. A few cars were haphazardly parked. The houses, behind small front gardens, towered Victorian, moderately spacious, and at first glance well looked after. A police car already stood at Gormley's front gate. Roadside trees were recently planted, though one or two old stumps remained.

The two pushed through, towards the front door, pillared Norman. A smart policewoman marched round on them from the back.

'Professor Towers?' she asked. She gave her name. Neither caught it. 'We'll have another look round. The curtains aren't drawn. I've only just arrived. Can't make anything out.'

The three peered in at the front windows, and failing to see the body, edged round the side, and then to the back. They could discover nothing untoward in either the kitchen or the two back rooms.

The WPC looked puzzled. Jon spoke. 'I imagine his study must be upstairs. That's where he would have written the letter.'

237

'The garage,' the policewoman said.

They stepped across. The doors were unlocked. They pulled one side open. The place loomed empty. No car. The policewoman switched on the lights for a final check. Shipshape and Bristol-fashion.

'Have you got the letter with you?' the policewoman asked. Towers produced it, watched while she read it.

'Are you sure that it's his writing?'

'Yes. Yes. I'm certain. Dr Winter will confirm it.'

She looked at Jon. Her eyes were pale blue, and her lips thin.

'Yes, it's his. I know it well.'

'You think his study would be upstairs?' she asked. 'Back or front?' She handed the letter over.

'I've no idea. Back, I imagine. It would be quieter.'

The policewoman walked purposively again to the garage, and wrenched one side of the door open, then the other.

'There's a ladder,' she called.

The men followed her over. Between them they moved the ladder from the wall. It looked like oak, weighed heavy and its two parts were separate. They assembled it against the back wall of the house.

'We'll try the small window first,' the police officer said. Jon, bemused, shivering slightly, thought that Gormley would most likely have chosen the room with the larger space, more light for his own. He said nothing. They moved the ladder a foot or two.

'Shall I?' Jon asked, pointing upwards.

'I'd better,' the policewoman said. She climbed steadily. Jon, one foot on the bottom rung, observed her legs, which were both elegant and sturdy in their black stockings.

She peered about from the top.

'Nothing,' she reported. She again checked carefully, then descended. 'The other one,' she ordered. The men moved the ladder across. 'A small bedroom. Not much used. Bed not made up. No furniture big enough to hide in.' She climbed again, without hurry. 'I can't see anything,' she shouted down. 'Nobody in here.' She moved a step higher, put her right arm in by a small pane she had managed to open, and reached downwards to the handle of the catch on one of the large sections. She struggled, withdrew her arm, dusted her uniform with the left hand. Again she looked carefully into the room, her face pressed hard to the glass, before climbing down.

'My arm's not long enough,' she said. 'You look to be about the right size. Will you go up and open that side? Then I could creep in, and look round and make sure.'

They heard a car draw up on the gravel in front of the garage but out of their sight.

'Who's that?' The policewoman took her foot from the bottom rung where she was testing the ladder for Jon. The three waited, looking towards the drive. Gormley appeared, staring at the open garage doors, and then to his left at the two men, the woman and the ladder.

'Gormley,' Towers said.

'What are you doing here?' Gormley replied, equably.

He wore a smart, fawn raincoat, herringbone grey trousers, highly polished brown shoes, and a brand new trilby hat. He might have been dressed for a wedding.

'Is this the Mr Gormley who wrote the letter?' the WPC asked. Towers nodded, as if stunned. He drew himself together.

'Your letter? The one I got this morning?'

Gormley smiled slightly.

'Yes,' he answered, then very evenly, 'I changed my mind.'

Towers stood speechless. The policewoman looked from one to the other. Silence.

'I shall have to make a report on this,' she said.

'It's too cold to stand outside. Be kind enough to come in.' Gormley said no more, but turned about, marched off to let them in by the front door, and leaving them standing in the hall, removed scarf and coat and hung them on the stand by the stained glass.

239

To Jon Winter, the next ten minutes stretched almost surreal.

The young woman took names, addresses, dates of birth, and asked a few questions. Gormley admitted without a tremor that he had written the letter, but gave no explanation why he had not carried out his threat of suicide.

'Did you write to anyone else?' Towers asked.

'That's my business.'

'It wasn't your idea of a hoax, was it?'

'Very far from it.'

Gormley delivered his answers without emphasis. The policewoman, obviously at a loss, asked Towers to hang on to the letter, and wished them goodbye. As she reached the door she turned and asked, almost motherly, if they'd manage. Jon and Towers thanked her. Gormley silently stood his ground.

'Shall we hear more from you?' Towers asked.

'I shouldn't think so, sir. Not unless there are developments. But that's dependent on my superiors.'

'Thank you.'

She let herself out. They heard the front door bang.

Towers now faced Gormley. 'Why didn't you let me know? You could have rung me. Told me to destroy the letter. Or pay no attention to it.'

Gormley did not reply. Jon noticed that he was still holding a shopping bag, which he must have carried from the time he left his car. Now he placed it on the table. The unfastened top fell slightly apart revealing what looked like groceries. Gormley slightly readjusted the position of the bag for no reason.

'You must be mad,' Towers spoke intensely, hissing.

Gormley raised his eyebrows.

'Think of the trouble and distress you created. Jon and I rushing down here.'

'You could have rung the police. That would have been sufficient.'

'Have you no sense of responsibility? A man of your age? You must be out of your mind. And your wife? Your

240

daughter?' Towers gibbered, seemed almost incoherent. He spat out short sentences of anger and accusation. Hands and lips trembled. His eyes bulged. Gormley did not even seem to listen with any attention, stood by the hat he had laid on the table, only half interested. Jon, taken aback by the stream of clichés from Towers, said nothing. In the end the professor stopped, realizing that he communicated with nobody.

They stood round the table, occasionally glancing at each other surreptitiously.

Towers collected himself, thought out a question. 'Is Mrs Gormley not at home?' he asked.

'No. She is not.' The voice indicated slight surprise at the question. No further explanation was forthcoming.

After a long, uncomfortable pause Towers let out a gasp of exasperation.

'We'd better be on our way, then,' he said.

'Yes.'

Towers waited, clearly expecting apology or words of vindication. He did not get them. He made for the door, like a ham actor.

'Is there anything we can do?' Jon asked, low-voiced.

'No, thank you.'

Gormley shook his head, sadly. Jon followed Towers out.

Once they were in the car, the professor's anger exploded. He swore, thumped on his knees with clenched fists. He muttered obscenities, ground his teeth, oblivious of his colleague who waited long enough for the frenzy to abate. Again Towers blew out fierce breath, but spoke now in a plain growl.

'He's mad, absolutely bloody mad.'

'Well . . .'

'It's the only rational explanation.'

'Seat-belt,' Jon said, flattish. Towers obeyed, fastening it clumsily, groping, even groaning. Once they were en route he did not stop talking until they reached the university car park, cursing, fluently accusatory, inhibitions shattered by

241

Gormley's lunacy. He set off for his room once they had arrived, almost running, saying nothing more, Gormley-fashion, as Jon locked his car. Smiling to himself the younger man watched the striding, scarecrow figure. He guessed the professor was searching out, rehearsing for a further audience.

In the next fifteen months, until Gormley took retirement, they heard not a word on the subject of suicide. Jennifer, his daughter, said to Jon that neither she nor her mother, still living away from Gormley, had received a suicide note. She could offer no explanation, but felt it unlikely that it was a hoax at Professor Towers' expense. If her father had said that he had changed his mind, he had changed it and that was that. She seemed embarrassed, as well she might, but her attitude to the incident was as oddly unusual as Gormley's. If her father sent out misleading letters to unbalanced enemies, that met with her guarded approval. Towers should have acted more circumspectly; he knew surely by this time what Gormley was like.

Every few weeks the professor asked if Gormley had mentioned his 'prank', as Towers now designated it. He never lost interest in the matter, even after Gormley had left. 'It has made me feel that I live in a world with only a veneer of sanity. I wonder who will do what next.'

Emma said bluntly that Gormley must be slightly insane, but then so were many apparently normal people in certain small parts of their life. She thought it a hoax, and warned her husband to be on the watch for the next instalment. They invited Gormley and his reconciled wife to their house, but the older people invariably excused themselves. Emma could never quite make up her mind whether the letter was meant merely to jolt Towers or to have a more serious effect.

The young couple set out on the second year of their married life. They both worked hard. The Ashley parents had apparently recovered, and father preached the Word as vigorously as ever. Diana said that the processes were now in motion to make her husband a bishop; one never quite

242

knew what political preferences were expressed. In fact Anthony Gregg was quickly elevated to a see in a northern industrial city, and Diana was heard to say that she would have to come to terms with her children's Yorkshire accents.

In the local newspaper one evening Jon, skimming, recognized the photograph of George Hookes, the good Samaritan with guns, who had let him into his house on the evening he had been chased by the muggers. Hookes had died leaving £200,000 almost entirely to charities; the major beneficiary was the Salvation Army.

'I wonder what they'd do with his guns?' he asked Emma.

'As you would. Sell them.'

Jon thought he saw one of the criminals, alone in the street. He could not be sure. The youth, wearing a baseball cap, strutted along the pavement, speaking to no one, looking into no shop windows. He stared into Jon's eyes as they passed, insolently, malevolently even, but without recognition, as at one of the tens of thousands of enemies.

Harold Winter, with permission, organized and paid for a first wedding anniversary celebration. Alma Franklin fetched in caterers, ordered wine. She seemed more than ever satisfied with life, walked round with dignity, claimed nothing, no status for herself that was not hers. She spoke of her employer as of a schoolboy of promise who needed careful watching, coaching, tuition.

'He's still working quite hard,' she informed Jon, 'harder than he needs. But he's not quite what he was physically. At night, he's more and more content to sit in front of the television. He regrets having to go out to meetings. He rarely goes down to his club. But I've made a small breakthrough.'

'What's that, then?'

'We've joined a dancing school. Every Wednesday. And a formal dance on the first Friday of each month.'

'Is he any good?'

'He's learning. He could dance a bit before we started, and he's even taken a few private lessons. And we sometimes practise at home. He'll be first-rate before we've finished with him.'

'Who's "we"?' Emma asked.

'His instructors and I.'

Friends walked up and down the garden, drank at outside tables, talked and shouted on the anniversary, or strictly, the first Saturday following it. Jon had a long conversation with Jennifer Snowdon, Gormley's daughter. Her husband was now a professor of medicine, and unlike his wife seemed barely pleased about his promotion. Jennifer confessed that her father was the same old humbug as ever.

'And your mother?'

'She's gone back to him. Nothing could keep her away. She had enough to invest in a little flat and keep alive even if the old man failed to offer any support, which was likely, though your dad thought we could make him cough up. But, no. Not she. Thyrza creeps back to him. Pleading. Grovelling on her knees.'

'And your father?'

'He sees it's to his advantage to have her there slaving over the kitchen stove for him. To tell you the truth, he's treating her rather better, but that's not difficult. The fact that she left home, even briefly, sobered him down, and my youngest sister, Catherine, who's a barrister, put it to him what he'd lose financially if he wasn't careful.'

'And is he keeping well?'

'Why do you ask me? You see him more often than I do.'

'I don't really. We pass the time of day. But have nothing that can be called a conversation.'

'There's no conversation with him nowadays, only monologue. About his enemies.'

'We invited him here, but he wouldn't come.'

'I'm surprised. You're the only one he says a good word for. And you're that kicking, young rugby-player.'

James Towers and his wife, invited late, were again impressed by the size of the Winters' house and garden.

They talked to guests in the professor's highest social style, even to Jennifer who gave nothing away. Harold Winter said Towers would be at advantage where no money was at stake. 'He reminded me of somebody on the stage. In the sort of play Alma and I like. Terence Rattigan or J B Priestley. Interesting. Something deep behind it, but not life today.'

Winter, slightly suspicious at first, had grown to like Lionel Ashley, but couldn't help concluding that the clergyman had wasted his gifts. 'He's really sharp, like Emma in many ways. He could have been something. An MP perhaps. A director of a company. But here he is preaching every Sunday to a handful of yokels, oddities, old women. And, worst, hardly being paid for it.'

'Don't you envy him?' Jon asked his father, mischievously.

'He'd be the last man I'd envy. He hasn't got enough.'

' "This night thy soul shall be required of thee." '

'Maybe. But until then I'd like a well-paid job and a comfortable life.'

'Whirling round the dance floor?'

'Don't you mock. I'm bloody glad I'm capable of still doing it. Some of my contemporaries are cripples if not corpses.'

Barbara Ashley, pleased for the occasion, no whit over-awed, spoke her mind to people. To Harold Winter she said, 'It must be marvellous to be able to give a gift like this lovely house to your children.'

'Child,' he answered, not quite sure of her.

'Don't you count Emma as your daughter then?'

'Emma's too good for Jon, and miles too good for me. She's great. I'm even a bit afraid of her.'

'Is Jon?'

'He may be. I'm never sure what he is.'

'They seem happy enough together.'

'I expect they are. But they've only had a year yet. Let's not boast.'

'You're a cynic.'

'Do you think so?' Harold answered. 'Perhaps it's my

job. I've seen some marvellously matched couples come to grief. Circumstances changed them, tripped them up, wore them down.'

'Lionel and I have been together over thirty years.'

'You're lucky. Or perhaps I shouldn't say that.'

'Why not?'

'You have beliefs, and principles that hold you together. Don't you?'

'They're important to us. But we're human beings with our ups and downs and bad days and depressions and set-backs. Even you must have your principles?'

'You wouldn't approve. Mere hedonism.'

They looked down the length of the garden and watched Emma and Jon walking up together hand in hand.

'Look at them,' Barbara said. 'They're happy.'

'Perfect, but what will they be like in forty years' time, when they've just retired?'

'Will it depend on how successful they've been? Or what their children are doing?'

'Your daughters aren't very alike,' Winter said, not answering.

'They're more similar than you might think.'

'Yes. But it's the small differences that count.'

Emma and Jon, pleased with themselves, glad to talk to each other for once, were laughing. The sun burnt his shoulders through his cricket shirt.

'Look at your mother and my old man,' he said.

'Do you think they get on?'

'My father, for all his faults and he has many, can recognize quality when he sees it.'

'What would have happened if they'd married each other? They'd both be quite different now.'

'We wouldn't be here to observe it, but you're right.'

'Better?' Em asked.

'Well. I can't answer that. Your mother has been influenced, very greatly I guess, by your father. The influence of my father would have been very different, and might not have suited so well.'

'Certainly she's pliable,' Emma agreed, 'but only so far. She's no feminist. She thinks that the woman's place is in the home. But that home includes the chapel, and its meetings, and the concerns of the congregation and so on. And all done for nothing. The Methodist Church is used to getting bargains. But it wouldn't have suited your father. He'd have wanted payment for what she did.'

'He didn't mind my mother doing a bit for charity if she felt like it. But he wasn't short of money, so he didn't need to lean financially in any way upon my mother. If he'd been not very well paid like your father, then I guess it would have been different.'

'I wonder if our children will talk about us in this way,' she asked.

'If and when we . . . '

'It often happens with married couples,' she said. 'That's what they think they want.'

'Do you?'

'Just now I feel completely happy, fulfilled, whatever the word is. I don't want change. At least for the present. But . . .'

'But,' He answered her with emphasis.

'It's marvellous,' Emma said, 'standing here, staring down a garden that's full of sunshine.'

'No rainbows wreathing?'

'Not that I notice. But, by God, Jon Winter, we're lucky.' She kissed him on the cheek, to the delight of a dozen observers. 'But now the first little urge towards change comes on me. We'll have to go and make sure our guests are being well looked after. So we'll part, my man.'

They looked round, noticed how many were watching them.

'The cynosure of all eyes,' she said.

'But for how long?'

They kissed. He made off for his father and his mother-in-law, she for a group of middle-aged lawyers and their elegant wives. Smiles crossed faces. The sun continued to blaze down. Alma's caterers emerged, a stately procession of three young women, with trays of iced drinks.

Professor Towers mopped his head with a well-ironed handkerchief. Lionel Ashley, conducting himself, hummed lines from Dr Watts as he often did when he exulted:

> The Lord pours eyesight on the blind;
> The Lord supports the fainting mind;
> He sends the labouring conscience peace.

The guests found their own content on this July Saturday afternoon. Shadows were short still. Many laughed loudly and knew why. Nothing of importance was changed, or learned, or even begun. Nobody expected it; nobody questioned. Minor problems were suspended. These seemed quiet times. As was proper.